COURT OF VICE AND DEATH

ALEXIS CALDER

1

Ara

The carriage halted, and I braced myself so I didn't launch forward. My heart raced as I stared at the endless blue of the water before me. This was really happening. I was sailing to Konos.

"Princess?" Vanth broke the silence he'd maintained for the duration of our journey.

I looked over at him. "What's going to happen to me? To all of us?"

His expression was full of sorrow.

"Never mind. Don't answer that. Perhaps it's best not to know." I smoothed my dress. "Shall we?"

He opened the door and climbed out before offering his hand. I accepted and exited the carriage with as much dignity as I could muster. My sandals sunk into soft sand and I breathed in the salty air. I hated that I felt instantly soothed by the scent. I should feel anxious about the water but I'd never been able to bring myself to fear the sea.

For a moment, I let myself stare at the endless expanse of blue. From here, I couldn't see Konos, but I knew it was out there, waiting for me. Calling to me like a dangerous lullaby, urging me to drop my guard and accept my fate.

I wanted to touch the water, to feel the foam on the waves. My insides tensed as I resisted the urge to finally know what the sea truly felt like. It wasn't the time. Maybe this was as close as I'd ever get.

The ship waited nearby, looming over the landscape like a dragon awaiting a knight to slay it. It cast a dark shadow over the sand, as if taunting me. Reminding me that I was small and helpless against the power of those from Konos.

I'd yearned to be a warrior, to help my people. But I was a fraud. I wished I had more strength. The ability to free my people as I had hoped. But that was a fantasy I'd never fulfill.

What would happen to us when we reached Konos? Would we all be slaughtered upon arrival? Or would we be thrown into cells, slowly starving as the monsters who resided there neglected our human needs?

I scanned my surroundings and noted the absence of any other life. No fishermen, no merchants, no tributes. No other ships, even. "Where is everyone?"

"The other tributes were loaded on the ship already," Vanth explained. "As soon as you board, we'll sail."

Guilt twisted. They'd waited for me. I hated that I'd

received special treatment while the others from Athos were already in there, trapped and terrified.

There had to be something I could do to help them. To help us all. On the ride over, I'd let myself wallow. Now that I was facing this ship, I knew I needed to maintain hope. I couldn't get the tributes off the ship before we left, but what if I could do something to save them once we arrived? What if we could break out and steal a ship? What if we could rally against our captors?

What if I could kill the Fae King and end all our suffering?

A chill ran down my spine.

If you kill the king, all the monsters die with him.

What did I have to lose?

If I killed the king, I could save us all.

My hands balled into fists, and I took a deep breath of the salty air. Human blood might be weak, but I wasn't even sure if I was exactly human anymore.

All this time, I'd thought the gods had ignored me, but what if I'd been presented with a path to do something greater? What if I could help my people from the shores of Konos?

While my thoughts swirled, I followed Vanth toward the ship. The red sails billowing in the breeze like flowing puddles of blood. There was no turning back once I boarded, but I knew this was where I was supposed to be.

Even if I could go back, I wasn't sure I'd recognize home right now.

My father was gone, and my entire life was a lie.

The only way through was forward.

If I ever returned to Athos, it would be because I'd

found a way to save my people. The thought made my stomach twist. I wanted that. I wanted to help them. I wanted the king to pay.

The plank vibrated under my feet as I left land, crossing over the water on my way to the waiting ship. It swayed slightly, reminding me that I was no longer on solid ground. My heart seemed to swell in anticipation despite the awful reasons for my being here.

The only way I was going to get through this was to focus on finding something I could do to help. If I survived long enough, I would find a way.

The plank was pulled in behind me and the crew immediately burst into action. I watched in fascination as they worked with ropes and called out orders. Vanth and I had to move several times to make sure we weren't in the way as they worked. It was organized chaos. A practiced dance. Each sailor falling into step as if they'd done this a thousand times. They probably had.

The sails caught wind, and we moved. It happened so fast it made my head spin.

There was no turning back now.

"This is your first time at sea, is it not?" Vanth asked.

I nodded, still taking in all the activity and movement around me. I knew I should be concerned, but I was too interested in what was happening on the ship. Too enthralled by the fact that I was moving away from land, away from everything I'd ever known.

"Come over here." He led me toward the railing and I leaned against it, staring out at the buildings of Athos and the palace high on the cliffs. It was getting smaller with each breath.

"Better view from this spot," Vanth explained.

I nodded, then turned my attention downward. Foamy water splashed alongside the ship as we cut through the sea. I wanted to look for signs of the monsters that lurked in the water, but I didn't want to lose out on watching Athos melt away.

"I know you're probably already plotting something," Vanth said.

I looked up from the water. "I have no idea what you mean." I hadn't yet had time to plot, but I would get there.

"You should know the king can't be killed. So many have tried. He's got protection you can't even begin to comprehend. It's an impossible task."

"What kind of protection?" I blurted out before I could stop myself.

He chuckled. "I knew it."

"I'm not plotting. I'm just curious." I looked back out at the city, growing smaller with each passing second.

"Just trust me on this, alright? If there was a way to get to him, he'd already be dead."

I turned, planning to ask Vanth another question, but instead, I saw Morta approaching. Vanth caught sight of her at the same time and murmured something under his breath before walking away, leaving me alone with her.

"You aren't supposed to be here." Her lyrical, haunting voice sent a shiver down my spine.

"I couldn't let you take my sister," I told her.

She grinned. "It's funny how people always think they can outsmart the fates, but that's not how it works, child."

"I'm not sure I believe in fate," I replied.

"That's because yours is so unusual." Her gaze was

somewhere far away, and I got the sense she was seeing something beyond my abilities. Something I wasn't sure I wanted to know.

"I'm not all that unusual. History is littered with bastard children who are tossed away as if they never mattered." I had to resist the urge to rub my chest to appease the pain growing there. My father's actions hurt more than I wanted to admit.

"There are also many who turned the tides and changed the whole world. There are too many ways your story could go. Unlike most, you have choices. The fates are not clear for you."

"Wouldn't that eliminate the whole idea of fate?" I asked.

She hummed, the sound an amused tone. "There are those who are players and those who blaze trails. You have a choice as to which path you walk."

"How?"

"You'll know when the time comes. You'll make a choice and the stars themselves will change," she said.

My pulse raced. "You're putting far too much weight on someone like me. I'm no hero."

"But you could be." Morta walked away, the sheer gray fabric of her dress billowing around her like impending storm clouds.

My brow furrowed as I watched her disappear behind a group of sailors. What was she talking about? And how could she think I would have so much power over my own life, let alone the world?

She knows.

The thought struck me as if from an external source.

As if it came from beyond myself. I gripped the railing tighter. Morta must know I wanted the Fae King dead.

And it sounded like she was cheering me on.

Resolve expanded within me, the feeling both intoxicating and terrifying. I knew what I had to do.

As I watched Athos fade from view, I knew that if the fates did have something in mind for me, I was on my way there. And Morta was right: If I was successful, I would change everything.

2

Lagina

Clouds of smoke rose into the sky, the smell of burning flesh mingling with the scent of death. The funeral pyres had been erected at dawn as I'd ordered and the burnings began at sunset. Ash rained down from the sky as if the gods themselves were crying over our loss. So many dead for no reason. It was a fool's errand, that fight. If my father and mother had asked my opinion, I'd have told them as much. But nobody informed me. I'd been just as in the dark as my other sisters, and now Ara was gone. My father was gone. My kingdom was in disarray.

I kept my posture strong as I watched the flames consume the bodies, knowing there were so many eyes on me. We'd told the people it was a group of rebels who'd attacked the Fae. We'd told them the strain on my father's aging heart was too much, that he'd perished alongside those he loved most: his people.

It was all bullshit.

The whole thing was built on greed. A man who became immortal and decided he wanted more. And now his children had to pay the price.

Sophia clasped my hand, her palm a surprising contrast to the hot grip Cora had on my other hand. My sisters had stepped up this morning, slipping into the masks we'd been taught to wear for the sake of our titles.

A priest chanted nearby. It should be Istvan doing the honors, but he'd fled the palace. Another loose end I was going to have to settle once the fires burned out.

Cora squeezed my hand, and I focused on the priest's words. It was an old prayer used in wartime when too many dead were sent at once. A plea for Charon to have patience as he ferried the deceased to the Underworld. I'd only ever read about it in history books. Hearing it performed sent a shiver down my spine. We shouldn't be at war. That was the purpose of the Choosing. We were to maintain peace, at least with the Fae.

Yet, I knew the war was just getting started. The Dragon King would be in Athos soon, the final piece in the game my father was making secret moves toward. I was lucky his advisors had shared with me last night. What else was I going to discover?

And how was I supposed to do this job without him by my side? It wasn't supposed to be like this. I was supposed to train for a few more years, then take over the role little by little. He was supposed to be there to answer my questions and offer guidance. Now I knew he never planned to leave. He'd have ruled forever if he could have.

My throat tightened, and I pushed the betrayal to the surface, allowing it to mask the sorrow. I'd inherited a broken kingdom with a precarious throne. I didn't have time for mourning right now. In three days' time, we'd hold the funeral for my father, as was the custom. I had to ensure that nobody would get wind of what he truly was before that happened. We were too weak right now. If a powerful noble wanted to make a move for the throne, this was the time to strike. I couldn't afford any signs of weakness or any cracks that would make my rule come into question.

As far as anyone knew, his body had already been taken to the catacombs. Someone else's cloth-wrapped form had taken his space in the family tomb. I didn't ask where it had come from, only expressed gratitude at the guards who'd so quickly moved to help. They'd been promoted to my personal guard immediately. Loyalty was everything moving forward. I couldn't risk any mistakes.

The priest finished his chant, and the cries of the families escalated. They'd remain here until the bodies were nothing but ash. In three days, we'd gather again and burn whoever was currently occupying the family tomb.

Out of the corner of my eye, I caught sight of Argus, my new head guard, walking toward me. His steps were hurried, his body tense. Something was wrong.

"Remain here until the crowd dwindles," I told my sisters.

"What's going on? Where are you going?" Cora asked.

"Back to work." I offered a smile, but no further explanation as I turned and left the balcony. Some might note my departure, but I'd remained for the official ceremony and if my sisters lingered, we could get away without offending the more pious citizens who demanded that we were to stand vigil until the flames burned themselves completely out.

Argus turned as I approached, falling into step beside me as we left the balcony and entered the palace. I noted how tense he still appeared. "What is it?"

"Something your mother found," he said. "This way."

My stomach twisted into knots as we continued down the corridor. While my mother would no longer hold an official title once I completed my coronation, she was still helping with the aftermath of the Choosing. Her job being one that was specifically well suited to her ability to cozy up with anyone. She could get even the most tight-lipped noble to spill their family's darkest secrets with a few bats of her eyelashes and a couple of glasses of wine.

If she found something, we were in trouble. I swallowed down the fear clawing its way up my chest and hoped we could fix whatever she'd found before word got out.

We paused in front of my father's study, then Argus opened the door for us. Two guards waited with my mother, between them stood Mythiuss. My heart fell into the pit of my stomach.

"Mythiuss?" I turned to my mother. "What is the meaning of this?"

She held up a pile of neatly folded letters. I could see my father's seal on them from here. My brow furrowed.

"I can't let it happen again," Mythiuss said, his voice gravelly and strained. "Your family is going to unleash a curse on the world."

"Letters addressed to every noble house in Athos. A few in Drakous, too," Ophelia said before shooting a glare at the healer. She crossed to me and set the letters in my hands. "They all say the same thing."

"They deserve to know," Mythiuss hissed.

I cracked the seal on one of the letters and read the note scrawled in the healer's tight, slanting writing. My eyes widened and my mouth went dry. This was exactly what we were afraid of. If these had gotten out...

I crumbled the letter in my fist. "How much did you know? When was he turned? Why did he do it? Who did it to him?"

I took a step closer, my sympathy and fear transforming into rage. This man threatened my family. His letter would have told everyone that my father had been a vampire. If the people knew, they'd come for all of us.

"You've known, but you've never told. Why would you do this now? Why break your silence now?" I held up the letter.

"Because of the creature growing in your mother's womb," he hissed. "She carries an abomination. A sin against the gods."

I glanced toward my mother, her face was pale, a protective hand on her slightly bulging stomach. Her child was half-vampire. What if the rest of us were too?

"Is he the only one?" I asked.

"It doesn't matter," he said. "Once the word is out, none of you are long for this world."

"Why not tell me what you know," I pressed. "You cared for him all these years. You know the truth. How long did he hide this?"

"Let me leave the palace and I will send you a letter answering all of your questions," he said.

"You know we can't do that." I could hear the touch of sorrow in my tone. How many times had he helped me through an illness or injury? He'd cared for all of us since we were children. Cared for my father when he was a child as well. "We can't let you leave this palace."

"Let me leave, and I'll tell you everything. All of your father's secrets. Like the name of Ara's mother."

"We do not speak her name in this palace, old man," Ophelia sneered.

My stomach tightened at the mention of my sister, and I threw a warning glare at my mother. I didn't care how lowborn her mother was, Ara was not to be disrespected. That was a line my mother could not cross.

Despite the fact that we'd grown apart in the last few years, our pasts connected us and I would never dishonor her memory. I still thought of her as my best friend. Nobody would fill that void. Especially after what she'd done to protect Sophia. "Ara's mother is not my concern. She's my sister and she's a member of the royal family. no matter where her blood comes from."

"He's going to tell everyone," Argus said softly.

I knew what he meant with that warning, even if I didn't want to believe it. "Last chance, Mythiuss."

The old healer locked his eyes on mine. "Athos is at the beginning of the end. You are going to rule over a kingdom of corpses."

I'm not sure how the blade ended up in my hands, but the look of surprise in Mythiuss's eyes as I shoved it into him told me everything I needed to know.

Nobody was going to take my reign seriously unless I showed them that I could be just as strong as any king.

3

ARA

I COVERED my nose and mouth against the sudden overwhelming smell of sweat and human waste as we reached the bottom of the stairs leading to the belly of the ship. It was dark, the few circular windows only providing minimal light. Each step sent a little splash around my ankles. The entire floor was wet, and I wasn't sure it was just water.

Faces turned toward me. Brows furrowed, eyes narrowed, expressions judging. I lowered my hand and tried to adjust to the smell. A quick scan of the room told me there weren't many tributes here. "He didn't take a hundred?" I looked at Vanth.

"He said there were enough dead and that the fourteen were sufficient," he replied.

It was a tiny victory instantly overshadowed by the mention of the dead from the failed rebellion. I understood the reasons behind wanting to eliminate the Fae delegation. I'd even tried myself. But the distance from everything had me questioning right and wrong; glory and its cost.

There had to be another way. Something else that could maintain peace without so many lost lives. They didn't need Athos to provide them with humans. They were powerful; they could do whatever they needed another way.

Morta's words swirled, and my chest tightened. I would force another way.

"We'll be in Konos in a few hours," Vanth said. "I have to go back up there. You sure you want to stay down here?"

"I'll be fine." It was better to be down here with my people than to stay above like the traitor they all thought I was.

"I'll see you when we arrive," he said.

There wasn't anything to say, so I simply nodded, then walked deeper into the cargo hold, taking in the faces of the tributes around me. I heard Vanth's steps receding and then the sound of the hatch closing behind him. I glanced back, feeling a little claustrophobic with the trapdoor shut. Maybe I should have stayed on deck.

"Where's your ambassador?" someone asked.

I turned and saw a young man with a huge slash across his cheek. Blood and dirt smeared on his face made it take me a moment before I realized who it was. "Belan? What are you doing here?"

Whispers were rising around me as the others in the hold were catching on to who I was. I ignored them and knelt down on the soggy floor next to the bloodied guard. "What happened to you?" I reached for his face to push his hair back so I could check his injury, but he slapped my hand away.

"Don't touch me, traitor," he hissed.

"Konos whore," someone spat.

So everyone knew I'd been with the ambassador. I let out a sigh, then set my hands in my lap when all I wanted to do was scream at everyone. I wanted to tell them I'd come here to save my sister. I wanted to tell them the attack against Konos has cost me everything.

But I knew reminding them that the royals were exempt from the Choosing wasn't going to win me any friends. So I sat in silence a long while, letting them whisper about me. Letting them speculate and chatter, letting them hurl insults at me under their breath.

"That's enough," I finally said, my tone even. "If anyone has something to say to me, say it to my face."

"Why are you down here with us when you can be with your new friends?" Belan asked loud enough for everyone to hear.

"She's why there's only thirteen of us down here," a woman said.

I hadn't actually counted, so I did a quick scan of the room. She was right. My chest tightened. Not only had they not taken a hundred tributes, they'd left someone behind since I was joining. Well, since Sophia was to join.

I hated that I felt a little rush of gratitude toward Ryvin, because I knew this had to be his doing as well.

"Is that true?" Belan asked. "You're a tribute?"

I nodded.

"What happened?" he whispered.

"You first," I replied. "How did you get down here? Weren't you at the palace for the ceremony?"

"None of us made it to the ceremony," he said. "They showed up at the barracks in the morning and hauled me away."

"You fought them." This time, when I reached for his hair, he let me. I pushed it aside and examined the slice down the side of his face. The blood had dried and was caked along a long cut that would need cleaning soon or risk infection.

"I told you I would." He offered a weak smile. "And I'm not done yet."

"I'm glad to hear it because I'm going to need some help." I moved my hand from his forehead. "We need to find out the Fae King's weakness."

"So they didn't break you?" he said with a grin.

"I'm going to break them," I replied.

"I can't wait to watch them all burn."

VANTH TIGHTENED the rope at my wrists. "I'm sorry about this."

The other tributes were also being bound, their arms tied in front of them just as mine were. Some were crying, while others wore distant expressions. Already walking ghosts. How much time did they have? How much time did any of us have?

The ride to Konos had gone almost too quickly. I'd hardly finished explaining the fight and my father's death to Belan before we arrived. While I was ready to get some fresh air, I wasn't ready to face the Fae capital.

We didn't know what happened to the tributes on Konos. The stories of the Fae Court were horrific enough that my imagination was already running wild. Would we be flayed alive? Fed to monsters? Kept in cages as food for the vampires? I swallowed hard, forcing the images away. My heart was thundering in my chest, my stomach in knots. It was difficult not to be afraid of what was to come.

The only thing I knew was that I had to survive this.

Vanth's fingers closed around mine. "You're shaking."

I glared at him. "I wonder why."

"Just do what they say and you'll make it through this," he whispered.

"Do I want to make it through this?" I wanted to save my people, and I wanted to see the Fae King pay for what he did to us, but there was a tiny part of me that wondered if it was worth the fight. I shoved that dark thought away. Of course, I was going to fight. I had to.

Before he could respond, someone was shouting from the hatch, calling orders for all the tributes to line up at the ladder.

"For once, just play the game, Ara," Vanth warned. He walked toward the ladder and started guiding tributes up. One at a time, my people awkwardly climbed, having to grip the rungs with their bound hands.

Belan was at the back of the line, and I joined him. He glanced at my hands. "I'm surprised they tied you up."

"I don't think they care much about my past," I replied. "Or who I slept with."

"I still think you can use that to your advantage. Having a royal on display will make them look good. Or feed their ego. You should use it if it keeps you alive," he said.

"Or if it gets me closer to the king," I whispered.

Belan smirked. "I'm ready the moment you tell me to go."

"We're going to figure something out," I promised.

"Keep moving!" someone shouted from the hatch.

The line inched forward as tributes ascended the ladder. It was a pathetic procession. We'd only been in the hold for a few hours, but most of the people looked as broken as if they'd been here for weeks. I wondered how many of them would survive the next couple of days. My chest tightened. Whatever I was going to do to help them, it would have to be soon. Most of them weren't going to make it long here. Especially if they treated us poorly. And judging by the bindings on my wrists, it was a legitimate expectation.

A red-clad Konos guard shoved Belan. "Up the ladder, now."

Belan bared his teeth but complied, gripping the rungs with his bound hands. As soon as his head was through the hatch, I grabbed the ladder and began my ascent.

We emerged into dim light, the constant dark cloud cover blotting out the sun. Lightning flashed and I could taste the charge, as if it hung around us, leaving a remanent of sparks in its wake. The scent of salt and brine filled my nose, mingled with something familiar. Something I thought I'd smelled before. I wondered if it was that lingering lightning. Who knew the magically created dark clouds around the island actually carried a storm with them? I wondered if it would bring rain as well.

The ship rocked and swayed as we were shoved forward toward the plank I'd taken when I boarded. I shuffled forward, doing my best to follow along with the group while also glancing around for any signs of Vanth. Or Ryvin. Even though I told myself I didn't want to see him.

My insides twisted at the thought. Where had the ambassador gone? Was he already off the ship? Returning to whatever luxurious home he resided in? Was he already lost in another's embrace?

Swallowing hard against the unwelcome jealousy, I tightened my jaw and strode forward, watching my steps as I made my way down the platform.

Churning gray water splashed and rippled under us as we slowly made our way to a wooden dock. The tributes had already been led away toward waiting carts, loaded in like goods headed to market. Or like lambs to the slaughterhouse. My breathing grew rapid, and I had to remind myself that I wasn't dead yet. I didn't know what was going to happen, and I had to stay alive as long as I could. It was the only option.

"I don't want to go," someone yelled through bursts of crying.

"Get in the cart," a guard hollered at a young woman with a long blonde braid. She was sobbing and pulling away from him, trying to free herself from his grip on her upper arm.

"I want to go home. I'm to be married. I'm to be

married..." she repeated the words over and over through her heaving breaths, tears streaming down her face.

"Not anymore," the guard hissed.

She yelled, a hollow, animalistic sound that could only be described as hopelessness in its purest form. My heart cracked for her, aching for her loss.

I took a step closer, wanting nothing more than to comfort her, but someone grabbed me and pulled me back. "Stay out of it." Vanth's voice in my ear made me tense. I wanted to resist him, but for some stupid reason, I believed he was trying to help me.

In my moment of hesitation, the woman broke free of the guard's grip and she sprinted to the docks. The guard followed, yelling at her as he chased her, but he slid to a stop just as she leapt into the sea.

I ran forward, but Vanth grabbed me around the waist, pulling me back before I could reach the edge. "Let me go!"

"Can you swim, Princess?" he said with a growl.

"Someone has to help her." I tried to fight my way out of his grip. "I can lean over the edge."

"Stop fighting me, Ara," Vanth snapped.

I struggled against him, even as I knew it was probably useless. There was no splashing, no sign of the woman trying to fight her way to the surface. But how could everyone stand back and do nothing?

That's when I realized they weren't just standing back, they were moving backward. Some guards were still pushing tributes into the carts, but the rest of them seemed to be holding their breath as they moved farther away from the docks.

Vanth pulled me. "That's not possible."

"What's not possible?"

He tugged me harder. "Back up, Princess."

I resisted. "Someone has to help her."

A bellowing sound, low and rumbling, vibrated the wood planks under my feet. Vanth's grip on me tightened, and he lifted me with ease. For a second, I was stunned by the fact that he'd let me fight against him when he could have simply tightened his grip and carted me away. But that thought didn't have time to linger because a massive creature burst from the water with an ear-splitting shriek. Jaws lined with hundreds of razor-sharp teeth opened wide, water and smaller sea creatures pouring from its massive maw. The monster plunged into the sea, silver scales glinting in the dim sunlight, a massive tail slapping the water as it submerged.

An eerie silence enveloped us, like a suffocating mist that absorbed everything around it. I could hear my heart pounding in my ears; my breathing was too loud. My hands were shaking, and I found myself actually grateful that Vanth hadn't released his hold of me.

Suddenly, the monster burst through the waves again, a dangling corpse clenched in its teeth. Bile crawled up my throat and my eyes widened as the creature flipped the woman's body into the air, then opened its jaw and tipped its head back like an expectant bird. Her mangled and broken form landed in the beast's waiting mouth and the monster clamped its jaws closed before sinking into the depths.

Water rippled in warning circles where it had been

and red bubbled at the surface for a moment before white foam washed it away.

"What the fuck was that?" I asked.

"Sea serpent." Vanth shook his head. "I haven't heard of one coming this close to shore in centuries."

"So we shouldn't see something like that again?" We'd all heard stories about the monsters in the depths, but this was the first time I'd ever seen one. "Are we safe on land?"

"Everything in Konos will try to kill you, Princess," Vanth whispered.

"Even you?" I challenged.

"I might be the only one here who doesn't want to see you dead," he said darkly.

I wanted to ask about Ryvin, but I couldn't form the words.

"Get in the cart. Do what you're asked." There was a warning in his tone and, for once, I complied without question.

My people weren't going to survive here. Even if they were given every comfort of home, Konos itself was a death trap for humans.

I wanted to be the hero, to end the king and save us all. But I'd seen battle, and I'd failed. I wasn't prepared for that kind of endeavor. But maybe I could get us off this island.

If the path my father had set in motion continued, we'd all be at war soon. A few humans who escaped would be the last concern for the Fae King. If we could get off this island, maybe we had a chance to survive.

4

Ara

The tributes were shoved into two different carts, Belan in a different one than I was in. I wondered if that was on purpose. Had they already noticed the two of us talking while we'd been in the hold of the ship?

The cart rolled and bumped, the bottom vibrating as we made our way over the rocky landscape. Cyprus trees, yellowed and dying, lined the dirt road we traveled down. We passed abandoned buildings and empty fields. Strange flowers dotted the landscape. They were bleached of all color, their petals like glass attached to muted green stems. It was as if the clouds covering the island settled around us, making the plants and other life gray and fading.

I shivered, pulling my knees closer to my chest. My mind continuously replayed the last few days. The stolen moments with Ryvin, the battle during the ceremony,

David's betrayed expression, my father wrapped in shadows...

Squeezing my eyes closed, I forced the thoughts away. I wasn't going to last here if I wallowed in the past.

My chest ached as guilt tightened around my ribs. I knew it was my fault. So much of it could have been prevented if I'd been more aware of the things going on in my own kingdom. How had I allowed myself to be so blissfully unaware?

I'd let go of court politics, tuned out the truth about how badly my people were faring, and blinded myself with my desire to get away. I'd chased escape; chased my own path, at the detriment of all those around me.

I wasn't any better than my father or the Fae King himself, but I could find a way to atone for what I'd done. I looked at the defeated faces around me. Dirty and terrified, they all seemed to have detached already from what was happening to us.

Closing my eyes, I thought about what I knew of Konos. Of their king. Were there any weaknesses in the stories we'd heard? Was there a way to get out of here? Any creatures who were sympathetic to humans who lived under the Fae King's rule?

"Is it true, your highness?" A quiet voice asked.

My eyes fluttered open, and I turned to face a timid looking brunette with huge brown eyes. Her cheeks were tear-stained, her hair mussed. "Is it true that the king is dead?"

I nodded.

"Is that how you ended up with us?" she asked.

I could feel the eyes of my companions on me and

glanced around, taking in their disheveled faces. There were eight of us in the carriage, crammed in like animals being carried to the market.

"The ambassador killed my father." I said the words more to remind me that he was my enemy. That I couldn't trust him, no matter what my body might desire.

A few whimpers or gasps sounded.

"Wouldn't that violate the treaty?" the brown-eyed woman asked.

"We violated it first. When our people attacked at the ceremony," I said.

"But we didn't attack. I didn't even know that was going to happen. Yet, I'm here. Why punish us?"

"I thought the royal family was exempt," A man said.

I met his stare. "I volunteered to come."

He scoffed. "Why would a spoiled royal do that?"

"Leave her alone," the woman next to me said. "We're all here now. There's nothing we can do about that."

"They must have wanted you gone," the man said. "You're nothing anymore now that your father is dead. Just another bastard."

"You're right." I locked my gaze on him, refusing to blink. "I'm the same as you."

"I heard the rumors," he sneered. "You were fucking one of them. Even that wasn't enough to save you."

I took in his torn and bloody tunic, his ripped trousers, and lack of shoes. He'd been through a lot before getting here. "You fought back when they came for you, didn't you?"

"Going to defend your new friends?" he hissed.

"No, I'm not. I'm glad you fought. We're going to need that kind of defiance to survive here," I said.

He scoffed. "If you think I'd do anything to help your time here be more pleasant, you're mistaken. I wasn't able to kill you outside the Opal, but I won't be run off this time."

My chest tightened. "You were there?"

"Yeah. I was there."

The moment of fear I felt staring at him quickly dissolved as I realized he'd been there, then he ran. "You left your friends when the fight got hard."

I'd nearly died defending the Konos delegation. I'd killed my friend to keep them alive. My throat tightened, and I fought against the pain that David's memory stirred. The regret. The deep abyss of knowing I'd made a mistake. If I'd killed Ryvin instead, my father would be alive and I wouldn't be here right now.

"Better that I ran to fight another day than what you did, traitor," he hissed.

I couldn't defend myself or my actions. Not anymore. Not after everything I'd seen and everything I'd done. Even after Ryvin had killed my father, I couldn't end his life. I was a disgrace.

It was going to take a lot to make up for what I'd done, but I was determined to see it through. "I can't change what I've done. But I'm here, aren't I? A prisoner just like you."

"Until you find another from Konos to throw yourself at. You're nothing more than a whore," he spat.

My hands curled into fists, my nails biting into my

palms. "At least I tried to fight for what I thought was right. You fled."

"What difference does it make now?" the woman next to me snapped. "None of us will survive this. The gods will determine our fates now."

"She has a point," someone else said.

Another man, also covered in blood, cracked his knuckles while he glared at me. I turned to him. "You have something to say?"

"Not to you, traitor." He spat on the ground.

These were the people I'd spent my whole life feeling loyalty to. The people I thought I was helping. They didn't want my help. Maybe they never did.

The cart stopped suddenly, causing all of us to slam into each other. I quickly righted myself and apologized to the brown-eyed woman next to me. She mumbled something so quietly I couldn't make it out, then offered a weak smile. Her hands were shaking, and I had a feeling if she had any tears left, she'd still be crying.

I wanted to say something comforting to her, to offer some reassurance or kind words, but I couldn't form them on my tongue. There was nothing I could say that wouldn't come out sounding shallow and forced.

The back gate opened and several Konos guards flanked either side, their red tunics the only spot of bright color against the desolate gray landscape. "Out."

Wordlessly, we stood and everyone filed out of the cart. I waited in the back again, taking in our surroundings. We were on a long driveway that stretched toward a high stone wall. I could see a massive palace peeking above the wall, but the details of the rest of the structure were hidden.

Cyprus trees along the wall stood like a warning. Their usual proud forms sagging and brittle. As if the very land they occupied was full of poison. Maybe it was.

I climbed down from the cart and fell into line behind the others, but a guard grabbed my upper arm. "I hear you used to be someone important." His lips brushed against my ear and I tensed as his hot breath warmed my skin. "I've never fucked a princess, but I'm not sure I want someone's cast offs."

"Let me go," I said through gritted teeth, tugging my arm away from him. To my surprise, he released me but it wasn't because I'd asked him.

Ryvin had his hand around the guard's throat, the man's eyes bulged, his face turning red as he clawed at the hands constricting his air.

Nobody moved, and all attention was on the scene unfolding between us. Ryvin's fingers tightened, his gaze fixed on the man in his grasp. But he didn't look angry. His expression was cold, impersonal, nearly devoid of emotion.

It was possibly even more terrifying than him being angry.

"You so much as look at her again, and I will pluck your eyes from your skull personally." His tone was flat, as if he was wasting his time by speaking to the guard.

He released the guard and shoved him away. The guard gasped, reaching for his throat as he scrambled back away from Ryvin.

With an exasperated sigh, he looked around. "The

king wants this one unharmed. So do try not to break her, understood?"

I opened my mouth, ready to say something to him as soon as he looked at me, but he didn't turn toward me. Shadows circled his feet, then climbed, swirling around him until he was swallowed by the inky tendrils. When they dissipated, he was gone.

"See? Told you he was her whore," one of the men from the cart said.

"Shut up," the guard, who was still rubbing his neck, said. "Get in the cage."

Two large cages pulled by a pair of massive white horses waited for us. We were shoved toward them. I tried to move so I could be in the same cage as Belan, but they kept us in the groups we'd arrived in.

"Where are we going?" I asked as the guard closed the gate behind us, locking us inside.

"To a celebration," he said with a grin. "And you're the main event."

I caught sight of Belan as the cages rolled down the road. He watched me, his expression impassive. My fingers gripped the bars, so tight my hands hurt, but I didn't let go.

5

Ryvin

The guards tensed as I stormed down the hallway. I wasn't in the mood to deal with this right now, but not even I could keep the Fae King waiting. He was going to be furious with me, but I could take it. Whatever punishment he had in store was worth the information I'd gained in Athos.

My thoughts wandered to Ara, and I shoved them away. She was a complication I wasn't ready to deal with. I shouldn't have let her come. I should have forced her to stay behind, but I could see the fire inside her when she'd demanded she take her sister's place. If I'd said no, she'd have found her way here anyway, and she'd be dead before I could figure out how to get her off this island.

Word would spread quickly about what I'd said to the guard who touched her. It would be enough for them to keep their hands to themselves for now. But it didn't protect her from the king. If he found out about my feelings for her, even I couldn't save her.

I paused at the doors to the throne room, taking a minute to banish her from my thoughts. I had to keep her out of my head. For so many reasons, the least of which was the way she distracted me.

Two wolf shifters stood in front of the doors to the throne room. Both of them flinched slightly as I approached, but they were trying not to show their fear. I allowed some of my darkness out, the shadows twisting and writhing around my hands and arms like snakes.

Hesitating for just a moment, I lifted an annoyed brow, silently questioning why they hadn't already moved into action. Eyes widening, both shifters turned toward the massive brass handles and pulled open the carved oak doors.

I glanced at the polished carving, so well cared for and meticulously maintained despite its age. Mangled bodies and proud warriors depicted the aftermath of a bloody battle. One that very few shifters walked away from alive.

They'd tried to rebel against the fae, seeking their own kingdom. But the shifters had their uses and the Fae King wanted them under his domain.

Creatures like me and my kind were unleashed, ending the lives of thousands of shifters in seconds. Now, they were rare. Few shifters without Fae blood survived. And the Fae King kept most of them as his guard. Even I kept Vanth by my side. They were too few to rebel again. If they did, it would mean the end of their lines.

I shoved the memory aside, my jaw tight. I was gifted

at killing, but I didn't have to make it hurt. That day, I'd been ordered to inflict as much pain as possible. The nightmares still plagued me all this time later. The difference was that I no longer felt guilt.

I'd told Ara it got easier to forget those you'd killed. It wasn't true. I'd lost track of how many lives I'd ended, but I used to count. It wasn't that it got easier, you just stopped feeling anything. There just came a point where you shut it all down. Closed off that part of you that cared about anyone or anything. That was the only way to move forward.

Imagine my surprise when I met Ara and felt something besides numb indifference for the first time in centuries. Gritting my teeth, I pushed her aside again. It was going to be harder than I realized to keep her from invading my thoughts.

My footsteps were silent across the black marble floor, my gaze already locked on the king himself. His amber eyes watched my every move. Jaw set, expression impassive, he sat in his gold throne, his long fingers gripping the armrest.

As I neared the dais, he stood, his sweeping crimson robes brushing over the floor as he climbed down to meet me. With his unblemished golden-brown, sun kissed skin and thick dark hair, he didn't look a day over forty, but he'd been alive for centuries.

He'd long ago perfected that ability to shut it all down. To cut off his emotions and feel nothing but whatever high he was chasing for his own selfish needs.

He was every bit the monster they said he was.

But then again, so was I.

"You wanted to see me?" I drawled.

"You went with the delegation to Konos. I told you that was not your place."

"Our spies were right, though. Had I not gone, you'd have a dead delegation and no tributes," I said.

He clasped his hands, his expression becoming the picture of calm. I knew that tell all too well.

"You wanted them to break the treaty." I suspected he was up to something when he suddenly changed the number of tributes back to one-hundred. We had never enforced that number, and fourteen had always been enough to satisfy the beast.

"I want to hear it from you. I want to hear how you killed hundreds of humans and revealed their king's secret. Tell me, Ryvin. Tell me how it ends up that you destroy our one link to Athos. Their king was easy to control. He would bend to anything we asked," he seethed. "The new ruler better be compliant."

"When were you going to tell me he wasn't human?" I countered.

"You didn't need to know," he snapped.

"You put that whole city in danger with a turned vampire at the helm," I pointed out. It was amazing there weren't dozens of the creatures feeding on their population. The fact that the king was able to kill his food and hadn't turned any was the only thing keeping the entire city from becoming just like Thebes. What had once been a glorious, advanced civilization of thriving humans was now a desolate wasteland of vampires desperate for food.

"If they fall, they fall. I'd like to see their blood and

salt save them when they're eating each other." A wicked grin spread on his lips. He'd like nothing more than to see all the humans gone.

If it weren't a requirement to appease the monster in the labyrinth, the humans would all be dead.

"Besides, if you were so concerned about keeping those flesh bags alive, you wouldn't have slaughtered most of them when they attacked you. A little extreme, even for you." His brows lifted, an unasked question lurking in that stare.

I knew he wanted me to tell him why I'd snapped. Why I unleashed everything I had. My magic was usually restrained, and I hadn't used that kind of power since the revolt. Few who lived knew what I was truly capable of.

He wouldn't get an explanation. Because I knew better. I knew I shouldn't have exposed myself that way. But I'd let her get to me. Ara had been in danger and I'd let my anger and my desire to protect her cloud everything else.

"If I allowed them to violate the treaty, we'd be obligated to go to war," I said simply.

"War has already started. The dragons are on their way to Athos."

I straightened. The dragons had always worked to keep out of all of this. They wanted nothing to do with the humans who'd spent centuries hunting them for sport. The wall kept the humans out and only those dragons with a death wish or a fascination with their bloody past visited the site. It kept the humans feeling threatened and resulted in the occasional dead dragon, but it didn't allow for any kind of alliance. How could this have happened?

"You didn't know?" He dropped his hands to his side. "You're slipping, Ryvin."

He walked toward the door where another pair of guards were standing. Both fae males wearing the crimson tunics of Konos. A color I was forbidden to wear due to who my mother was.

"Bring her in," the king ordered.

My heart kicked up, and my pulse raced. He couldn't know already, could he?

The doors swung open, and a pair of guards walked in, my sister Laera between them. I swallowed hard as relief washed over me, quickly replaced by guilt. The fact that my first thoughts had gone to Ara reminded me how dangerous she was. And how much risk I was putting her in by simply letting her into my mind.

"Nice to see you back where you belong, brother," Laera sneered.

She walked into the room, her steps elegant and graceful. She practically floated across the marble floor, her red dress skimming the ground like a pool of blood in her wake. Fitting.

Unlike me, she was permitted the color of Konos. Just like me, she was illegitimate, but her mother was fae. Mine was not.

Laera flipped her silver hair over her shoulder and set her violet eyes on me. She was every bit her mother's daughter. If the Court of Vipers still stood, Laera would inherit the crown. But it, too, had fallen, just as every other house and court had come under the control of the Fae King.

"My contacts tell me you got to know the king's household well while you were away. Servants, nobles, and even one of the princesses." She was the embodiment of everything her court was known for. Spies, lies, and deceit.

While she could live in the shadows, I could wield them, but my power was death itself. My job came after she'd exhausted all she could doing hers.

Our father had created a perfect set with us: spy and assassin.

"No wonder you were too busy to notice that they were preparing for the dragon delegation to arrive." She stopped right in front of me, her smile mocking. "So many humans to bed."

"You do your job, I'll do mine."

She chuckled. "So grumpy. Human girls didn't do it for you, did they? Yasmin's been waiting for you, why don't you go pay her a visit after this so we can all move on from your gloomy expression."

"My sex life is not your concern," I replied.

"Enough," the king called. "The dragons will reach Athos soon, and we must be prepared. I'll need both of you working together so we can put a swift end to the war ahead."

"I've already sent my best spies to watch the delegation from Drakous. We'll know the second they arrive at Athos. And our man on the inside will get what we need from the palace."

"Good." The king turned to me. "You will prepare

your men for battle. We have a chance to weaken the dragons enough to claim their city for our own. They're the final holdout, but the time has come for us to bring them under our control."

"We can't hold Drakous," I replied. "We failed last time you tried that."

"That was before." He smirked, and I gritted my teeth, resisting the urge to throttle him. Before. Before he'd stolen Nyx's magic, making him into the monster he was today.

"And what of the gift Ryvin brought back with him?" Laera asked, a sadistic smile on her lips. "Will she be the monster's meal today?"

Of course she already knew Ara was here. I wondered which of the sailors on the ship had been in her employ.

"What gift?" The king looked intrigued.

"One of the princesses from Athos," I replied flatly, careful to keep any emotion out of my tone. I couldn't allow any feelings in or Laera would pick up on them. She always did. "The dead king's favorite. A reminder of what happens to those who disobey."

The king grinned. "And here I thought you were losing your touch. She could be useful as a bargaining chip in the war ahead."

"Or we could toss her to the beast now," Laera suggested. "Send them back her head as a warning."

It was taking everything I had to keep my emotions neutral. "While watching her scream as she's eaten would be helpful to keep the other tributes in line, she could be worth keeping alive for a while. The new queen does care for her. We could exploit that if needed."

"Killing her might be enough to remind their new ruler about the power we hold over Athos," the king said. "Do what needs to be done, Ryvin."

"Send Laera, she enjoys watching the carnage." I waved my hand dismissively.

"No. You insisted on being part of the Choosing so you will see this through. Let the princess from Athos see what happens to those who cross us." The king turned, walking away from me before he even finished speaking.

I balled my hands into fists, tamping down the rising shadows. It was getting harder to hide how I felt about the king, but I wasn't about to lose my temper today. "Of course, your highness."

6

Ara

A HUGE CIRCULAR coliseum appeared like a stone giant at the end of town. If there was sunshine, it would cast most of the homes in shadows. Instead, it loomed over the city as ominous as the ever-present storm clouds.

"They're taking us there, aren't they?" someone asked.

"They're going to kill us all for sport," another said.

My stomach was in knots. I had no idea what they were going to do with us, but my palms grew sweaty in anticipation. It couldn't be over yet. It couldn't end like this. We needed more time. I needed time to get the tributes out, or at least make the king hurt.

What if Vanth had been lying to me? What if I could kill the king if I could just get close enough? It wasn't like anyone from Konos had ever been honest with me.

It wasn't like anyone in my entire life had ever been honest with me.

The thought made my chest ache as memories of home raced through my mind. I already missed my sisters so much it hurt. Whatever I was about to face, it would be worth it if my sisters were safe. Lagina was smart. She'd figure out how to fix things. And Sophia might have a long life ahead of her because I was here instead of her.

The tributes around me were making panicked sounds and whispered in desperate conversations. I was too focused on watching the coliseum grow larger as we approached to make out their words, but it was clear we were all worried this would be the last thing we ever saw.

An arched entry was guarded by several males in crimson Konos tunics. They stepped aside as the cart neared. I looked at them as we passed, hoping to find any signs of what we were about to find. They wore bored expressions, revealing nothing.

As soon as our cart passed through the archway, an eruption of applause sounded and my chest tightened with anxiety. Thousands were staring down at us from the stands surrounding us, their cheers deafening.

I tore my gaze away from the crowd, my heart racing as I scanned the circular ground. There was no indication of what was coming. From every direction, all I could see was dirt. No weapons or cages or creatures.

There were other archways to enter, though. And all of them were covered by closed gates.

I swallowed hard, my hands tightening into fists. "Whatever comes, we need to work together." I looked at the tributes around me. "Okay? We're stronger together."

"What would you know about that, Princess?" One of

the men sneered. "If they asked me to slit your throat to save my own, all I'd need is a weapon. Where were you when they were selecting us from the slums?"

"I'm here now." I glared at him. "And I'm telling you, if we are divided, we're all going to die."

"Then I'll go down with your blood on my hands." He grinned, showing a toothless smile.

None of the other tributes said a word. I clenched my jaw, then looked back just as the second cart was rolling through the gate. My eyes found Belan's. He nodded as if understanding what I'd been trying to say here. We had to fight back, but we were nothing compared to the creatures who called Konos home.

The memory of Ryvin leveling the battlefield flashed before me, and I shivered. They had so much more power than us. If they sent someone like him, we had no chance.

My blood ran cold.

What if they sent him? What if I had to watch him as he killed us all? What if that's what he was warning me against?

The other cart rolled to a stop next to us and I heard the metallic sound of a gate slamming closed. My pulse raced. We were locked in here.

The man driving our cart climbed down and threw a dirty look at us before walking toward the center of the ring. The other driver followed him, then they both dropped to a knee.

I scanned the crowd, looking for the king's box, and found an empty section of seats complete with a pair of thrones. Trumpets sounded, and the crowd roared even louder, making me wince.

A figure emerged, moving toward the thrones with a familiar steady gait. He was clothed in black leather armor, his dark hair windblown and wild.

If there was any more of my heart to break, it might have right there. He'd told me he was important, but let me believe he didn't have the kind of power to make changes with the Choosing. He'd reduced the number to fourteen, but he was still here, in the Royal family's box, staring down at us tributes as if he held our lives in his hands.

His eyes found mine, and all the air left my lungs. I felt like I was submerged underwater, helpless to tear myself from him even as I was being pulled deeper under.

Finally, he looked away and I sucked in a breath, resisting the rising betrayal that was burning my insides. I had done so much I shouldn't have with him. I wanted to blame him, but I'd let him. I could have walked away. I should have walked away. Instead, I continued for more like a woman starved.

I studied my feet, noting the layer of dust and dirt that coated the exposed skin. Anything was better than seeing him. If I was about to die, I didn't want him to be my last view.

The trumpets stopped and the screaming of the crowd dwindled until it was eerily silent. My fingernails bit into my palms and I forced myself to look at him again. I hated the little flutters that rose in my chest when I saw him, even as I was fighting to hate him.

Maybe it was better if this was the end. How was I supposed to live with myself after all I'd done?

"People of Konos, please welcome our new tributes from Athos," Ryvin's voice boomed.

The crowd cheered again and an icy chill ran down my spine. Why were they so excited to see us? What were they waiting for?

Ryvin lifted his hands, and the noise died down. "As is our custom, we will give one tribute the chance at freedom before we take them to their new home."

I straightened, then glanced around at my fellow tributes. Everyone stood tense and focused, none of them breathed.

If there was a chance of getting out of here, I could go back to Athos and make sure Sophia was safe. I could help Lagina with anything she needed. I could find a way to help with the dragons when they arrived. Maybe end the Choosing once and for all.

But I'd be abandoning all the tributes here.

Not that any of them wanted me here.

I glanced toward the other cart, where Belan's gaze was fixed on Ryvin with an intensity I'd rarely seen from such a young guard.

Grinding and clanking echoed, and the crowd roared. My heart thundered as I watched a slice in the ground in front of us begin to expand. It was a trapdoor, widening by the second.

The smell of death and decay floated from the earth, the tributes around me gagging and covering their mouths. I stopped breathing through my nose and swallowed down the rising bile.

I knew in my bones what that hole led to. The stories were told to all the children in Athos. Sometimes even used as warnings to teach us to behave. If we didn't, the beast from Konos's labyrinth would peel our flesh and drink our blood and chew on our bones until nothing was left.

Every hair on my body stood on edge.

It wasn't a myth. None of it was a myth.

"In the center of the labyrinth below, you'll find a portal that will take you anywhere you wish to go. Back to Athos, off for adventure in Drakous, even travel to the other continents if you wish. Simply reach the portal, speak your destination, and you'll be whisked away," Ryvin drawled, his tone bored with a malicious edge. It was a mocking kind of tone I'd never heard him use.

I glared at him. So this was who he truly was. Back home with his own people, he could let down his guard and finally show me who he was.

"This is your only chance to leave Konos. If you choose to stay, you'll be our guests for the rest of your short human lives. You will be fed and cared for, but you will remain here until your time comes to an end." Ryvin looked past me as if he was avoiding me; his attention turned to the other cart of tributes. "Any takers?"

It was a trick. It had to be. There was no way any of us would survive.

"Maybe we should try it," someone said.

"Don't listen to him, it's a trap," I said. "There's no way we'll survive whatever is down there."

"If you haven't noticed, we're not likely to survive anything that happens here," someone hissed.

"Speak up. Whoever asks first gets this chance. Only one of you," Ryvin called.

"Don't do it," I begged. "Don't."

I turned to the other cart and shouted, "It's a trick!"

Belan caught my eye, his jaw set, his expression intense. I could tell that he thought the same way, but it looked like he was fighting himself to keep from volunteering.

"Fuck this," the man with no shoes said. The whole cart rocked as he stood. "I'm not going to sit here with the rest of you on this gods-forsaken island."

"They're not going to let us out of here alive," I hissed. "You do realize they gathered here for a show."

"Hey! I'll do it. I want out of here." The barefoot man walked toward the back of the cage and a guard I hadn't noticed opened it for him.

"Don't," I tried again. "Don't be an idiot. You're going to end up dead."

"We're all dead already, Princess." He leaped from the cart, then sauntered toward the gaping hole, stopping before he reached it. "What's the catch?" He called up to Ryvin. "What's down there?"

Ryvin's lips curved into a cruel smile. "I can't go ruining all the fun."

"So you expect me to jump into a pit to face an unknown threat for a chance at escape?" The man rested his hands on his hips.

"Just get back in the cart, you idiot," I called.

For just the slightest second, I thought I saw Ryvin look my way, but then his attention was back on the man. "You won't be unarmed."

A pair of guards walked past our cart and stopped in

front of the man. Each held two weapons. A sword, a dagger, a mace, and an ax.

"Choose one," Ryvin said.

The man grabbed the sword. "The portal is at the center of the maze?"

Ryvin nodded.

The man walked to the edge of the hole and looked down. "How deep is it?"

"Last chance," Ryvin warned.

The ground shook, and the doors began to move, the gaping space growing narrower. The crowd roared, then started to chant, urging him to jump.

Jump. Jump. Jump.

The hole was quickly closing, and I gripped the railing so tight my knuckles went white. "Get back in the cart."

"Make your choice," Ryvin declared. The man's face was red and slick with sweat. He looked around frantically, glancing from Ryvin to the tributes in the carts, then around at the crowd before turning to the hole again.

His hand shook, and he took a step back. He had to get back in the cart. He had to walk away. There was no way he'd defeat the monster.

The man's whole body tensed, then he let out a cry as he raced toward the sliver of blackness leading to the pit below.

He leaped, disappearing into nothing right before the doors slammed together, sealing him below the surface.

The audience went wild, their cries drowning out all thoughts, all other sounds.

Suddenly, our cart moved, and I realized the driver was taking us out of the ring. He was shouting something, but I couldn't hear him over the roar of the crowd. The other tributes opened their mouths to speak, but all communication was swallowed by the unrelenting roar of the thousands of people around us.

We were dragged out of the carts before the gate and roughly shoved into an enclosed box of four rows of seating. Before I could even figure out if this was something we could escape from, the ground shook again.

Bracing myself on the railing in front of me, I watched in horror as the entire floor of the colosseum split in two and began to recede, revealing a lower level below the ground.

Icy dread spread through my body as I found myself staring in horror at the labyrinth we'd all heard about. Twisting paths of black stone and crumbling earth, mostly leading to dead ends. But there, in the center, was a blue glow. It had to be the promised portal.

"It's real," the woman next to me whispered.

"He's all talk," a male voice said quietly in my ear. "He'll never survive."

I glanced over to see Belan. "Was he a guard at the palace?"

He shook his head. "No, but I've seen him brawl. If he can't fight dirty, he won't win."

"I have a feeling the only way out of this place is fighting dirty," I said.

"You're probably right. But the problem is if everyone fights dirty, it'll mean the last man standing is the best fighter. That's not Clayton."

I swallowed hard and scanned the maze, searching for him. I found him at the end of the maze, as if they'd magically placed him at the start. One hand gripped the hilt of the sword, the other reached out, brushing through the air as if he was unable to see.

That was how the stories went. Absolute darkness. We could see him, but he appeared to be blinded. Was that how they achieved the dark? Was he ever going to see again? Or was it magic closing off the dim light of the shrouded sun?

Clayton was a brute and had no problem spitting venom at me, but he was from Athos. I didn't want anything to happen to him. "What if he did it? What if he made it?"

"Wouldn't that be something," Belan whispered.

7

Ara

Gripping the rail in front of me, I watched wide-eyed as Clayton navigated the labyrinth. From the way he wildly reached ahead of him and shuffled along, we could tell that he couldn't see anything around him.

"Do you think they blinded him? Can he even hear us?" Belan asked.

"I'm not sure." I looked around at the crowd and noted their wild cheers. They were screaming and chanting and enjoying every moment of this lost human creeping through the tunnels.

I turned back to Belan. "Maybe it's magic? Maybe it's sealed off somehow."

The cheers died down to a general chatter as Clayton continued to explore his surroundings. He'd walk until he reached a wall, then turn, moving forward slowly until he reached another. He'd hardly progressed at all from his starting point.

"If he can't see, he won't know where the portal is." I looked at the glowing light in the center of the maze. For all of us, it was a beacon of light, an obvious destination. But if he couldn't see anything, he wouldn't even know if he arrived where he was supposed to go. Would it come into focus for him as he got closer?

Clayton lowered his blade, letting it drag on the dirt alongside him as he walked. He was already tired from his progress, or he'd decided there weren't any immediate threats.

"Pick up your weapon," I called. "Don't drop your guard." I was nearly certain he couldn't hear me, but my insides were twisting with anxiety just watching him lower his guard as he continued forward.

"He's going in the right direction," someone said hopefully.

Indeed, he was making progress toward the center of the maze. A momentary flicker of hope warmed my chest. What if the creature who was supposed to dwell within the labyrinth wasn't there for some reason? What if it was sleeping or simply not hungry?

I scanned the lines of the maze, searching for any signs of movement or anything that looked like it might house something living. No matter how many times I visually traced the paths, the only living thing I saw was the human man making his way closer to the center.

I reached for Belan's hand and gripped it, squeezing. "What if he does it? What if he makes it through?"

The guard by my side didn't respond, but I could practically feel the tension radiating from him. From all of us from Athos sitting on the enclosed benches.

Suddenly, the crowd erupted. A wild roar of approval surrounded us and I released Belan's hand and jumped to my feet, leaning over the railing to get a better look at what had caused such a reaction.

Movement on the opposite side of the labyrinth.

Something massive that nearly blended in with the dark earth around it. When it stilled, it was so perfectly matched to its surroundings that I couldn't find it. Then it moved again, and I began to make out its shapes.

The creature was massive. Easily twice Clayton's size. It walked like a man, with large fur-covered legs and a wide, muscular torso. Furry arms swung back and forth as it lumbered forward, moving toward the unsuspecting human. Claws glinted in the faint light.

Then the monster turned down a path, heading toward us, and I got a look at its face. The head was that of a bull, massive and snarling with gold eyes that glowed like stars in the sky.

Shivers ran down my spine.

This was the creature of legend. The monster who would eat through bone and enjoy devouring human flesh. The creature that was the most feared on the entire island of Konos.

"He has no idea what he's walking toward," Belan said quietly.

I swallowed hard as I turned my attention back to the unsuspecting human. Clayton's sword was still loose by his side and he had picked up his pace a bit, but his steps didn't seem worried. It was as if he'd accepted the maze as the threat. He dragged his fingers alongside him, shifting his weight and turning as soon as he approached a dead end. If he had any concerns about a monster hunting him, he wasn't showing it.

But the monster was on his way, navigating the maze as if he knew every twist and turn by heart. He probably did.

"I can't watch this," someone behind me said, her words coming out in-between heavy pants.

"Turn around!" someone else screamed.

The monster was getting closer, and Clayton's choices seemed to be taking him right to him.

I couldn't hear the tributes anymore. The crowd's roar was too intense, and all conversation was swallowed by the cacophony.

Belan's hand clasped mine, and we squeezed each other tightly as we watched and waited. Each step brought Clayton closer to the monster's path. Even if he could somehow reach the center to get to the portal, there was no way he'd survive an interaction with that beast. It didn't matter if he was blind in the labyrinth, it didn't matter how good his weapon was. He'd need a whole crew of fighters to have a chance.

It was getting harder to breathe. The crowd was insane, their cheers escalating to levels I didn't think possible. I tore myself from the inevitable slaughter to look around. The stands were full of people who looked almost human at first glance. But if I looked a little more,

I could see the pointed ears, the horns and antlers, the variety of skin and hair colors that far exceeded any I'd seen in Athos. Blue, green, violet, gray, orange... the colors would be beautiful if I didn't know how dangerous each of them was.

Then I found myself looking for Ryvin. He was slouched in a massive chair. A throne that was probably reserved for the king when he attended the spectacles. His body was relaxed, his expression bored. He'd seen this a hundred times. Maybe even more. This was just how things were for him.

He didn't care if another human died, and why would he?

A collective gasp, then a change in the cheering sent me back to the maze just in time to see Clayton realize he wasn't alone.

Belan shouted something in my ear, but the noise was so intense I couldn't tell what he said. I glanced at him, but when I caught his eyes widen in horror, I went back to watching the labyrinth.

Clayton had his blade raised, swinging with an accuracy that told me he could probably see at least a little bit. The creature swiped at him, making Clayton dodge and move, avoiding the first few blows. The human tried to attack, lunging and swinging, but never striking the monster. The creature of the maze was always one step ahead of him, able to twist or move just enough to avoid each strike.

With each attempt to attack, Clayton was getting slower. He always missed, then was knocked back with a shove or swat by the massive hands of the monster. Back and forth, attack and miss. Then a shove.

From our vantage point, I could tell the creature was playing with him. Like a cat batting around a dying mouse before going in for the kill. He could end this any time he wanted, but he was giving the audience a show.

Bile crawled up my throat.

How was this entertaining? Clayton didn't stand a chance. He'd not landed even one blow against the monster.

Suddenly, his sword sliced across the creature's midsection and it let out a bellow that could be heard over the crowd. My whole body tensed and shivers spread over my skin, leaving a trail of goosebumps. The sound was like the Underworld itself opening and releasing its most gruesome beast.

Perhaps that's where the creature had come from.

Chanting erupted around us, the crowd urging the beast to end the fight. Kill him. Kill him. Kill him.

I'd never felt so small my whole life. My breathing was shallow, and I retreated within myself, trying to shield my emotions from the inevitable. This was the punishment that awaited us humans. We were disposable. Helpless. Unable to defend ourselves even when provided with a weapon.

It was everything we'd been warned about coming true in front of our eyes.

The creature bellowed again, and the crowd responded with an answering cheer before returning to their chanting.

Belan's hand gripped mine tight, and I kept my gaze glued to the scene, unable to look away.

The beast grabbed Clayton and lifted him. The human swung wildly with his weapon, the monster leaning away from each strike effortlessly. Then it reached a massive hand out, still gripping the large man in his other hand, and yanked the sword away.

Clayton flailed, twisting and turning, his hands on the beast's, trying to break free of his grasp. The monster dropped him suddenly and before Clayton could scramble to his feet, the creature's huge hoofed foot slammed into the man's chest, pinning him in place.

My heart was in my stomach, my eyes wide, my fingers digging into Belan's hand. This was it. I could just barely make out the crimson around Clayton's lips, he was bleeding from his mouth, which meant his chest had probably been crushed under the monster's hoof.

The creature leaned down, and I stopped breathing. I couldn't hear the crowd anymore, only my own fear and anger like a roar in my ears. My blood was cold, my whole body tense. It was as if I could feel what was coming.

I glanced at Ryvin and took in his calm indifference as he watched the scene unfold. His eyes found mine and for a moment, we stared at each other, unblinking. There was no emotion in his expression. No sense of recognition, nothing left from the moments we'd shared in Athos. No remorse or concern for the atrocity happening before him.

He'd shut it all down. I don't know how I knew it, but I did. He'd turned it off. All his feelings, all his emotions.

It was easier that way, wasn't it? To feel nothing rather than feel everything.

I narrowed my eyes, throwing him the dirtiest look I could manage. Fine. Two of us could play that game. If he was going to shut it all down and be the villain he told me he wasn't, I could too.

If it meant keeping my cool enough to help the rest of my people avoid this fate, I could close it all off too. I could find a way to resist the fae. And then I would kill their king.

Ryvin returned his attention to the maze, and I took a deep breath to steady myself before doing the same. I would be just as closed off as him. If it meant finding a way to get off this island, I would do anything it took. I had to beat the fae at their own game.

When the monster tore Clayton's arms from his body, there was nothing left in me to respond. Icy numbness spread through me, my body practically shutting down to protect me from feeling. From reacting.

The beast lifted the torn arms in the air, hoisting them like some gruesome trophy. I released Belan's hand, letting the numbness spread, refusing to let it get to me. This was on purpose. They wanted us broken. They wanted us scared. If I let myself feel, I'd never resist. I'd let fear rule my decisions. I refused to bend to them.

Clayton was screaming even though we couldn't hear him. His head thrashed from side to side, blood pouring from the stumps where his arms once were.

The monster dropped the arms, then grabbed the still breathing man, lifted him in the air, then tore him in half effortlessly.

Someone behind me threw up, and I turned to watch Ryvin. He wasn't in the chair anymore. Balling my hands into fists, I made myself watch as the monster feasted on Clayton's remains.

They were going to pay for this. I would make sure the king suffered for what he'd done to my people.

8

Ara

Except for quiet sobbing, the tributes were silent as we were shoved back into our cages. The roar of the crowd continued as we rolled away, and I tried not to think about what they might be watching now.

"They won't let us leave," Belan said quietly. We'd managed to get into the same cage this time.

"No, they won't," I agreed. "But they haven't killed us yet. Now we need to figure out why."

"You think they have something worse in mind?" he asked.

"Worse than being ripped to pieces and eaten?" I lifted a brow.

"Why else would we still be here?" he asked.

I shook my head. "I'm not sure."

The other tributes in the cage with us didn't speak. All of them were pale, and some were shaking. One of the men had vomit drying on his tattered tunic and the woman sitting in the corner was pulling at her hair, grabbing chunks of it as she rocked back and forth.

Whatever they had in store for us, none of them were going to last long. I looked at Belan as Vanth's warning came to mind. The wolf shifter hadn't given me any reason to doubt him, other than the fact that he was from Konos. I'd been betrayed by so many around me, but I had a feeling his warning about the king wasn't because he was trying to protect the king. He'd seen me fight and fail. My training was limited, and I knew I'd be no match against a centuries old fae.

"I'm not sure how we take out the king," I whispered.

"Don't give up, that's what they want from us," he said.

"That's not what I mean. Someone gave me a warning," I explained. "Told me he was impossible to kill."

Belan's expression darkened. "Your ambassador? He sat up there gloating while his monster tore one of us to pieces. You can't trust a word he says."

"Not him. One of the other guards. He said if the king could be killed, someone would have done it already."

Belan breathed deeply through his nose, his jaw set.

"You know it's true," I said. "If he had a weakness, some enemy would have exploited it. Nobody stays in power that long without amassing enemies."

"I won't be food for that creature," Belan said.

"I don't want any of us to be." I glanced around, making sure nobody was listening to us, then leaned closer. "If I can't find the king's weakness, we have to get our people off this island before something worse happens."

"How?" Belan asked.

"It's possible the fae will be distracted." I was angry at myself for not thinking of it sooner. If Lagina followed through with meeting the dragons, the war might come to us. Why bother with a small group of humans when there are greater threats? "My father was in talks regarding an alliance to take down the fae."

Belan's eyes widened. "The dragons?"

I nodded slowly. "It might be our best bet. If they do attack, we have to move fast. Get everyone out."

He grinned. "That's the first good news I've heard since they came for me."

"So you're in?" I asked.

"Of course I am. What do you need from me?" he asked.

I glanced around at the tributes around us. Nobody was listening to me. They were too wrapped up in their own thoughts. I had no idea what was in store for any of us, but I needed them to maintain hope. To fight for their survival long enough for us to return to Athos.

"I need you to befriend them." The other tributes wanted nothing to do with me. I was an outsider, I knew that. "Help keep up morale. Give them hope. Help them stay alive."

Belan's throat worked. "I was trained to fight, not comfort."

"I know. But it's our best chance." I offered a weak smile.

"What if they're driving us to our deaths right now?" he asked quietly.

"Then none of it matters. But I don't think that's the case. I think Clayton was a warning to keep us from doing anything they don't want us to do."

Belan's gaze was somewhere far away, beyond the bars of our cage. He was silent for several breaths, then he turned and nodded. "Alright. We run as soon as we can."

I squeezed his upper arm gently. "Thank you."

I was surprised that we were going away from the heart of the city. I thought we'd be tossed into a dungeon in the palace or somewhere close by. Instead, we were traveling over the stone road past shops and homes. Each passing moment was taking us farther into the outskirts until the road changed to dirt and buildings became sparse. I caught sight of farmland and sheep grazing. Groves of massive olive trees that made those we had on Athos look like shrubs. I caught the scent of citrus mingling with the ever-present salt of the sea.

Despite the lack of sun, there were things that grew here. I wondered if they have the same fruit we had on the mainland or if it was different given the magic held by those who lived here.

Finally, I saw more buildings ahead, but I realized as we approached, they were all abandoned. Crumbling and ancient, the structures looked like they had once belonged to a whole village. Now, they were left to the elements. Vines climbed some of the walls and creatures had built nests in the rubble. A temple stood at the heart of the buildings, a few lonely columns of mismatched marble chunks stood precariously in an incomplete circle.

I wondered what this place used to be or why it was left to rot. Why not clear it away or move new families in?

"Wonder if this was where the humans used to live," Belan said darkly.

I shivered. "Maybe. Whoever it was, they haven't been here a long while."

Once we emerged from the abandoned town, I could see a massive building in the distance. Lush lawns and gardens sprawled around it. Those strange transparent flowers were intermixed with deep red peonies. A stone walkway led to a grand entrance lined by columns that supported a balcony on the second floor. The white walls were bright and freshly painted, the blue roof an homage to Athos. It was the only blue roof I'd seen on any of the structures in Konos. Everything else was washed in red.

"That must be where they're taking us." I stood and gripped the bars, straining to get a better view. The house was massive, but isolated. Behind it I could make out more of those enormous olive trees, but no other signs of homes or buildings.

"Wonder why it's so far from the city." Belan got to his feet next to me, peering out between the bars.

"So they don't have to see us or mingle with us, hopefully," I replied.

"Maybe they'll just dump us here and then leave us alone," he said.

"I doubt we'll be that lucky."

"What is that?" One of the other tributes asked,

moving next to me. "You think they have dungeons in that house?"

"Maybe that's where they're going to cook us," a woman suggested.

"I don't think they'll bother with cooking us," someone else replied.

I glanced at the tributes in the cage with me. Color had returned to their faces, and they looked less numb than they had been. Using what I hoped was a confident tone, I faced them and said, "Whatever it is, we can handle it."

"Look what happened to Clayton," the man commented. "We can't handle that."

"Clayton was an idiot," Belan retorted. "He didn't have to volunteer. He did that to himself."

The cart stopped, and I stared at the massive building. It was almost as large as the palace I'd grown up in.

"Out," a gruff voice called.

I turned to see a guard opening our cage. The gate swung open with a creak and the guard stepped back. "Now."

Nobody moved. All the tributes were frozen where they stood. I glanced at Belan, then walked forward. "Where are we?"

"Tribute house," the guard said. "This is where you'll live while you're here."

"Does that mean there are past tributes in there?" I asked.

He laughed. "Oh, no. Only a few tributes ever see the end of the nine years. If you do, they'll have other plans for you."

I scowled at him and his easy dismissal of human lives. It was fine, though. I didn't plan on any of us being here that long. Lagina and I might not have seen eye-to-eye the last few years, but I knew if she had a chance to go up against Konos, she'd take it.

"Do you think they're going to kill us?" The brunette asked as they corralled us toward the massive house.

"Not right now," I assured her. "They'd have done it with the audience earlier. No point in killing us with nobody to watch."

Her face paled, and I realized my words weren't as comforting to her as they were to me. "It's going to be alright."

She didn't look like she believed me and I tried to think of something else to say, but we were nearly to the building. A sprawling portico wrapped around the structure, a set of double doors open at the center of the building, exposing the interior. I could see several figures waiting for us. They weren't dressed in the tunics I'd seen on the guards or any of the delegates from Konos.

As we neared, I realized they were all dressed in white peplos or tunics. Each of them wore a smile on their faces and waited patiently with their hands behind their backs. Their eyes were downcast and their postures were relaxed, the same way servants had held themselves at the palace in Athos.

Our group stepped into the massive portico, then filed into the foyer, our dirty sandals leaving a trail of dust on the pristine marble. The space was airy and open with a view of a courtyard just beyond a large sitting room. Twin staircases led to the second floor, one on each side of the sitting room.

"Welcome to the Tribute House," a woman with pale green skin and mossy hair said, spreading her arms wide as she spoke. "This is where you will reside from now on. Your home while you are our guests. Each of you will be assigned your own personal servant. They will help you prepare for the feast tonight and will provide you with anything you wish."

The tributes around me whispered and looked around, most of them seeming suspicious of this news. Why would Konos give us such luxury? What did they gain from it?

"Princess Ara?" A feminine voice called, and I turned to see a small woman with light brown hair and huge brown eyes. She had delicate features, her tiny, pointed nose and chin making her look even smaller than she was. Like the other gathered servants, she was dressed in a simple white peplos.

She curtseyed. "I'm Noria, and I will be taking care of you."

Part of me wanted to snap at her, but she didn't have anything to do with my being here, and I knew she had no say in the choices made by her king. The best thing I could do would be to befriend her. Servants heard everything. "Nice to meet you, Noria."

Out of the corner of my eye, I noticed the tributes being swept away, following their assigned servant up the stairs. I glanced around for Belan and caught his eye. He nodded once, then walked away, following the others up the stairs.

I turned, expecting to follow them, but Noria moved in front of me. "You will use the royal suite." She extended her arm, indicating a hallway near the stairs on the right.

"I don't need any special treatment." I was already struggling with some of the tributes seeing me as an enemy. It was going to be challenging enough as it was to get them to believe me when I tried to help them get away from here. I didn't need the fae setting me aside even more.

"The king insists," she said.

"What if I don't want to use the royal suite?" I asked.

Her eyes widened, then she blinked rapidly. "We don't disobey the king." She inclined her chin toward the hallway. "Please. They're expecting us."

"They?"

She took a step forward, then waved her hand, asking me again to follow. I didn't want to get her in trouble and I had a feeling there wasn't much I could do to change this. Reluctantly, I followed.

9

Ara

THE ROOMS WERE DRIPPING with luxury to the point where they made everything I'd grown up with seem lackluster. The walls were painted with stunning murals in bright reds and golds. The curtains were made of lightweight shimmery silk. The same fabric was used for the linens and pillows on the bed. Everything deep crimson and shining gold.

Glass spheres hung from the ceiling, flickering lights glowing from them. They didn't look like candles, but I wasn't sure what was making them glow. I wondered if it was magic. A shiver ran down my spine at that thought. This wasn't a normal palace, this was Konos. Even if Noria seemed nice and the room was beautiful, I couldn't drop my guard.

"Why do the royals have rooms here if this is where the tributes live?" I asked, as I followed Noria past two plush couches situated on either side of a massive fireplace. Carved wood around the hearth showed scenes of battle, complete with mangled bodies and severed limbs. My upper lip twitched, and I had to swallow back my disdain.

"It used to be the queen's palace," Noria explained. "Past kings and queens each held their own courts and had their own homes. They didn't live together."

We stepped into a bathing chamber, complete with large copper tub, marble counters with mirrors and gold sinks. Like the rest of the space, it was luxurious, and every feature was of the highest craftsmanship and most expensive materials.

"Does that mean the king and the queen are a love match?" It was the only reason I could think of that might have caused them to change their traditions.

"Oh, no." Noria started the water in the tub. "I think it's because our current queen used to be a queen in her own right before the Fae King claimed all the other courts."

My insides twisted as I watched the tub fill with water. "That's enough."

Noria's brow furrowed.

"I don't want the tub too deep." I walked over and shut the water off. "This is enough."

"You're filthy." Noria's eyes swept down, then back up, taking in the dirt and dust from my journey here.

The thought of even climbing into that tub was enough to make my skin crawl. "It'll be fine."

She nodded. "Would you like me to help you undress?"

"No, I'll do my own bath. You can go. I prefer to bathe alone," I said, hoping she couldn't see the shaking of my hands.

As soon as she left, I took a few steadying breaths, then faced the tub. There wasn't much water in there and I had to remind myself a few times that it wasn't deep enough for me to go under.

Carefully, I leaned over and touched the water. It was warm. Magically heated directly from the faucet the same way it did in Athos. While magic wasn't accepted in Athos, someone long ago had worked out a way to have it applied to our water systems. As far as I knew, it was the only way we used magic regularly in Athos. I wondered if the people who'd attacked the fae realized that was where their warm water came from in their homes.

There was something comforting about the fact that the water was heated the same way here as it was at home. Even though the idea of getting into a tub made my chest tight with anxiety, it was familiar. And as far as I knew, everything in Konos was already trying to kill me, so the chances of the bath being the cause were slim. At least that's what I tried to tell myself.

Gritting my teeth, I made myself undress and step into the shallow water. Once I was in, some of the anxiety eased. It was far too shallow for me to go under.

Quickly, I grabbed a bar of soap that had been left for me and got to work cleaning every inch of my skin.

No matter how much soap I used or how hard I scrubbed, I didn't feel clean. Bruises marred my wrists and several had bloomed along my ribcage. Based on how achy everything was as I moved, I knew there were more that I couldn't see.

Until this point, I hadn't allowed myself to feel anything. I'd been running on fear and anger and a need to survive. I hadn't even slept in over a day, yet I didn't feel tired. I couldn't relax enough to allow myself the luxury of sleep.

The water cooled quickly, and I was shivering as I rinsed the last of the soap bubbles away. After I dried off, I walked back into the bedroom.

Noria had added a vase of purple flowers on the small table in the corner. The lights glowing around the room were brighter than they'd been before, and the room almost seemed cheerful. Almost.

"Would you like me to do your hair?" Noria asked, her tone quiet but eager.

Nodding, I allowed her to help me into the peplos, then sat down on a stool in front of a small vanity. "Can you tell me anything about what I should expect tonight?"

She paused, her fingers stilling in the middle of the braid she was plaiting into my hair. "I've never been to any of the celebrations for the tributes."

"I'm sure you hear things. Know things. What will they do to us tonight? Will there be another monster?" I asked.

Her fingers moved again and she quickly worked her way down, tying off the end of my braid with a ribbon. She let out a long breath. "Not tonight. The creature needs to be fed at least one human every year. The rest of the year, they can feed it anyone who upsets the king."

"Why one human a year?" I asked.

"I've already said too much."

"Please. I could use some help. Anything." I found her eyes in the mirror and watched her pause her movements in my hair.

Her shoulders slumped. "That creature hasn't always been here. It was created as a curse. Tied to the king as punishment."

I straightened. "What do you mean tied to the king?" Was that the missing piece? The way to get to the Fae King?

"I'm not sure how the magic works," she said.

"What did he do? How is it punishment?" I couldn't see how it was negative for the king if he was simply feeding the monster. It didn't seem like it was harming him.

"I am not privy to all the details," she said, her posture stiffening.

"I didn't mean to make you uncomfortable," I said. "What can you tell me?"

She returned her attention to my hair, her fingers twisting the strings effortlessly. "It must eat at least one human every year or it will die."

"Only one?" Why take so many of us and why only every nine years if they needed one each year? Why not grab one human each year from Athos to appease the beast?

"It must be a volunteer," she said. "The human has to enter into the maze willingly."

My eyes widened. Ryvin had asked for volunteers. Clayton had jumped in on his own. Nobody made him.

"Why make us watch then?" There was no way another tribute would risk entering that maze now that they've seen what happened to Clayton.

"You'd be surprised what a person will do after years of living here," she replied darkly. "Each year, someone always volunteers. The king makes sure it happens."

"I don't understand. Nobody would do that after seeing what that creature is capable of." I shook my head, completely confused by what I was hearing. None of it made sense.

"The beast serves two purposes. It is a punishment for anyone who crosses the king, but it's also a ticket out of here. The portal at the center, it's real." She resumed her work.

"They count on desperation." I swallowed. "What exactly is it that they're going to do to us while we're here?"

She leaned closer, lowering her face so she could whisper. "They provide everything and anything your heart desires except your home. Luxury can only mask homesickness for so long. Humans don't belong here. They can feel it. There's this urge to flee that calls out in their very bones."

I could hear my heart pounding in my ears. She didn't say it outright, but I could catch what she wasn't saying. Humans don't belong here. "You know about me. About my father?"

"Word travels fast, Princess." She straightened, returning to her task.

"What exactly did you hear?" I asked.

She finished the braid, then removed her hands from

my head. "I heard what your father was, but you're not a vampire. You'd have gone through the cravings already if you were."

My brow furrowed as I considered her words. Perhaps I'd imagined that she's categorized me differently than the human tributes. If I wasn't part vampire, what else could I be? Maybe I was simply human. The thought should have been a comfort, but I felt oddly unsatisfied by the notion.

With practiced movements, she added color to my cheeks and kohl to my eyes. "You should stop worrying about things you can't control and focus on survival. If the king likes having you around, you could live a long, happy life here."

"I have no interest in spending the rest of my life with the Fae King," I replied.

She returned the makeup to a small drawer. "When I was young, The Prince of Vipers tried to kill the king's monster. He was certain the beast was somehow the key to taking down the king himself."

"Is it?" I straightened, feeling flutters of hope cautiously rise in my chest. Was the monster the answer I was looking for?

"We'll never know. The prince wasn't the first to try to slay the creature, but he got closer than anyone else ever had. We all thought he might actually do it. Nobody tried the things he tried. I remember watching him, holding my breath while he left that trail of thread behind him. Such an optimistic boy to think he would need that trail to find his way out. He really thought he could do it..." She sighed. "But even with help from the king's inner circle, it wasn't enough. The beast can't be slayed. The prince never stood a chance."

She took a deep breath, then closed her eyes for a moment as if recalling the memory. When she opened her eyes, she looked very far away. "The king destroyed their entire kingdom the next day, then he didn't stop until he'd taken control over every other Fae Court."

I let her words sink in, adding them to the minor knowledge I had about the Fae King. My whole life, he'd controlled all of the Fae, Vampires, and Shifters. He'd always been the one ruling over Konos and Telos. Only the dragon shifters were beyond his reach.

I'd never thought about how that came to be or the fact that those he ruled over might not want to be under his control.

"They resisted, didn't they?" I asked. "The other Fae Kingdoms and the shifters and vampires."

"The vampires never cared. They easily pledged their allegiance. The others..." she shook her head. "It was centuries of warfare. The bloodiest time in our history."

Somehow, knowing that the shifters and the other Fae Courts didn't want to be under the rule of the current king gave me hope. Did my father know this? Was that why he thought he'd have a chance to win with the dragons by our side? If the other courts could be convinced to help us, would we be able to finally defeat the king?

My stomach twisted. What if they didn't know this? I had to get out of here and get that information to Athos. It could be enough to change everything.

10

Ara

Noria led me to the courtyard at the center of the house. It was enclosed by two story colonnades, their Doric columns painted bright scarlet. Paper lanterns in jewel tones hung from strings across the open space, illuminating the evening with cheerful colors that reminded me of home.

It was achingly similar to how parties were set up in Athos. Like the party we'd held to welcome the delegation. An event that should have been treated as a time of mourning was transformed into a festive scene. As if we were happy to hand over our people to Konos.

Hadn't I done the same thing? That was the night when I'd met Ryvin and I'd handed over most of myself to him that evening, even if I didn't know it at the time.

Pushing the thought away, I scanned the courtyard from my space near the entrance. It wasn't completely like home. Much of it was different than the parties in the palace, but it held a familiar touch that I couldn't place. Something about it was almost comfortable.

Couches in jewel tones lined one side of the space while servants in various states of undress wandered between them, offering libations from gold trays.

Smoke wafted up from hookahs sitting on a few of the tables. A fountain stood in the center of the room, ruby liquid pouring from the trumpet shaped flowers circling the top into a pool that resembled blood. Servants brought gilded pitchers to the horrific centerpiece, filling them with the liquid before returning to their rounds.

Small tables in front of the couches held drinks and platters of sweets. Larger tables were set up along the back, as if ready for a banquet to be served on them, even though nobody was yet sitting on the cushions that took the place of chairs around each of them.

In the very back of the courtyard was a raised platform with a long table. Behind the table were several elaborately carved chairs.

Thrones.

My blood ran cold. I hadn't yet seen the Fae King, but it was a matter of time before he arrived. How would I feel when I finally set eyes on him? Was his appearance terrifying? Or would I find him so beautiful that I'd forget that I wanted to kill him?

I glanced around, searching for the tributes in the crowd. Were they all safe? Had we lost any others? So far, I'd seen two of our fourteen torn apart by monsters. And we hadn't even yet met the king himself.

I lingered in the entryway, taking in the scene and

looking for familiar faces. The dimly lit room was overflowing with people. Some of them clearly fae with their pointed ears. Beings that appeared human save for the antlers or tails they bore wandered between couches, taking sips from golden cups.

A small green creature with spindly fingers and long legs stopped in front of me, locking solid black eyes on me. It blinked, its eyelids moving vertically instead of horizontally. I swallowed, unsure of how to react. The creature took a sip from its cup while it regarded me, then continued on, stumbling as it walked.

Out of the corner of my eye, I caught movement and turned to see Belan walking toward me. My shoulders slumped in relief. At least he was alive. And he appeared well cared for. He wore a green tunic trimmed with a golden leaf pattern and his dark hair was clean and shining. There were no signs of injury or mistreatment that I could see.

I stepped forward to meet him. "Are you safe? They didn't hurt you, did they?"

He shook his head. "No. So far, everyone I've talked to is fine. I was worried when they took you somewhere else. They didn't do anything to you?"

"No." I lifted the skirt of my peplos. "Just dressed me up and sent me here."

A servant stopped in front of us, holding a platter filled with cups brimming with scarlet liquid. She was wearing a gold skirt that covered her hips. Across her chest was a pile of gold necklaces that covered most of her bare breasts. "Wine?"

"No, thank you," Belan said, moving slightly in front

of me to prevent me from taking a glass. He watched as the servant walked away, then turned to me. "The others started drinking it and they got very comfortable here very quickly."

"Fae wine." We'd all heard the stories, but I supposed the others figured there was nothing left to lose. They must not have cared if they slipped into complacent oblivion.

"Have you seen the king yet?" Belan asked.

"No."

"They say he'll be here tonight."

"Then we'll start learning everything we can about him," I replied. "Listen to gossip, especially from servants. We need anything we can find."

"I'm not sure he'll be our greatest concern when it comes to escape. Especially if you're correct about the distractions," Belan said.

"What do you mean?" I glanced around, half expecting to see guards charging us simply for having this conversation.

"Most of the tributes have never seen luxury like this before," he said. "They're not going to risk giving this up if it means they might die at sea."

"I know. But they'll tire of it, eventually. They'll get homesick." I recalled what Noria had told me. "They count on us wanting to go home so they can have volunteers for the maze."

Belan's brow furrowed.

"That's why they told us we could win our escape," I explained. "The monster needs a willing human."

Belan's face paled.

"We'll have to be ready as soon as the opportunity arises. You have to get them to trust you. They won't listen to me." I wanted to say more, but pounding sounded, echoing through the large room, drawing all eyes.

A procession of red clad drummers marched in through a side door. Their flowing crimson tunics were trimmed with fine gold thread and they wore black leather sandals that wrapped around strong bronze calves.

None of them had the pointed ears to designate them as fae and they all showed signs of age on their faces. A few of them even had gray streaks in their dark hair. I wondered if they were human. Past tributes who somehow survived, or some of those few humans who existed in the cities now dominated by monsters. The guards had told us that none of the past tributes lived long, but what if they had? Was that what we had to look forward to? The off chance that we'd make the fae happy enough that we could work for them for the rest of our lives?

The musicians formed a line along the back wall, continuing to play a lively, upbeat rhythm. They looked straight ahead, toward the crowd. None of them moved their gaze, continuing to stare blankly ahead as if watching something in the distance. I shivered. There was something unnerving about those expressions. They didn't have any spark. It was as if they were puppets, moving along to someone's orders without thought of their own.

Suddenly, the people lounging on couches began to rise. Then they lowered their heads. The room felt charged, the taste of an impending thunderstorm coated my tongue. It was as if pure power had entered the room, that increasingly familiar scent I'd caught a few times mingled with the incense and smoke of the hookahs.

A chill settled over the room as the drummers moved aside, allowing a new procession to enter through the doors. The hair on my arms stood on edge. Even Belan dropped his gaze, but I continued to stare defiantly as the Fae King walked into the room.

He was tall and handsome, with golden sun kissed skin and long midnight black hair tucked behind his pointed ears. Even from where I stood, I could make out his amber eyes and cold stare. His gaze skimmed over me, an amused smirk tugging on his lips before he continued forward toward a table at the back of the room. He was clothed in a red tunic of a deep rich fabric that shimmered when it caught the light, taking on an iridescent pearly sheen. The cuffs and hem were trimmed in gold that matched the gold of his sandals and the gold crown set atop his dark hair.

I stared at him, anger seething through me, my hands shaking with rage. This was the creature responsible for the near destruction of all humans. He was said to have more power than any being save the gods themselves. Yet, he continued to torment us by stealing my people away rather than do something good for the world. If he only needed one human a year, why go through all this?

I was supposed to fear him. And since leaving Athos, I'd felt so much hopelessness, so many thoughts of surrender, so much fear. Yet, looking at him now seemed to wash those feelings away. My purpose here was clear. My confidence restored. I would not go down easy.

The drummers were still playing, but their sound was lost on me as my vision tunneled in on my target. If he was the key to saving humanity, I would do what it took to get to him. I knew the stories. I knew how deadly he was. How powerful. But everyone had a weakness. It seemed his monster was his.

I wanted to end him.

I wanted to watch him suffer the way Clayton had suffered. If I didn't have the strength or power to make it happen alone, I would do everything I could to help Athos and the dragons defeat him.

The king moved with flawless grace, his smile cold and calculated as he blandly took in the gathered crowd. He was as handsome as the rumors said, but I only felt disgust while looking at him.

Movement caught the corner of my eye and I allowed myself to look away to see what had drawn my attention. Several figures were emerging through the same door the king had taken. First was a beautiful woman with silver hair and deep brown skin. Unlike the king, she wore a dark green peplos that made her look like a burst of life among the sea of crimson.

Her violet eyes scanned the room with sharp precision. When she found me, I caught a momentary glimpse of something that looked like amusement in her expression. There was nothing warm about that look. Despite the momentary smile, she was pure predator. I knew I'd be insane to cross her.

The gold crown on her head was in the shape of a

serpent, open in the middle with the tail on one end, the hissing mouth, complete with fangs on the other.

She might be more dangerous than the king himself.

Behind her, a younger woman entered. She was practically the mirror image to the older woman. Stunning silver hair, gorgeous deep brown skin, violet eyes that seemed to be able to see into your very soul. On her head was a circle of gold, a snake, smaller and less pronounced than that of her mother's, but a serpent crown just the same.

Her red peplos pooled around her feet, her movements carrying it across the floor like a puddle of blood. She didn't look at the crowd, instead keeping her gaze forward, her expression pure boredom. As if she'd done this a thousand times and hated every minute of it.

I couldn't help but wonder if it was the same expression I wore every time my father made me attend royal events I didn't want to go to. My chest tightened, and I shoved the pain of him away.

Then my eyes caught on the last figure and time stopped.

Ryvin strolled into the room as if the whole world revolved around him. My pulse raced, and I stopped breathing. He was clad in black from head to toe, the only color being the circle of gold on his head.

Ice ran through my veins, and all the air from the room was gone. My chest tightened and betrayal slammed into me like a punch.

I was frozen, completely stunned as the pieces began to fall into place. As he took his place next to the Fae King, his eyes found mine. There was no flicker of acknowledgement, no softness. Only the sharp, focused stare of a predator.

My shock melted into rage, hot and angry; my insides a mixture of fire and ice, seething and stunned all at once. Ryvin had lied to me.

He'd lied to all of us.

He wasn't just an ambassador.

Ryvin was the Prince.

"Did you know?" Belan whispered.

I shook my head as I balled my hands into fists so tight I could feel my fingernails biting into the skin. I welcomed the pain. "No."

"Now you know just how devious they are," he said.

All that time, even as I resisted him, I had still thought that maybe it was real between us. Even when I watched him casually allow a monster to devour one of us, I'd still resisted my feelings. I thought that maybe I was the asshole for pushing him away.

Turns out, all my warnings were justified. I'd been nothing more than a way for the Fae Prince to get what he needed to harm my people. He'd used me.

Nausea rolled through my insides when I realized I'd done the same to him. That was what we were. A pair of spies sent to seduce the other for our kingdoms. I'd fallen for it, just as he had. We'd both played the other. We were both guilty. I'd let my father use me as a pawn in his game. Had Ryvin done the same?

"Don't let your emotions cloud your goals, Princess," Belan said quietly.

"They won't." I let it all in then. All the anger I felt at my father's betrayal, all the rage I'd built up over the years of being treated as lesser, all the hate I felt for the way the fae used my people for their twisted harvest.

My vision blurred as the rage flooded in. I had turned off my emotions, tried to cut everything out. Now, I welcomed all the things I'd tried to send away. The darkness Ryvin had sensed.

I knew it had always been there, simmering below the surface, but I'd never let it out. I'd fought it, afraid of what it might mean if I were to release it.

"I'm done being afraid of the fae." I leaned into the anger and betrayal. It made it easier to forget the way I felt around him. Easier to focus on finding a way to save my people.

That was all that mattered right now. I had to force my emotions away. I wanted to let the anger drive me, but I couldn't risk losing control. I let it simmer just below the surface, just out of reach. Enough to remind me of what had been done to me, but not enough to make me act irrationally.

I could do this. I could help my people and get us home. Nothing between Ryvin and I mattered. As soon as I could, I'd be away from this island and I'd never see him again.

11

Ara

THE DRUMMING CEASED and the room was deathly quiet. Nobody breathed. All the heads around me were still bowed, even the tributes from Athos were showing respect to the Fae King. Their enemy. My enemy.

The King found me again, his feline smile dared me to speak. I knew better than to push things that far. At least not yet.

He took a step forward and began to speak, "Tributes of Athos. You are among the rare few humans who will get to experience the luxurious life of the Fae. Your sacrifice for your people to keep the peace between us is the most noble thing anyone can do. Your life here will help us all to remember about the commitment our two kingdoms made long ago to protect one another."

My jaw hurt from clenching my teeth. Needing a willing human every year was a terrible curse, but it didn't require all the fanfare and production that his every-nine-years Choosing demanded. I knew it was more than that. Requiring us to send our own kept us fearful of him. Kept us complacent. Learning that he had enough power to swallow all the other kingdoms and courts around him showed how strong he was. He didn't need the pageantry he held with Athos. It was probably because he enjoyed tormenting us. It made me hate him even more.

"On behalf of myself and my family, welcome to our kingdom. I look forward to getting to know each of you in the coming weeks." He smiled, a cold expression that didn't reach his eyes. "Now, please, sit, enjoy yourselves. This celebration is for you."

String instruments began to play from somewhere behind me and it was as if the room let out a collective breath. People returned to their distractions. Some of them took seats at the long tables, which were now piled high with delicacies, while others remained on the couches, too dazed on Fae wine to even notice what was happening.

It was right back to the way things had been when I arrived. Human and Fae guests alike were in their own worlds, blindly enjoying the luxuries around them without care. It was familiar. Something even I'd participated in. How often had I shut everything else out so I could simply exist without the weight of expectation?

Eating, drinking, touching... it was as if I'd walked right into the Fae version of the Black Opal. It would be so easy to sip the wine and let myself forget Athos and my father and the danger my sisters were in. The danger I was in.

I kept my eyes on the king, on Ryvin, on the whole royal family. They sat in ornate chairs and servants brought food and drink directly to them. After a moment, they were eating and drinking and speaking to various people who freely approached their table.

Except for Ryvin.

He didn't touch his food or his cup. He simply stared at me, his expression blank. I held his gaze, willing him to feel the anger burning within me. I was never going to forgive him for his deception.

The younger woman sitting next to him, his sister presumably, tugged on his sleeve and he finally turned his attention toward her, breaking his hold on me.

"Excuse me, Princess Ara?" A red-clad Konos guard was standing next to me. I'd been so focused on Ryvin I hadn't even noticed his approach. I looked over at him, my brows lifting in silent question.

"I was asked to find you. The king requests your presence."

I glanced at Belan. He nodded once, and an understanding seemed to pass between us. At least I knew there was someone here who had my back, but it was probably best for him to stay away from me if he was to earn the other tribute's trust. "Watch out for the others. Say what you need to about me to get them on your side."

He nodded. "Good luck."

I took a step toward the guard. "After you."

My heart raced and my stomach knotted as I approached the table where the royal family waited. Just as I arrived in front of the king, Ryvin stood, then left without a word. Coward.

"Princess Ara, how wonderful to meet you," the Fae King drawled.

My eyes snapped to him, hoping he hadn't noticed the glare I'd shot his son at his departure. I fixed a smile on my face. "It's my honor, your highness." I dipped into a small curtsy, hating myself for even that little show of respect.

"You are a bit of an anomaly, my dear," he said. "We've never had someone ask to come to Konos as a tribute."

Chin held high, I waited, knowing there was nothing I could say that would help me. He already knew the story, I was certain. There was no sense in replaying it in front of his court.

"Get her a chair. She's a princess, she should be at our table." The king waved his hand toward his queen and princess, indicating he wanted me to join them at his left.

"You are too kind, your highness," I replied, knowing that Ophelia would be proud of how I was speaking to him. Proud of how I played the part like a practiced courtesan.

Servants quickly added a chair next to the princess and after a brief inclination of my head toward the king, I calmly walked to my new place.

I wondered if perhaps I could befriend the princess. Get her to share information with me about her father and their court. Maybe I wouldn't have to go through the king himself.

A servant held the chair out for me and I sat, allowing them to push me closer to the table. A shining gold plate was set in front of me, then several servants came by, loading fruit and bread and meat onto the plate. Someone set a cup in front of me and filled it with fae wine. I could smell the enticing scents of the wine and the food and my mouth watered. I couldn't remember the last time I ate.

Was the food safe to consume? I was going to be here a while, so I'd have to eat eventually. I knew the wine was too dangerous, at least that was Belan's speculation, and I had every reason to believe his guess was valid.

Something sharp poked my side, and I sucked in a breath before looking down to see a blade poised just below my ribs. Red painted fingernails gripped the handle. I looked up at the smiling princess, her violet eyes glinting with malice.

"This is your only warning, Princess of Athos. I have eyes everywhere and if you so much as breathe wrong, I'll know. That plotting you've been doing with your little friend over there?" She inclined her head, and I followed the movement. She was staring right at Belan. My stomach clenched.

She leaned closer to me, lowering her voice to a whisper, "It ends now. You're ours. Consider Konos your home until the gods take you to the Underworld."

My pulse raced, but I worked to keep my expression blank. Taking my eyes off Belan, I turned to face her. "You shouldn't underestimate me."

"Oh, I don't, which is why I'm warning you now."

"Why do you care, anyway?" I asked. "I can't imagine you spend this much time watching all the humans your father steals."

She smirked. "You're different. You've still got some fight in you. But don't worry, darling, it won't last long."

"You don't know anything about me," I hissed.

"I know everything about you. Your love of your sisters, your heartbreak at your father's betrayal, the way you killed your own best friend to save my brother..." she clicked her tongue. "Must have been something when you found out who he really was."

My jaw tensed and I balled my hands into fists. It was taking everything I had to resist attacking her right here. If she knew all this, Ryvin had told them. He'd betrayed me in every way. How could he tell them about David? Guilt squeezed around my chest. I'd made the wrong choice.

I'd made so many wrong choices.

She set the knife on the table between our plates, then took a long sip of her wine. "I know your kind, Princess. Loyal to a fault. Willing to sacrifice everything for those you love. And I'm going to give you some free advice: everyone will always let you down. There's no such thing as love. It's weakness. Your mind's way of leveling the playing field and distracting those who are too strong. That love you feel for others? It's your death sentence. Turn it off if you want to live."

"You're wrong," I said. "That might be how the fae see the world, but that's not how things work for us humans."

"Us?" She chuckled. "You sure you belong with them?"

I swallowed hard, a trickle of doubt making me feel itchy. After Noria's comments, I wasn't sure of much of anything anymore. I hated that she'd alluded to the fact that I somehow belonged in Konos. "I don't belong here, if that's what you're insinuating."

"No, I don't suppose you do," she agreed. "But I know you don't belong in Athos. Not after everything you've done."

"I did nothing wrong." I made mistakes, but they were all about trusting the wrong people. I wasn't about to do that again.

She shrugged, then sipped her wine again. She hadn't touched her food, but she shoved the plate forward and a servant grabbed it, carrying it away.

My fingers twitched, tempted to reach for the glass. There was a part of me that longed to shut it all out, to feel the numbness provided by wine. How often had I done that in Athos? Downed one drink after another until I didn't have to hate myself or let the uncomfortable questions surface? I'd been so good at shutting everything else out. I couldn't do that anymore. It was time to be stronger.

The princess set her glass down, then retrieved her knife, stashing it somewhere on her person. What I wouldn't give for a weapon of any kind. I glanced at the silverware next to my plate. Perhaps I could steal that from the table.

"Well, as lovely as speaking with you is, I have other things to do." She stood, then leaned down so her face was right next to my ear. I tensed. "It will upset my father if I kill you without making a spectacle out of it, but I won't hesitate to kill your friend. One wrong move, and his time is up. Perhaps it already is."

She stood, then looked down at me. "I can't guarantee

how long he has, but I can promise that I will end him the second you give me a reason. It's been a long time since I flayed a human alive. I rather miss the screaming."

"Well, it's nice to know all the rumors about your court are true," I said with mock politeness.

"You haven't even scratched the surface of what this court is like."

"Things must be quite boring around here if you're wasting those talents on someone like me."

She made an amused humming sound. "You might have anyone with a penis fooled, but as a female who is always underestimated, your games don't work on me. I know how dangerous you are and I'll be keeping an eye on you. There's nowhere on Konos you can go that I won't know every detail."

"You'll be wasting your time." I picked up a fig and popped the fruit into my mouth, deciding that eating was worth the risk. Especially since I was already being threatened. I had nothing to lose. Which meant I had every reason to follow through with my plans. The princess was right, very few would take me seriously. I might have a chance to find the king's weaknesses after all.

Chewing slowly, I met her stare, those strange, beautiful eyes boring into me as if trying to read my thoughts. I resisted the urge to shudder. What if she could read my thoughts? I was going to have to be extra careful around her.

I swallowed, then offered my sweetest smile. "I suppose, if you're going to watch me, I'll have to come up with some way to entertain you."

Her brow furrowed, then amusement made her lips quirk into a smile. "I look forward to it, Princess."

She walked away from the table, leaving me just two empty chairs away from the king. He didn't seem to notice that both his children had left. There was a constant stream of visitors coming to speak to him while he ate, keeping him distracted. I tried to listen to their conversations, but they were too quiet. Perhaps I could gain another dinner invitation and sit closer? The thought made my stomach twist into knots. I wasn't sure I wanted to sit closer to the Fae King, but I'd do whatever it took.

I made myself eat even though I wasn't feeling hungry. The tributes and the members of the court were oblivious to everything around them, lost in their own pleasure. At least most of them were.

Aside from Belan, I only counted two other tributes who were staying away from the fae and watching the debauchery around them with cautious expressions. I studied their features, knowing they were my best chance at allies out of the tributes who'd come with us from Athos.

Wine flowed freely and food was constantly provided on trays carried by servants. A quartet of musicians played lively tunes, creating a festive atmosphere among the colorful lights and lively guests.

I wanted to scream at the humans who'd so easily slipped into the diversion. I wanted to tell them to stop drinking the wine, to stop imbibing from the hookahs, to stop making out with various creatures.

Several women were naked, rolling around on the

couch with a pair of fae males. One of them had small antlers sprouting from his fair hair. The other's skin was tinted blue and his fingers were connected by webbing.

What were these males going to do with them once they'd had their fill? And would these women regret their actions once the wine wore off?

Someone came by and removed my plate. Then, with practiced efficiency, everything was removed from the table and then the table itself was carried away, leaving the king, queen, and me sitting on the ornate chairs staring at the party unfolding in front of us.

The king stood, and a hush fell over the room. "Please, no need for that. Enjoy yourselves. Stay as long as you like."

The music returned, and the people went right back to their various activities. The queen stood, so I followed suit, my years of etiquette practice kicking in without thinking.

"Princess Ara, please enjoy the party," the king said. "I hope we'll see each other again soon."

I forced myself to bob into a small curtsy. It was the only time he'd spoken to me since inviting me to join his family, and I wasn't sure what to make of it. Had he asked me up here so his daughter could threaten me?

She seemed like she might even be a greater threat to me than the king himself. He had no interest in me, whereas she'd marked me as a threat.

After the royals left, I weaved my way through the mass of people, most of them now free of all their clothing and rubbing against anyone they could find; fae or human. Twice I had to shove someone away for grabbing me as I passed.

Finally, I found my way to Belan. The relief in his expression was obvious as the two of us moved toward the wall and out of the way.

"What happened up there?" he whispered.

"They heard everything we were talking about," I warned. "We can't discuss anything."

He ran a hand through his hair, then glanced around as if looking for spies. It would be impossible to know who was reporting to the princess. It could even be one of the tributes. Everyone had a price. Some weren't even that high. I had a feeling many of the tributes would be chasing the feeling the fae wine was giving them. Maybe it wouldn't be as hard as I imagined to get a volunteer to leap into the labyrinth.

"So now what?" he asked.

"We play the game. We do our best to survive and I figure out how to make this happen," I said, hoping he could catch my unsaid meaning. "We both look for things that might help us, but we can't discuss it until we figure out a place that's safe to meet."

He nodded. "Okay." His eyes darted around the room. "It's not going to be easy to help any of them."

"We'll do the best we can," I said, following his line of sight. Most of the tributes looked so happy. They'd so quickly warmed up to being captives, but they'd miss home soon enough. Likely once the wine wore off, and they recalled what they'd done while under its influence.

Belan gave my hand a quick squeeze. "Be careful"

"I'll see you soon," I promised.

He walked away, disappearing into a mass of people who'd started dancing to the increasingly upbeat music from the band.

I scanned the room, trying to decide where I could go to blend in without being pawed at. Then I noticed one of the women who'd been hesitant to join the fray, fighting against a male who had his arms around her. She was struggling and pushing, but he was so much stronger than her.

Without thinking, I pushed my way toward her, just as the male pulled her through a door. I followed, spilling out into a hallway. He was fast, already hauling her through another door.

I raced toward them, desperate to help her, to save her the way Ryvin had once saved me. If he'd not shown up... I pushed the prickle of fear away, knowing that if I let myself go there, I wouldn't have the strength to help her.

Bursting through the door, I yelled, "Let her go!"

The male had his mouth on her neck and shoved her aside at my intrusion. Blood covered his lips and dripped down his chin. His fangs were covered in crimson and his eyes were wild. "You interrupted my meal."

The woman was crying, her hand pressed to the wound on her neck.

"She isn't on the menu," I hissed.

"Are you offering to take her place?" He strolled toward me, dragging his tongue over his fangs. "You smell amazing. Different."

What I wouldn't give for a weapon right now. Any kind of weapon.

12

Lagina

Torches flickered against the inky black. Stars dusted the sky, the moon a sliver above. This place had scared me when I was a child, but I wasn't a child anymore. In a week's time, I would officially be crowned as Queen of Athos. I didn't have room for fear.

The wide marble steps led toward the towering columns surrounding all four sides of the temple. I'd never been permitted inside the naos, the inner sanctum was reserved for priests and priestesses and the king himself.

But I didn't care what the gods said.

I needed answers.

Leaving my sandals at the top of the stairs, I entered the naos. The marble was cool under my bare feet. The floors gleaming and shining in the golden light from the burning vats of oil at each corner of the rectangular space.

A massive statue of Athena towered over me, her gold painted tunic shining against the white interior.

"You can't be here," a voice called.

I spun to face him. The coward who'd run the second my father's life was taken. "I'm the new Queen of Athos, as I'm sure you well know, considering you ran before my father's soul reached the Underworld."

"He won't make it to the Underworld. Not with that death. Not with what he was," Istvan said.

"You knew." It wasn't a question or even an accusation. It was acknowledgement that the priest had helped conspire with my father. "You helped him hide it."

Other than Mythiuss, the priest was the only other threat. My mother had been searching for information for days. It seemed my father had been very careful about sharing his condition. Istvan was the final loose end.

I hadn't practiced with a blade in years, but the feel for it came back far too naturally. As if it had been just last week I'd sparred with Ara rather than two long years. I'd humored her at first, training on occasion to spend time with her. But my schedule grew more complex and her abilities quickly surpassed mine.

My fingers rested on the hilt of the sword, the one still red with the old healer's blood. Using it against Mythiuss had broken something in me, but it also gave me confidence that I could be the queen my people needed.

I hated what I'd done. I hated what I had to do now, but my sisters were in danger. The entire kingdom was in danger.

The shame of Mythiuss's death weighed heavy on my heart, but I knew he'd have brought nothing but danger to my family. I'd already lost too much in the aftermath of Konos's visit. I refused to lose more.

I pulled my weapon from its sheath. I would not allow these men to rally the people of Athos against me and my sisters. I would not allow Ara's sacrifice to be in vain.

The priest took a step back. "You can't do that. Athena will never forgive you."

I glanced toward the goddess, then looked back at the priest. "Athena will understand."

"I'm on your side," the priest sputtered, sweat beading on his forehead.

"Then why did you run?" I asked.

"Because I thought the Fae Prince was going to stay and claim the throne for himself."

I froze, gripping the weapon tighter. I wasn't a fighter. Not like Ara. But I was angry, and I was done with being a pawn in a game I was shielded from. It was my father all over again. Telling me one thing while planning something completely different while I was out of the room. "What are you talking about?"

He grinned, that devious smirk that I saw whenever he whispered something into my father's ear. How often had I felt that cold chill down my spine simply from his presence?

I pointed the sword at him. "Explain."

"The ambassador was not who he seemed." The priest took a step forward, his turquoise robes dragging over the shining floors. "You will need my help, your highness. I have eyes everywhere. I can guide you, just as I guided your father."

"Take another step toward me and I paint the floor in your blood," I said through gritted teeth.

He quirked a brow. "I always thought Ara was the bloodthirsty one."

"Clearly you don't know us well as you think you do. Now, stop wasting my time."

A gust of wind blew into the temple and the fires flickered, casting dancing shadows across the floors and over the massive columns. My hair whipped across my face, but I shook my head, clearing it from my eyes without taking my gaze off the priest.

"The ambassador was the Crown Prince of Konos. And he could have ended all of us. His powers make his father look weak. Some say he's more than just Fae, he's something else. Something darker. Something far more dangerous. Why do you think the king sent Ara to entertain him? If he was a mere ambassador, why would your father risk her life? Didn't you wonder how hundreds of our men ended up dead in minutes? That shouldn't have been possible."

"That's impossible." Why would the Fae Prince himself come to Athos? "My father wouldn't have kept that from me."

"There is so much he kept from you. But I can help you. Tell you everything. Make sure you know all the secrets he was hiding." Istvan's voice is almost a purr.

I swallowed over a lump in my throat. Ara had gone with him. With a creature capable of killing all of us effortlessly. Was she even still alive? Were any of the tributes alive?

Ara was the best of us. She was devoted to Athos. Devoted to her sisters. Despite the way the rest of the world treated her, she never faltered. My throat tightened. I would never see her again. I couldn't even remember the last thing I said to her or the last time the two of us had spent time together doing something that wasn't steeped in protocol and etiquette.

I owed it to her. I would be the queen this city needed. For Ara.

"Why would I trust you?" My hand started to tremble, and I had to fight the burning in my arm. The sword was heavier than I thought it would be and I wasn't used to the weight.

"Because I'm not a good man. I'm selfish and power hungry, and therefore, predictable. If helping you keeps me living in the palace," his hand covered his throat, "and keeps my head where it is, I'll be loyal."

"Until someone with more power comes along?" I scoffed.

"Who could have more power than you?"

"Your flattery doesn't work on me. I'm not my father," I snapped.

"Which is why you'll succeed where he failed." The priest lowered his hand and took a step forward. "With my knowledge of Athos, and your drive, we can return the city to its former glory."

I stared at him, his words rushing past me. "I see no value in glory. Look where it got us so far."

"We can bring Ara home."

My breath caught for a moment, then I tightened my jaw before narrowing my eyes at him. "Don't play games with me."

"He was dying, and he called in a favor, willing to risk being turned at a chance for immortality. That's why your father did it. It was that or death," Istvan offered. "I was there while he went through the change, watching in case he needed someone to end him. You know there's always that risk, that you'll become a mindless monster instead."

I sucked in a breath and lowered the weapon. Mythiuss hadn't been willing to tell me details, leaving me to question my own blood. "When?"

"During the Choosing, eighteen summers ago." Istvan took a step back and the sword in my hand fell to the ground, clattering against the stone.

"You're certain?"

He nodded.

"Who else knows?"

"I swear, I've never told a soul." The priest placed his hand in the middle of his chest, a sign of goodwill.

I believed him, even though I knew I shouldn't. "Eighteen summers?"

"Yes. One of the delegates from Konos was willing to do it for him in exchange for something. He never told me what, but it had to be something important," he replied.

I should be concerned about what my father gave to someone from Konos, but the only thing I could think about was the date. The timing. The implication of what that meant. "Sophia?" If Istvan was telling me the truth, and my mother had been faithful…

"You're going to need help with this," Istvan said, his tone quiet and calm. "I have eyes everywhere. People who can be trusted. I can guide you, help you."

The back of my eyes burned, and I blinked back the urge to cry. Sophia was so innocent. How could she be one of those monsters? "It's impossible. Sophia can't be one of them. Tell me my mother was with someone else. Anyone else."

My father's infidelity was well known, but my mother had a reputation for being faithful. I couldn't imagine she could hide a lover, but right now, I was hoping that was the case.

"Half-vampires are rare, but they exist," he said. "I've heard stories of them in Telos."

My knees were weak, and I struggled to stay on my feet. It was what we'd feared since hearing the news about my father's secret, but I didn't think it was possible. How could any of us be half-vampire and not know? Shouldn't we know?

"And my mother's baby?" I asked.

Istvan nodded. "If he survives, he will also be a half-vampire."

I narrowed my eyes. "You're the soothsayer. You tell me how this plays out."

The priest suddenly looked ancient, well beyond his years. He opened his mouth, then his eyes flicked to the side and his body tensed. "We are no longer alone."

I followed his gaze and noted several priestesses approaching cautiously.

"High Priest, has something happened?" A young blonde woman walked into the naos, the rest of the women behind her staying in the shadows of the columns.

"Why has an outsider breached our sanctuary?" The woman looked terrified, and I had to wonder how long she'd been here, isolated from the rest of the world.

"This is our new queen," Istvan said, no sign of hesitation in his tone. "She came to pay her respects to the Goddess before she officially accepts the crown. She honors us and Athena with her presence and will honor the goddess during her reign."

My eyes moved to the statue and for a moment, I was overcome with the heavy weight of the crown I'd inherited. A crown of lies and deceit; vice and death.

I couldn't help but feel like I was heading right into the same path my father had walked. One that would lead me to my demise.

All I could do was try to reverse the damage my father had caused. And the first step was the meeting with the dragons. They couldn't find out the truth about my father.

The acolytes gathered seemed to relax a little. "You chose Athena as your patron?" One asked, her eyes shining with unshed tears.

"Who else would I choose?" I asked, hoping they'd leave soon.

"Perhaps you can go and prepare an offering to Athena in the name of our new queen," Istvan suggested.

The women hurried away, none of them looking back. I wondered how they'd learned to obey so blindly. Years of living here, forced to take orders. Was that how I looked? All that time following my father? Meanwhile, I was blind to the truth behind his movements. The game he was playing in meetings I wasn't permitted to attend. The immortal rule he was preparing for.

I shivered, then sent the thought away. It was difficult to let myself feel anger for him because the grief always accompanied as its twin. I'd recall the meals and holidays, private lessons where he showed me things meant only for the king's eyes, meetings with guards and high-ranking nobles, quiet moments with my sisters.

What had been real and what had been for show? I'd always thought I knew him. I thought he truly wanted what was best for our kingdom.

I didn't know him at all.

Istvan moved closer to me, lowering his voice to a whisper, "What's it going to be, Your Majesty? Kill me and hope the gods forgive you? Or gain an ally who can help you return glory to Athos?"

I glanced at the priest. "Who else knows?"

"Mythiuss," he whispered, keeping his tone low even though the others had left.

"He's dead," I replied.

"Good." Istvan's eyes met mine. "Then it's time for us to get to work, making you the most powerful ruler Athos has ever seen."

"And Ara?" I asked.

"All of Konos will pay for what they've done," Istvan promised.

13

ARA

"I really can't leave you alone, can I?" A bored voice drawled.

I whirled, already knowing who I was going to find. Anger prickled under my skin. "I had it under control, *your highness*."

"Sure you did." Ryvin said from his place leaning against the doorframe.

"When were you going to tell me?" I hissed.

He shrugged. "I didn't think it was relevant."

"You're a liar." I balled my hands into fists. That furious energy I'd felt toward the vampire was shifting to Ryvin. He'd let me get so close, but he'd hidden who he was.

"Don't even pretend you weren't hiding secrets of your own," he said.

"I never lied to you."

The woman next to me was still crying, her sobbing getting louder and more uncontrollable by the second. I turned my attention away from Ryvin. I'd deal with him and his betrayal later. "She needs a healer. This bastard nearly ripped her throat out."

"I was within my right to feed on her," the vampire hissed. "She gave me permission."

Ryvin took a step into the room, and the vampire flinched. "There are rules, Zacharious. That human doesn't look very willing to me."

"She was startled by this whore," Zacharious spat, pointing a finger at me.

Ryvin lifted a brow. "Careful with your words, old friend."

I ignored the insult and stepped in front of the woman, putting myself between her and Zacharious. "You dragged her away kicking and fighting."

I moved closer, daring him to touch me. That part of me I'd unlocked, that darkness that was fueled by rage and pain seemed to want a fight. It practically simmered and hummed under my skin, a dangerous, swirling storm of energy waiting for release.

The vampire growled, inching closer to me by the second. "You think just because you fucked the prince that you're special? I hate to break it to you, darling. But you're not the first princess he's brought home."

His words were like a punch to the gut, but when I turned to the Prince, he was already in motion.

Ryvin was a blur. A flash of black fabric and twisting shadows so quick, I was still registering that he'd moved at all when the vampire's body hit the floor.

Wisps of twisting black shadows undulated and pulsed, circling Ryvin before spreading out, slithering over the ground until they'd consumed the fallen vampire.

Zacharious screamed. A spine-chilling, desperate, primal sound that split through the room. I winced, covering my ears. The sound faded, and I dropped my hands just in time to hear ragged breathing coming from the convulsing form. The vampire's back arched, his fingers desperately trying to grab hold of the ground under him as his gaping mouth bubbled over with blood. Eyes wide, terror flashed, as if the monster never expected he'd meet this kind of death.

Perhaps this vampire had done things like this before. Maybe he was used to taking what he wanted without repercussions. I had a feeling the woman he'd dragged in here tonight wasn't unusual. And deep down, I knew she'd be dead if I hadn't followed.

"She's just a human," the man sputtered. "She's nothing."

I was so tired of having to cower in fear of these monsters. So tired of them thinking they could take what they wanted. So tired of feeling helpless. So tired of not being part of the change. I wanted to claim some kind of power. To stand up for myself and others like me. To defy the monsters. To fight back.

Something dark and angry seared through me and I let out a scream as my body heated, pain tearing through my chest as energy exploded from me. I felt like I'd released a piece of me that had been caged my whole life; it was like taking my first full breath of air. Until now, I'd been trying to breathe under water, only gaining a fraction of what I was supposed to have.

An explosion sounded as the vampire burst into pieces. Blood sprayed, bits of flesh and pieces of his body flew around the room. Panting and overwhelmed, I wrestled with the conflicting emotions bursting to life. I was relieved and elated; nauseous and terrified; energized and exhausted.

Almost as quickly as the feelings came, they crashed down around me as I realized what happened. I was covered in warm, wet goo. Blood and guts and whatever else had been inside the creature. Closing my eyes, I held my breath, disgusted.

Distantly, as if from somewhere far away, I could hear screaming. Panting, that darkness began to recede, more exhausted than I'd ever been in my life.

My eyes found Ryvin's, and he looked at me as if he'd never seen me before. There was something else in his expression. Not fear, not surprise, even. More like awe. Maybe even pride.

"So that's what your darkness has been hiding, Asteri," he said.

"What happened?"

"You made him explode." Ryvin's tone was amused.

I shook my head, then glanced at my hands. Blood and bits of flesh clung to my skin. "No, that's not possible."

Even as I said the words, I could feel the truth of it. Had I really done that? My stomach lurched, and I fell to my knees.

Everything I'd eaten came back up. I felt Ryvin's

hands smoothing back my hair as I retched. Not like it mattered, I was covered in entrails as it was. The thought made my stomach clench, and I continued to vomit long after everything had been emptied.

Finally, I caught my breath and wiped my mouth before realizing that I'd simply wiped more blood on myself. I shuddered, and resisted the urge to throw up again.

I stood on shaky legs, ignoring Ryvin's hand on my back. I wanted to shove him away, but I was worried I might fall over without that support. My eyes found the remains of the vampire. There wasn't much where he'd been laying. A puddle of blood and some bits of flesh. The rest of him was flung around the room and covering everything, including all of us.

Then I remembered why I'd come in here in the first place. Stepping away from Ryvin, I approached the woman. She was shaking, her face pale. Blinking slowly, her wide eyes scanned the room. Bits of skin and other parts of Zacharious clung to her hair and stuck to her face and shoulders. She didn't seem to notice.

"Are you alright?" The wound on her neck wasn't seeping blood anymore, which I took as a good sign, but she would still need someone to look after her.

"Let's get you out of here," I said, taking another step toward her, "get you all cleaned up."

Her eyes seemed to refocus, and she shook her head. "No. Don't you dare come near me." She retreated. "I saw what you did. I know what you are. You're just like them. You're a monster. You're a traitor. You're one of them."

"No, I came in here to help you." Now my hands were

shaking as her words struck me. As the last moments of the vampire's life pushed their way into my mind.

I'd felt that anger build. I'd wanted him dead. My whole body felt numb. What was going on here?

"You're all monsters! All of you!" The human woman screeched. She was shaking, crying, completely and totally frantic. Then she ran, aiming for the door.

Ryvin moved with his unnatural speed, cutting off her exit. Shadows swirled around her, then dissipated. She crumpled to the ground, and I waited to see her chest rise and fall, waited for some sign that she was alive. She didn't move.

With a gasp, I looked at the prince. "What did you do?"

"She would have told everyone what she just saw," he said. "You think your people would welcome you back into the fold once they find out?"

"I was trying to save her," I said.

"And I'm still trying to save you. Even if you're doing everything in your power to get yourself killed." Fury flashed in his expression, but it didn't feel like it was directed at me. "It's not just them. Your people. If my father knew..."

"Your father, the king?" I sneered.

He spoke through gritted teeth, "We're not starting that again. You have no right to hold that against me when you were hiding this." He gestured to the floor, where the pile of goo that was once Zacharious gleamed in the flickering light like some kind of gruesome work of art.

"It's impossible. I couldn't..."

He lifted a brow.

"I couldn't do that." I kept saying the words, as if it would change what I already knew. My hands shook.

Somehow, that was my doing. It didn't make any sense. It was impossible. Whatever had torn apart the vampire wasn't Ryvin's dark magic.

That had come from me.

The door slammed and I started, turning as if expecting to see the king's crimson robes sweeping into the room. The lock clicked, and I realized Ryvin had locked us into the room.

Heart racing, I took a step back. Away from the mess I'd made. Away from the male who'd saved my life more than once.

Even knowing how dangerous he was, I'd never felt threatened by him. Until now.

"Why did you lock us in here?" I asked quietly.

"I can't have anyone finding you with them." He inclined his head toward the mess on the floor. Two dead. Because of me.

He moved toward me with slow, graceful steps.

I swallowed hard. "If you're going to kill me, just do it." There was no point in trying to fight him. I knew what he could do. If he wanted me dead, I didn't stand a chance.

Something like hurt flickered in his expression, the change so subtle, I might have imagined it. He froze. "How could you think I'd ever harm you?"

I stepped back again and my heel bumped into the fallen human woman. I recoiled and carefully stepped over her, swallowing down the rising bile.

When I reached the door, I tested the knob, but it didn't move. "I don't even know who you are. You lied to me about your title. You sent that man into the Labyrinth with a fucking smile on your face."

"I might wear a different title here, but you know how little the title defines someone." He closed in on me and I backed up until I was pressed against the door. "And you, of all people, should know that we are often called to do things we don't want to for the sake of our positions."

His arms caged me in and I tensed. "You weren't supposed to be here. I told you not to come here. And I promised myself I'd stay away from you."

"Then go. Leave me be." Heat was building in my chest, and tingles skittered down my arms. I hated that I still reacted to him. I had bigger issues to worry about.

I should be reeling about the power I'd summoned. Concerned about the dead vampire and the dead human tribute.

But all I could do was recall how Ryvin's hands had felt when they caressed me. How his lips had felt against my own.

Something was so wrong with me.

He was right about the darkness. I was a monster. No better than the fae I'd hated my whole life.

"Why did you hide yourself from me?" he asked. "How did you hide from me? I could sense a sliver of something that wasn't human, but nothing suggesting this kind of power."

"You know as much as I do," I replied, my words coming out a little breathless from his closeness despite me doing my best to reel in my feelings.

"That wasn't vampire. You're too old, if you had vampire blood, you'd have shown it by now," he said. "What are you?"

"Why would you even care?" I hissed.

"You can deny our attraction as much as you want. But you can't deny the fact that if my father finds out about this, you're in more danger than I can save you from. He collects power. And if he can't have that power, he eliminates it."

I sucked in a breath as I recalled the threat from his sister during dinner. "The princess. She said she's watching me."

He dropped his arms to his side, then ran a hand through his hair. My brow furrowed. He actually looked worried. Ryvin, who could kill hundreds without effort, looked concerned at the mention of the princess.

"Your sister?"

He nodded. "Half-sister. You and I have more in common than you realize."

I pressed my lips together as my thoughts went to my own sisters. Were they safe? Had they managed to rebuild enough protection to keep the people from coming after them? Was Lagina holding things together in her transition to queen? Was Sophia still alive?

My chest ached thinking of them. I would give anything to know if they were okay. "Is she like you? With the shadows?"

He shook his head. "She's something else. Deadly in her own way."

The look of concern in his expression softened my disposition enough that I felt some of the fight toward him easing. "I really don't know what happened or how I did that."

Once the words were out, fear clawed at my chest. Would I do that again? What if I hurt someone I cared about? And if I had that power within me, what did that make me?

Was I even the same person I'd been before I'd walked into this room?

Ryvin grabbed hold of my hand and I pulled it away. More afraid that I would hurt him than anything else. Not that I was willing to admit that to anyone.

"Fine. I haven't earned your trust yet, I get that. But you have to listen to me. You can't cross my sister or hide anything from her. You don't have the skills to hide from her." One corner of his lips quirked in the faintest smirk. "Yet."

"I am not going to let your people kill mine," I said.

"Are you so sure there is a division between mine and yours anymore, Princess? That magic you just wielded says otherwise. It places you squarely in the Fae Kingdom. If anything, you're more of Konos than Athos."

I shook my head, even though I'd already been comparing myself to them. It was different coming from him. Made it too real. "No."

"Do us both a favor and keep that contained for now." He tucked a loose strand of hair behind my ear. "Can you at least do that? I'd like you to still be alive when I return."

"Where are you going?" Something that felt an awful lot like panic roared to life. The thought of being on this island without him was impossible. Even if I couldn't allow myself to be near him again, I wanted him here with me.

I wanted more than that, but I knew I couldn't act on that. Especially not with the princess's warning and this strange power I'd unleashed.

"I have to do something for the king, but I'll return soon." He glanced behind him at the bodies we'd left behind and let out a heavy sigh. "I'll take care of this, and you need to blend in. And please, Ara. For once, just do what they say and don't go looking for trouble."

"What if it comes back?" My voice was a whisper. "I don't want this. I didn't ask for this."

He cupped my cheek with his large hand, then leaned down, pressing a gentle kiss to my forehead. I closed my eyes, allowing myself this moment to ignore all the messy things between us.

His breath was warm against my forehead. "I'm going to help you through this. I swear it to you."

When he pulled away, I felt more alone and empty than I ever had. Shoving the thought away, I opened my eyes. "Why?"

"I told you. I will always keep you safe," he said.

And gods spare me, I believed him.

How many times had he shown me he wasn't going to harm me? "Why can't I stay away from you?"

"Maybe you aren't supposed to stay away," he suggested.

It was so complicated. The two of us together wouldn't work. I needed to leave Konos and save my people. He was the future ruler of the entire Fae Kingdom.

Me being with him would put his entire life in jeopardy. I couldn't bring myself to do it. "You know we can't."

"Let me worry about that. Just try not to die while I'm away, okay?" His silver eyes almost glowed, and I got the sense he was amused by me.

"You know I can't promise that."

He grinned. "You got this. Try to keep your emotions under control and avoid stressful situations until I return."

"I'm stuck in Konos with my enemy, and you want me to avoid stress?" It didn't seem possible. I'd already seen enough to have me on edge, and I knew it was only the beginning.

"Please, trust me on this. Don't go see the other tributes. Give me three days, okay?"

I opened my mouth to object, but his lips met mine, silencing me. I let myself melt into his kiss before remembering that we were both covered in blood that didn't belong to us. I pulled away. "I can't."

Hurt flashed, but he nodded. "Three days. Play the game. I know you can do that. I've seen you become whoever you have to be to survive. Don't quit on me now."

"Alright." I could give him that much. If only because I didn't want to risk hurting anyone.

Or having the other tributes see me unleash that kind of magic. The dead woman was right, I was a monster. But I wanted to help them and if they feared me, they weren't going to let me help.

Suddenly, a dark little thought nuzzled into my mind.

What if this magic was enough to change all our fates? What if it was enough to save us all?

I knew the Fae King was powerful, I knew I couldn't kill him with normal means. He was too strong, he'd be able to defend my attacks. But I wouldn't even have to touch him if I could figure out how to use this.

Maybe there was a silver lining to having such a deadly power. I reached for the doorknob as a million ideas and questions raced through my mind. What if this changed everything?

"Ara?"

I turned and looked at the bloody male standing in the center of the room, his expression serious. "Even that magic isn't enough to kill the king. You'd end up showing your hand, and he'd either recruit you to work for him, or he'd kill you."

"Don't worry, I'm not going to kill *your* father." That night came flooding back and my chest ached. Another reason I had to keep up my guard with him.

"I'd be the first one to tell you to go for it if I thought you could get away with it," he said. "I don't give a shit if he dies. But I do need you to live and right now, there's no way you could kill him and survive."

"Right now?" I asked, my pulse racing.

"At some point, you're going to have to stop fighting me and realize we have the same goals."

"You want the fae dead, too?" I was skeptical. Even if he wanted his father gone, it would just put him in charge. What did I really know about him? What if he was just as brutal?

Then Mila's body on the dining table flashed into my

memory. My father had been responsible for that, but I wasn't like him.

I glanced toward the pile of what remained of the vampire and wondered if perhaps I was more like him than I realized.

"We are not our parents," Ryvin said. "You don't have to trust me, but give me this time. Just three days. That's all I'm asking. Then I'll tell you anything you want to know."

I nodded. "Three days."

When I opened the door, Noria was standing outside, waiting for me. Her eyes widened when she took me in. "What happened?"

"How did you know I was here?"

"I summoned her," Ryvin said before turning his attention to the servant. "Take her to her room. If anyone other than Vanth comes to see her, notify him immediately. He'll watch over her while I'm away."

Noria nodded. "Of course, your highness."

I bristled at her use of his title. That was going to take some getting used to.

He grabbed my wrist, and I turned to look at him. "I need you to trust me, Ara."

"Three days." I tugged my arm from his grip, then stepped into the hallway. I didn't turn back, but I heard the door close behind me.

Everything was so much more complicated than I realized. Everyone had lied to me and now it was as if my own body had been part of the ploy to hide things from me. I didn't even know who I was anymore.

14

Ara

The party was still in full swing as we crept down the hall, hoping nobody would see me in my current state. Ryvin had stayed behind to clean the mess, but there was no hiding the blood covering me.

Smoke billowed from the door and I peered inside, unable to prevent my curiosity from winning over the urgency to get back to my room. The courtyard glowed orange and pink and green through the haze. The lights from the paper lanterns flickering above, making the smoke into colorful clouds.

The Athonians and the creatures of Konos were tangled into groups on the couches, or otherwise occupied. None of them were clothed. I scanned the room for Belan and found him in a corner, watching the madness unfold. He appeared to be the only human who wasn't letting themselves get lost in the madness.

"Princess," Noria urged. "We have to get you cleaned up."

I turned away from the scene and followed her toward the room I'd been in earlier. As soon as the door closed behind me, everything flooded back into my mind. The way the vampire had exploded, the look of terror on the human woman's face, the way the power had felt coursing through me... It was too much.

I felt like I was carrying so much extra weight. My shoulders slumped. Everything felt harder, like moving through mud. How had I even made it back to this room? I wasn't even sure if I had the energy left to wash the blood from myself.

I shuddered. There was no way I was going to leave vampire goo all over me. With concentrated effort, I made myself move. My hands trembled as I reached for the fibulae holding my peplos in place. Noria set her hand on top of mine. "Let me help you."

I dropped my arms to my side and stood silently as she unclasped the fibulae. My dress fell to the floor, and I was too exhausted to care. Following Noria, I shuffled toward the bathroom and watched as she began to fill the tub with water. "Not too deep."

She let it run a bit longer, then turned it off. It was barely enough water to clean myself, but the thought of sitting in a full tub was too much.

Suddenly, loud footsteps sounded and the Fae Princess stormed in, pausing at the doorway to the bathroom. I covered myself quickly, a burst of energy I didn't think I was capable of rising through me. "Do you mind?"

Noria handed me a towel, and I quickly wrapped it around myself.

"What happened." It wasn't a question. It came out as an accusation. The princess stood in the doorway, her eyes scanning my naked, bloody form.

"The prince just told me you tried to stop a vampire attack yourself?" She crossed her arms over her chest. "You have a death wish, don't you?"

I couldn't mask my surprise at the fact that Ryvin had told her, but then his warning came to mind. She'd find out eventually, this allowed him to control the narrative. Not knowing all the details he'd shared, I kept quiet.

"I have no interest in your life, but my father seems to think keeping you alive for a while is some kind of fuck-you to Athos. If it were up to me, you'd already be dead." Her upper lip curled in disgust.

"Are you finished?" I fixed a bored expression on my face. I wasn't going to let her get to me.

"I should kill your friend for this," she sneered.

"You won't touch him," I said through gritted teeth.

"Get yourself cleaned up. You smell like death." The princess shot a look at Noria. "Don't let her go anywhere without an escort."

As soon as I heard the door close, I dropped the towel and climbed into the nearly cold water.

Goosebumps prickled down my arms and legs, but I wasn't about to add more water. There was no reason to linger. The water turned red as I used my fingers to rub off the blood and chunks that I didn't want to think about.

"If you're going to use such little water, we should

drain it and fill it again," Noria said. "You won't get clean bathing in blood."

I wrinkled my nose as I took in the state of the water I was sitting in. She was right. It was more blood than water. Silently, I pulled the plug and let the water run down the drain. Noria turned the faucet on and I shifted to the back of the tub, watching it carefully.

"I know most from Athos can't swim, but it's not that deep," Noria said.

"I'm not worried about that," I replied.

She turned the water off, then handed me a cloth and a bar of soap that smelled like fig and honey. "We can drain it again after you scrub everything off."

I soaped up the cloth slowly, the momentary energy already fading. When Noria reached for it, I didn't resist. She worked the soap into a lather and began to scrub.

She was surprisingly gentle, and we were silent while she lathered up every inch of my skin. "We need fresh water again."

I pulled the plug, and she waited patiently until it drained before filling it again. Anxiety squeezed around my chest as the water ran into the tub, only easing once she shut the water off.

"Does she know you report to the prince?" I asked.

"Princess Laera?"

I nodded.

"She knows. It's impossible to hide anything from her. Everyone in this palace reports to someone else." She turned the water on again and I tensed. "We need to rinse your hair."

Reluctantly, I watched as she filled a pitcher with water.

"How did you come to be in his service?" I asked, mostly to distract myself from the water being poured on my head.

"We all make choices when our loved ones are in danger," she said, lifting a brow. "I know that's how you ended up here. Word gets around fast."

"I couldn't let them take her."

Noria lathered up my hair. "It's why I asked him if he'd assign me to you."

Her confession surprised me, but I recognized the mournful hint in her tone. Whatever she'd been through, she'd lost someone very dear. At least my sisters were still alive. For now. "I'm sorry for your loss."

She hummed, then turned the water on again to fill the pitcher. She moved slowly and never left the water running long. We were silent while she finished rinsing my hair and when she helped me out of the tub, I couldn't see a speck of blood anywhere.

I still felt like I was covered in it. I wasn't sure I'd ever be able to wash the blood from my soul. The things I'd done couldn't be erased. When it was my time for my journey to the Underworld, I had a feeling I was going to be judged harshly. And I'd deserve it.

I'd killed someone. Again.

Only this time, I didn't feel any guilt.

And I hated that I couldn't find it in me to regret my actions. He deserved it. I knew he did. But who was I to pass that judgment?

Noria left the bathroom, and I stood there with the

towel wrapped around me, letting my thoughts wander. It wasn't just that I'd killed someone, it was how I'd killed them.

I stared down at my hands, fingers splayed, palms open. Whatever I'd done to make him explode was beyond my control. It was as if my rage had ripped him apart. What kind of magic was that? It wasn't like anything I'd ever heard of, and it was dangerous.

My tongue felt thick as I swallowed hard. Where had that power come from? If it wasn't from my father, that left one option. But my mother had been human, hadn't she?

I didn't know anything about the woman who'd given birth to me. I only knew the rumors that swirled, but they'd all been focused on my father's end. Whispers about how he'd fallen madly in love with her. Stories about how he'd nearly abandoned his wife and child for that whirlwind affair.

The only thing that I really knew was that my mother had died. I wouldn't be able to ask her any questions and I wasn't sure if anyone alive even knew who she really was. Did Ophelia know?

I dropped my hands to my side and shook my head. If the queen had known my mother wasn't human, she'd have used that against me. I was on my own with this.

Ryvin's words echoed through my mind, reminding me that if I wasn't human, I didn't belong in Athos. Was he right? Did I belong more in Konos than the kingdom I'd grown up in? Even the princess had hinted at it. She must have sensed something in me. Did that mean she knew more than I did? Was it possible she had information about this strange magic in my veins?

Were there fae here who had magic like this? Was it possible my mother had been fae?

A shiver ran down my spine.

Nothing in my life made any sense anymore.

Noria walked in with a nightgown draped over her arm. "You'll stay here tonight, but tomorrow they've requested you move into the palace."

So that was how Ryvin intended to keep me away from the other tributes. I hadn't gotten to ask him why he wanted me to avoid them, but part of me was grateful. The last thing I wanted to do was lose control of whatever magic I had wielded and accidentally harm a human.

I shook the thoughts from my mind and went through the motions of getting ready for bed. By the time I dismissed Noria and stared into the darkness of the room, I was even more confused.

Even before I arrived in Konos, everything I knew had been unraveling. And all it had done since I arrived was get worse.

Sound filtered in from beyond my door, people talking or walking by, even music. The Tribute House was coming to life, the others already out and exploring rather than staying holed up in their rooms.

I needed to join them. I needed to start getting my bearings and learn anything I could about the island and the king.

Quickly, I pulled my nightgown over my head and

tossed it onto the bed. My door swung open and Vanth stepped in, his eyes nearly bulging out of his head. I stood there, totally naked, blinking at him. "Um, knocking?"

His face went crimson and he exited, quickly closing the door behind him. He waited a few minutes before knocking.

I had pulled on a pair of trousers and a tunic that I found in the back of the wardrobe. "Come in."

Vanth walked in, his cheeks still flushed. "I'm so sorry. I will knock from now on." He rubbed the back of his neck and avoided making eye contact.

"It's fine." His obvious embarrassment let me know he hadn't done it on purpose.

He cleared his throat. "Well, I'm supposed to make sure you're not getting yourself into trouble."

"It's that obvious, is it?" I asked.

"You're probably almost as much trouble as Ryvin," he said.

I lifted a brow. "I think I need to hear some of the stories you have on him."

"Oh, no. I like my head where it is, thank you."

"Do you know of any particular weaknesses among the fae?" I asked, making my tone light, as if I was joking.

He chuckled, clearly seeing right through my attempt to pass it off as a joke. "You're going to get me in trouble."

"I'm not trying to get anyone in trouble. I'm just trying to learn about this place. We don't have magic in Athos."

"How about I give you a tour of the grounds?" he suggested.

Away from the prying eyes of the other guards and staff. "Can we go to the beach? I want to touch the water."

"Is this your way of trying to scope out the ships?" He looked skeptical.

It was now, and I was a little annoyed I hadn't thought of it myself. Mostly, I was curious about the water and hoping that with some distance from the palace, Vanth might open up a little. "I've never felt the sea. I want to know what it's like."

"You want me to call a carriage, or can you ride?"

"I can ride." It had been a while, but the thought of that kind of freedom was too good to pass up.

I followed Vanth out of the room and I looked around the house, hoping to catch a glimpse of the other tributes. With Laera's warning, I was afraid to risk speaking with Belan, but it would be nice to see how he was doing this morning.

The sitting room was empty, but servants crossed through it to get to the courtyard beyond. They carried trays of fruit and honeyed pastries. Some had flagons in hand, along with gold glasses.

I followed them toward the courtyard where the remains of last night's party were nowhere in sight. The lanterns, couches, and tables were gone. Instead, lounge chairs and large round poufs were clustered around the space. Some in full sun while others were shaded with large swaths of fabric tied to the columns.

Several tributes lounged and ate, some of them entwined in the arms of fae. None of them even noticed that I walked past them. Their eyes were glazed and lazy smiles played on their lips. The brunette who'd been so terrified yesterday was taking a sip of wine from a goblet held to her lips by a gold-skinned fae male with pointed ears and long gold hair. His gilded skin shimmered in the sunlight. She didn't seem to have any concerns about him. Or about anything.

"What's wrong with them?" I whispered to Vanth, who hadn't left my side.

"They'll be like this as long as they continue to drink the wine," he said.

"I should tell them. Or stop them." But I couldn't tear my eyes from the brunette. She was so afraid yesterday. Now, she looked like she was in paradise. How could I take that from her if this was all she had to look forward to?

"Are you sure that would be a good idea?" Vanth asked. "Some people can't tolerate it here. Even some of the fae are rarely without a glass in their hand."

I tucked that information away, wondering what else I was going to learn about the fae.

15

Ara

Horses were already waiting for us when we exited the Tribute House, a pair of Konos guards in crimson tunics already mounted on steeds of their own. I frowned, knowing there was a good chance that they were here to report on our movements. They kept their distance from us, watching from afar, but not interacting with us. Somehow, that made it worse.

"Friends of yours?" I asked, glancing at the guards.

He scowled at them. "I don't have any friends who wear red."

My brow furrowed. Most of my memories of anyone from Konos came with the crimson tunics. But Vanth was always dressed in black. Just as Ryvin was. When they'd come to Athos, most of them had been in black, but I did see some in red.

It had been a while since I'd been on a horse, but I

Court of Vice and Death

was hoping it was one of those things you didn't forget. I approached the honey-colored mare Vanth directed me to and let her smell me before patting her. "You are beautiful."

"Her name is Saffron," Vanth said. "I think you two will get along just fine. You rode in Athos, right?"

"It's been a while. But I spent a lot of time riding when I was younger. Usually with Lagina." I turned away from him so he wouldn't see my reaction as I forced back the dull ache in my chest. I wasn't sure I was ever going to get over the pain of losing my sisters.

He helped me onto the horse and I settled in, breathing in the familiar scents of fresh air and horses. I might be in Konos, but their horses smelled the same as the ones I'd grown up with in Athos.

Vanth mounted his horse, then took off at a trot. I clicked my tongue and fell into pace beside him. My honey-colored mare was responsive and sweet, taking my direction easily. As we left the Tribute House behind us, Vanth picked up the pace gradually, and my mare kept up, steady and confident with her steps.

I didn't need to turn around to know the guards were following us, but I was curious how much distance they gave us. After a few minutes of silent riding, I risked a backward glance and was surprised that they weren't right at our backs.

"Why the comment about red tunics?" I asked.

He looked over at me, then returned his attention ahead of him. "It's the color of Konos."

"I know that. But why would that matter? You're from Konos," I said.

"I'm not permitted to wear red," he said. "Some of us aren't."

"Why?"

"I'm not fae."

I thought back to the time in Athos. Most of Ryvin's men didn't wear red. None of them had when we'd gone to the Black Opal. I knew Vanth was a wolf shifter, as was Adrian. Orion had been a vampire, but I didn't know what the others were. "I always thought all the creatures under the Fae King were part of Konos."

"Well, we might exist under his rule, but we aren't fae. And he won't let us forget that," he replied. "Though some vampires are permitted."

"Ryvin doesn't wear red," his name passed through my lips before I could stop myself.

"As I said, only fae are permitted to wear the color of Konos."

"But he's the prince." It didn't make sense. How could the king's son not be fae? Did that mean the king wasn't actually his father? He did tell me the princess was his half-sister.

"His mother wasn't fae," Vanth said.

"But his sister's mother is?" I asked.

"Turns out human kings aren't the only ones who stray," he said. "Though, in Ryvin's case, his mother should have been queen. The king betrayed her in the worst possible way."

"What happened?" I asked.

Vanth glanced back, then looked at me. "That's all I can say."

Frustrated, I pressed my lips into a tight line and let

the new information I'd gained play through my mind. If Ryvin wasn't all fae, what else was he? Could he be part human? Was that why I felt such a connection with him? Maybe we were the same. Maybe that's what I was.

I hadn't let myself really dwell on my newfound power. As far as I knew, Ryvin was the only person who knew. Had he told Vanth?

"Why are you the one guarding me?" I asked. "Ryvin must trust you."

"We trust each other enough. But I'm not here for him. For what you did for Adrian, and for me. I will do whatever I can to keep you alive. He knows that."

We rode in silence for a while and I took in the landscape around me. We rode through fields of tall, dry grass and over rocky empty spaces littered with the occasional spindly shrubbery. With the overcast sky, everything seemed duller than it probably was. I wondered what this place looked like before the Fae King. The stories said he was the one who brought the constant cloud cover.

Vanth picked up the pace, slowly, as if easing me into it. I kept up, and each increase in speed made me feel lighter. We were moving quickly, racing across the desolate countryside, and I found myself smiling. The salty wind blowing through my hair was like freedom. The kind I hadn't experienced in years.

Finally, we slowed, just as the sea came into view. Panting, heart racing, I worked to catch my breath as I drank in the sight before me. Waves crashed against the rocky shore, white foam trailing in the sand as they retreated. We were so close I could hear the water as it moved, the sound like music in my soul. From my perch in the palace in Athos, I couldn't hear the sea. Now, it was as if I was surrounded by it, joining the sound of my heartbeat to the sound of the water.

Vanth climbed off his horse, then helped me down. He looked back to where the guards were waiting, still mounted on their steeds. "You can hold the reins for us for a bit. The princess wants to get closer."

"I don't think that's a good idea," one of the guards said. "We were asked to stay with you."

"Did I ask your permission?" Vanth replied.

"No, General." The guard tensed.

"Watch the horses. We're going down to the shore." Vanth guided our horses over to the waiting guards, then returned to where I waited.

We made our way down a rocky incline toward the beach and with each careful step closer to the water, tension seemed to unspool in my chest. There was something about the sea that emptied my mind and sent my worries away.

"It goes on forever," I said, taking in the endless expanse of water.

"It's more impressive when you're out there and you can't see any land. Just water in every direction," Vanth said. "Makes you realize how small we are and how much is out there."

I glanced at the wolf shifter, wishing I knew more of his story. It wasn't my place to ask. Especially since I wasn't planning on staying long. "You've seen a lot, haven't you?"

He nodded.

I stepped closer, my sandals offering little protection

from the jagged rocks. We were so close to the water, and I desperately wanted to touch it. I hesitated, only a step or two away from where the water washed ashore. My whole life I'd been warned against the sea. It held so many dangers. Including the water serpent I'd seen when I arrived in Konos.

"Careful, Princess," Vanth said. "I'm guessing you can't swim."

"I won't go far," I promised as I sucked in a breath and took those last two steps.

The water was cold, and I gasped as it licked around my ankles before pulling back. Reaching down, I dipped my fingertips into the water, then lifted them away. When I rubbed my fingers together, I could feel the grittiness of the salt left behind.

The water lapped at my ankles again, the wave that came in was larger, splashing up my calves. I laughed in surprise. It was like a heartbeat. Rolling in, then receding. Like breathing. As if the sea itself was alive.

The next wave was larger, the water coming to my knees by the time it made it to me. Vanth grabbed my shoulders and pulled me back. "Tide is rising. Can't have you swept away."

I moved back, already missing the feel of the water on my feet. Out of the corner of my eye, I caught movement and turned. Narrowing my eyes, I peered out toward the depths. "Did you see that?"

"See what?"

A flicker of movement. A splash. Then a massive wave roared to life, heading right for us.

Vanth grabbed me and lifted me off the ground. He

pulled me up onto a large boulder as the water crashed around us, covering the area we'd been standing. My heart raced as I looked at the pool of water around us. Another wave came, and the water rose, deeper than it had been.

"This isn't normal," Vanth said. "We need to get out of here."

Our rock was an island now, surrounded by rising water. "What's happening?"

"I'm not sure. I've never seen this before." Vanth still had one arm around my waist and I wasn't about to tell him to let go.

For the first time ever, I found myself afraid of the sea. Of course, this was the closest I'd come aside from the trip to Konos, but it still surprised me. Even when I heard stories of the creatures in the depths, I couldn't bring myself to feel fear. From my vantage at the palace, it had always brought comfort.

Something swam past us. A massive serpent undulated just below the surface, parts of its long snakelike body arched and dipped, breaking the water enough to show off its opal colored scales. It shimmered in rainbow colors despite the lack of sunlight.

Despite the fact that I was fairly certain that I was about to be eaten, I was in awe of the grace and beauty of the beast as it swam around us.

Vanth shifted his position so he was mostly in front of me now, blocking me from where the serpent was swimming in slow circles in front of us. He pulled a blade from its sheath, and I set my hand on his. "No. Put it away."

"You don't know what that thing is capable of," he said.

"Your weapon isn't going to kill it, anyway. You'll probably just make it more angry," I pointed out. "But it hasn't hurt us yet. Don't give it a reason."

"It's not like us. It can't think or speak. It's an animal. One of the worst of the sea. And this might be the same one that already tasted one of your fellow tributes."

My breath caught. The sea serpent from arrival. "I thought they were rare and lived where it was deeper? Why would it come so close?"

"I don't know. Maybe it's hungry," he said.

"I don't think so." The initial fear had passed and now I found myself simply curious about the monster. It wasn't the same feeling I had while watching the beast in the labyrinth. This creature seemed like it was moving with the waves, flowing with the water, part of the sea. It didn't feel like it was a threat.

I pressed my hand onto Vanth's. "Please, put your weapon away."

I felt his fingers tense under mine, but after a few heartbeats, he complied with a grunt. "Fine."

Then I moved his hand from my waist and crouched down on the rock so I could see into the water better. Without its massive jaw open and all its teeth on display, the creature looked rather harmless. More like a large, beautiful snake, practically dancing through the currents below.

I reached out, touching my fingertips to the water. Vanth grabbed me and pulled me back. "What are you doing?"

The creature leaped from the sea, sending water roaring toward us as it let out an ear-splitting shriek. Vanth reached for his weapon, aiming it toward the creature. The monster roared, whipping its metallic tail, knocking us from the boulder into the frothy water.

Cold enveloped me as I submerged, dipping below the churning surface. I kicked and paddled, but every time I tasted air, another wave crashed into me, knocking me under again. My lungs burned and my chest tightened with fear. I tried to find the ground so I could jump, or reach for a rock for some leverage, but I was moving so fast I couldn't grab hold.

Something slithered past me and I tensed, knowing it was the serpent coming for me. This was not how I expected things to end. I reached down to grab a dagger but realized I was unarmed. Cursing myself and my lack of planning, I kicked wildly, trying to move myself toward air or away from the monster or both.

The monster's scaly body tightened around me, squeezing my middle. I opened my mouth to scream on reflex and water filled my mouth. My lungs were on fire and my vision darkened. My arms went limp and my eyelids grew heavy. I was going to drown. After all this, the sea was what would finally take me.

Suddenly, I was coughing and sputtering and gagging. Air burst into my lungs, painful and wonderful at the same time. I was back on the rock where I'd started and the water was receding, the serpent disappearing back into the depths. The rock was still surrounded, the water too deep and too dangerous for me to cross to shore.

Still coughing up water, I looked around for Vanth

and found him, weapon drawn, facing the oncoming creature.

"Stop! Don't hurt him!" I didn't care if I sounded insane for crying out to the monster, but it was the only thing I could do from my perch.

The serpent's head turned toward me, its long body writhing as it moved, the scales shining in the dim sunlight.

"Over here, beast!" Vanth called. "It's me you want!"

The creature ignored him, swimming toward me instead. My heart pounded, and I sucked in air rapidly, hoping I wasn't about to go under again.

As the serpent approached, it moved slower, the undulation of its long body a graceful dance. It circled the rock, diving in and out of the water, the entire length of it surrounding me before it slowed, emerging from the waves to peer at me.

The creature's huge green eyes locked onto me. It seemed curious, rather than dangerous. Vanth was still making noise, but I wasn't paying attention to him. I was too entranced by the monster in front of me.

Kneeling down, I met its gaze, finding that I was no longer afraid. Slowly, I reached a hand forward. The serpent lifted its snout until its nose bumped the palm of my hand. It blinked twice, then dipped under the water.

I stood, watching as it swam back out to sea. In its wake, the water receded until the sand emerged around me, but I was still staring out after the creature. It was long gone, and everything looked the way it had, but I couldn't tear my eyes away. What had just happened?

I'd seen that monster eat a woman, yet it had simply looked at me. As if it was saying hello.

"Ara! Don't move," Vanth called.

I shook myself from my thoughts and turned to see the shifter racing toward me, weapon still drawn. Climbing off the rock, my feet sunk into the wet sand. Vanth was in front of me before I could take another step. "Are you hurt? What happened?"

"I'm fine."

His eyes scanned me, looking at every part of me. I could tell he didn't believe that I was unharmed.

"I'm alright. It didn't hurt me," I assured him.

He blew out a long breath, then ran a hand through his hair. "I thought you were dead. It was right there. Right in front of you."

The sound of the waves crashing against the shore was the only sound for a long while. I wasn't sure what I should say, and it seemed like Vanth was also at a loss for words. Finally, he sheathed his sword. "We should get back."

The guards who'd followed us reacted quickly when they saw our disheveled states, racing toward us. "What happened?"

"Sea serpent," Vanth said.

"That's impossible." The guard's eyes were wide. "How close was it?"

"Came right up to shore," Vanth said.

"We have to inform the king immediately," the guard said. "Something must have angered Ceto."

"So it seems." Vanth said as he offered me his hand to help me mount my horse.

I climbed onto Saffron's back, then looked down at the soaking wet shifter. "You think it's Ceto's doing?"

"I'm not sure," Vanth admitted. "Whatever is going on is probably larger than all of us."

My stomach was in knots the entire ride. Ceto, a goddess of the sea, was well known for using her influence over monsters to attack ships. But I'd never heard a story about her sending her creatures this close to land. There was always a risk, of course, because her influence covered the entire expanse of the sea.

I'd long ago decided that the gods weren't interfering with us in any way unless it was for their own sick amusement. If Ceto was sending her monsters to Konos, it was possible she was just getting started.

16

Ryvin

Water dripped in the distance, but everything inside the cave was damp. The gray rock had been claimed by life long ago. Green algae and curious blossoming plants clung to every surface. Foamy water splashed over the edges of the pools scattered over the ground. It would take seconds for the tides to rise and flood the entire space, sealing me into a watery grave.

While Konos had been bleached of most life when the clouds arrived, the sea had remained unmarred. The gods had punished Konos for my father's misdeeds, but the sea was spared.

"You're not welcome here, Prince of Death." The voice was an echo that engulfed me, threatening to swallow me whole and pull me into the depths of one of the pools.

"I am not here on fae business." This cave was the gateway between realms. The entry point into the

Ocean Kingdom. It was also forbidden for any fae to enter. My mixed blood kept me alive long enough to reach this place, but it wasn't enough to guarantee safety.

"We do not answer to you or your father." The voice was so loud I winced. I could feel it in my bones.

It was a warning, reminding me of the power the Queen of the Sea could wield. But I wasn't here for her, I was here to speak to another who occupied these waters. Someone who could provide answers.

"I came for an audience with Ceto," I replied. "I have a question for her."

"Ceto doesn't speak with the likes of you," the voice hissed.

A wave rolled through the pool nearest me, spilling over the edge and splashing onto my boots. I held my ground, determined not to show fear. "This is important. She will want to hear what I have to say."

"Why would a goddess wish to speak with you? Your tainted blood is an insult to all who dwell here."

It wasn't my mother's blood they despised. It wasn't even that the Ocean Kingdom valued purity. Plenty of their kingdom had half-children without any concern.

No, her issue was specifically against my father's blood.

Water splashed around my ankles, the pool continuing to rise, slowly flooding the cave. If I lingered, I would be swimming out of here. Or I'd be drowned and never leave.

"I am not my father," I reminded her.

"We have kept an eye on you, Princeling. You are your

father's weapon. He wields you against his enemies, using your power as his own. Just as he did with your mother."

Her words were like a knife in my gut. It was true, I'd played the role for so long I didn't even know who I really was. Everything had changed after the rebellion, but nobody knew my plans. Not a single soul.

So often, I'd been tempted to share with Vanth. But even though I knew we had the same goals, I couldn't guarantee he wouldn't turn against me.

My father's influence was too great and Laera's powers too strong. If she penetrated Vanth's head and found out, it would be over before it started.

The water was up to my knees now. I didn't have much time. "I need to know if there's any record of anyone else with powers like Ceto's."

I wasn't sure if it was in my imagination, but the water seemed to stop rising.

"Who?"

"I need to speak to Ceto," I repeated.

The water rushed in, and my breath caught as the cold crept up my thighs. "What would you do if someone had that power?"

"It's impossible," the voice replied.

The memory of Ara standing in front of Zacharious flooded in, but the part that I couldn't let go was that moment of sheer terror in her expression. Her fear over losing control and hurting someone. Of hurting me.

My heart seemed to twist, the knowledge that at least some part of her truly desired me was almost too much. But the thought of her losing control and harming herself, or getting killed for what she possessed, was what brought me here.

Taking a chance, I dropped to one knee, the water rushing in around my chin. I lowered my head in submission. "Please, your highness. This is personal, and I will owe you a favor." I hated this. I hated using this, but I had to find answers.

Water covered my mouth and I lifted my chin, coughing and sputtering, yet I remained on my knee, hopeful.

Just as water reached my nostrils, it began to recede, returning to the pool it had started from.

Dripping wet and shivering with cold, I maintained my position. I'd never gone to my knees for anyone. Not even my father.

There was only one person who could get me to do this, and with the power she'd unleashed, she was in danger.

We both were.

If my father found out everything I knew, neither of us would live to see another day.

"Stand up, Princeling." The voice was normal now. Beautiful, feminine; the kind of voice that would lead a sailor gladly to his death in a watery grave, but it no longer commanded the entire space as it once had.

I rose, then tried to mask my surprise at seeing the Ocean Queen herself standing in front of me. She was tall and graceful. Her skin a pale green, her hair the deep green of the algae around us. She wore a peplos the color of the sea, its shimmery, pearlescent quality catching the dim light through the holes in the cave above us.

"If you want me to contact my sister, I need to know what this is about," she said. "I do not easily welcome her to my kingdom's borders."

I knew what I was asking. Ceto commanded and created all the monsters that lived in the sea. Where she went, the creatures followed.

With the queen living so near Konos, it was rare we saw the larger, more deadly monsters near our shores. At first, I'd dismissed the sea serpent sighting the day the Tributes arrived as coincidence. After Ara used the blood in Zacharious's veins to blow him apart, the pieces started to fall into place.

The magic she'd used was so unfamiliar, there was little to compare it to. Only Ceto's powers were like what I'd seen. Add in that Ara might have attracted the sea serpent on her crossing from Athos, and I was nearly certain the goddess had sired a child that she'd hidden in the one place where she'd remain undetected.

I'd been able to sense something different about Ara, but with all the humans around, it was difficult to identify what it was. If she'd grown up here, or in Drakous or Telos, someone would have scented her.

And she'd be dead.

"I watched someone unleash power like Ceto's." I swallowed, waiting for the queen to respond.

"Which power?"

"Blood control."

The queen's expression darkened. "Are you certain?"

I nodded.

"You know what must be done. We can't have

someone with that ability. Ceto is forbidden to have children," the queen replied. "Who is it?"

"I can't tell you. Not until we know for certain," I said. "I need to find out if Ceto had a child."

"You must bring the child here and I can tell you if it is of Ceto's blood," the queen said.

"No."

"You seek my help and you know what the repercussions are. You know what this magic can do, Prince of Death."

"It might be enough to release my mother." Saying the words out loud sent a chill down my spine. It'd been my plan for so long, yet it still terrified me. My father was dangerous enough. My mother, with her true power restored, made my magic nothing more than parlor tricks.

The queen grinned, showing her pointed teeth. She was beautiful, but those teeth were a reminder of how deadly she was. As the Queen of the Sea, she held power over all the creatures that lived there. And many of them were just as deadly as she was. "So that's why you so confidently walked into this portal?"

"I told you, I am not my father."

"You found out where she's being held?" The queen asked.

I nodded. My trip to Athos had proved worth the time. I'd suspected for years, but I couldn't venture to the human city without a reason. The Choosing had been my cover, giving me access to places I couldn't go without causing war.

"And you think Ceto's progeny can aid your quest?" She looked skeptical.

"They're keeping my mother in Athos." It explained why my father protected the human city from others. Why he cared if they collapsed. His tributes were a ruse, a way to maintain power and keep the humans feeling like they were purchasing the protection. While the beast required human offerings, we could find humans other ways.

All of it had been explained in the original treaty I'd found in the Palace at Athos. The human royals didn't care as long as they kept their power.

The queen frowned. She was the Queen of the Sea, limited to the saltwater expanses, forbidden to travel into fresh water. But Ceto and her monsters could go anywhere.

If Ara could command them, it could be exactly what I needed to finally free my mother.

"And what happens once your mother is free?" The queen asked.

"I can finally put an end to my father's reign."

The queen's gruesome smile spread wide, and her eyes took on a hungry sheen. "I can taste the destruction already."

"How do I speak with Ceto?"

"There will be a ship waiting for you outside. It will take you to my sister," the queen replied.

I lifted a brow. "Am I to trust that you won't send your people after me once I'm on the open water?"

She sighed, as if annoyed that I'd called her out. "Fine." She made a circular movement with her hand, leaving a glowing trail in her fingers' wake. A shiny gold hoop hung in the air between us.

I reached for it, having heard rumors of such gifts, rarely bestowed, and never gifted to one with fae blood.

"While you wear this bracelet, none of my kingdom can harm you. Wear it well, Princeling, or I will come for you myself."

"Thank you," I replied.

"You know the child must die once she's served her purpose. I cannot allow any of Ceto's children to live."

I tensed, then gave a quick nod. "I understand."

Her body went transparent, then crashed to the cave's floor in a rush of seawater pouring into one of the ponds.

17

Ryvin

The island was a fortress. As soon as you stepped foot off the sandy beach, impenetrable trees and vines blocked your path. There was no way anyone would survive if they were dropped on this island. Unless they were invited.

Trees bent, parting to show a path that cut through the dark green foliage. A nymph emerged, her bare feet traveling down the path as if she memorized every rock or uneven pile of dirt. "You are not supposed to be here, Prince of Death."

I didn't react to the title, one that I despised but had earned by my own bloody past. Lifting my arm, I showed the gold band. "I need five minutes with Ceto."

The nymph's lips twitched when she saw the bracelet. She could probably sense its magic, which was why I wasn't dead or left on the beach alone.

"She's not interested in visitors. Especially not from anyone with the blood of the gods in their veins."

"I'm not the one who put her here," I reminded the nymph.

"Yet, you seek her when you need something. Just like all the rest." The nymph turned, and the jungle closed in around her, blocking my entrance to the path.

I raced forward, knowing this was my only chance to speak with the goddess. "It's about her daughter."

The trees stopped moving and so did the nymph. She turned slowly until she was facing me. "Ceto is forbidden to have children. Everyone knows that."

"I'm guessing that's why she abandoned her with a father who tried to sell her to the fae," I spat out, my words like venom. If Ara's father was still alive, I'd kill him again just to watch him suffer for how he discarded her in the end.

"The goddess is very busy."

"I'm sure she is." I didn't hide the sarcasm in my tone. "I'm guessing she left her daughter to be raised by humans in the hopes that she would survive. The Ocean Queen knows."

"Because you went to see her," the nymph hissed.

"I did. But I didn't know how to get to Ceto myself." It had been a gamble, but I already knew Ara was running on borrowed time. Getting the Ocean Queen on my side before she found Ara on her own bought us enough for me to fix things so I could save her. It was my only chance.

"Wait here." The trees swallowed the nymph and I

was left on the sand, the sound of the waves crashing against the beach the only sound.

Sweat rolled down my temples, and I resisted the urge to remove all my clothes as I waited in the blistering sun. The water was starting to sound like a song, calling me to its depths so I could cool off.

Finally, the trees rustled, and the vines slithered away like snakes before the plants shuddered and divided to reveal the pathway again. A different nymph was standing in front of me. Her long, graceful limbs the same color as the bark of the trees, her hair the color of bright spring greens. She blinked a few times, her head tilting from side to side as if studying me. I waited, knowing it was best not to startle a nymph. The last thing I needed was for her to return to her tree form before she could take me to the goddess.

"Ceto will see you, but you must abandon your weapons on the shore," the nymph instructed.

I did as she asked, removing my sword and daggers, letting them drop to the ground.

"The tunic and trousers must go as well. We can't have you hiding anything." She tossed me a simple woven long tunic. "Undress."

I hesitated, then removed my clothing, noting that the nymph was watching me very closely. I wondered who had come to this island with something hidden in their clothing to require such a process, but I wasn't going to ask that now.

Finally satisfied, the nymph nodded and gestured for me to follow. We were silent as we traversed the path. The trees groaned and creaked, as if they might return to their usual place at any moment, crushing us between them without concern.

The walk was long enough that I was breathing heavily and damp with sweat by the time I could see a building in the distance. The nymph stopped. "That is her home. She will meet you in the courtyard." Silently, she melted back into the trees, the female form stretching and extending until an impressive tree stood in her place.

I knew many nymphs avoided being around other creatures. Especially males. I didn't blame her after all the stories. "Thank you for your help," I told her, even if she couldn't hear me in tree form. At least she'd kept the path open for me and didn't make any of the trees strangle me or rip me to pieces.

The rest of the walk took longer than I anticipated, the home looked so much closer than it was. The sun was low on the horizon and long shadows covered the grounds outside the house by the time I arrived. It was still sweltering, and I had to stop to catch my breath and wipe the sweat from my brow before I made my way to the courtyard.

Ceto was already waiting for me. A pitcher and two glasses sat on a table in front of her. She poured one, not even looking up at me. "I wondered who would find her first. She got more time than I thought she would." She extended her hand, offering me the cup.

The goddess was just as beautiful as any that I'd met. Deceptively stunning. The kind of beauty that caused so many mortals to blindly follow to their own deaths. That's what she was; death. Not the same form as I was, but I knew better than to underestimate her. I might wield death, but she commanded an army of creatures that could take out even the most thriving civilization. She'd done it before. She could do it again.

I accepted the glass and gratefully drank the cool water.

"Sit. Tell me of my daughter. What is she like? Is she happy?" Ceto's tone was concerned and curious. It took me off guard.

I settled into the chair across from her and finished my water. "May I?" I gestured to the pitcher. She nodded.

After filling it again and taking another sip, I set the glass down. "Her name is Ara, and I think she was happy. For a time."

"But not anymore?"

I shook my head. "No, not anymore."

"Your doing?"

"Partly," I admitted.

Ceto hummed. "So what's the request? You need me to attack a city or find you some sunken riches or you'll tell the other gods where she is?"

"I think the other gods already know. And if they don't yet, they will soon enough. She summoned a sea serpent and accidentally blew up a vampire."

The goddess filled her own glass, then took a long drink before setting it down. She traced her finger through the condensation on the side, then looked up at me. "Does she know?"

"About you? About what she is?" I shook my head. "Not yet."

"I'm not asking about that. I'm asking if she knows how you feel about her."

Court of Vice and Death

I wasn't sure how to respond to that. "She might."

"How very unfortunate for both of you," the goddess said sadly.

"I'm not here to talk about me. I'm here about her," I replied.

"Liar. You're a man. It's always about you."

I sighed. From what I'd learned from my father and the rulers I'd met through the years, it was difficult to argue with her. Most of them were blinded by their own ambition. And there was a part of me that was doing this for selfish reasons. I couldn't let anything happen to Ara. How much of that was because I wanted her in my life?

"You were in love with him. Her father, weren't you?" I changed tactics, pushing forward to get the information I needed.

"I thought I was. I even told him who I was. What I was." She grinned. "He liked that. Liked the power I held, the possibility it might afford him. When I realized he cared more for the power than for me, I left."

"And you left your child with him," I added.

She returned to the condensation on the glass, drawing shapes with her fingertip. Her expression was guarded, her mouth in a tight line.

"Why did you leave her there?" I asked.

"I know what happens if a child of mine shows any bit of magic. I know the fear my brothers and sisters have about a child who can control all forms of water and the creatures who call it home. It was safer if nobody knew," she said.

"Her father knew."

"I thought he was different."

"You weren't the only one who thought that." The pain on Ara's face when she was faced with the betrayal flashed through my memory. I tightened my hands into fists. What I wouldn't give to take that pain from her.

"Is she with you, then? I heard she was going to travel to Konos."

I nodded. "She came as a tribute. To save one of her sisters," I explained.

"Stupid girl. Perhaps it's best if they find her and end her now. If she's so quick to help others, she's in for a lifetime of disappointment."

"She'd disagree with that," I said.

"If she's on your island, your father will figure it out. And likely sooner rather than later," she pointed out.

"I know. That's why I went to your sister."

"Yes, I know. The part I don't understand is how my child is still alive. The Ocean Queen has come for every one of my children. Most of them before they even had a chance to show magic." Ceto's face was hard. "I learned my lesson. I hid this one. She'd be protected still if not for you."

"I'm trying to help her," I said.

"By telling my sister?" Ceto shook her head. "The kind thing to do would be to make her death painless. My sister will give her no such death. She'll use her to teach me a lesson."

"I know where my mother is," I said.

Ceto sucked in a breath, then she blinked a few times while her surprised expression melted into a knowing smirk. "You're going to use my child to free her." She shook her head. "You are just like all the others. You'll use her, then allow her to be hunted down when she's no longer of use to you."

"I won't let them find her."

"There's only one way you could make that happen. And that's only possible if the stars themselves aligned for you."

My jaw tightened and I could almost see Ceto working out the details herself. She shook her head. "Does she know?"

"I haven't told her," I said.

"You're going to break her heart when she finds out," Ceto said.

"But she'll live," I replied.

"There are things worse than death," Ceto reminded me.

I swallowed hard. "I know."

"You might be half-god, but I will kill you if you get my daughter killed." The goddess stood. "It should be her choice, you know. If you take that from her, it will break her. You don't know what that does to a person."

"I know exactly what it does. I've seen it happen."

"Then you know what you're setting her up for. What you're asking her to sacrifice," Ceto said.

"I'm asking her to live a life free of being hunted by the gods," I said.

"When she sees you for what you are, tell her to find me. She'll be welcome to have sanctuary here."

I swallowed hard. When this was done, Ara might need that. There was no way she was ever going to look at me the same way again.

18

Ara

My hair was still soaking wet when someone pounded on my door. Noria handed me another towel. "Wait here."

I stood silently in the bathroom, having just rinsed the saltwater off me at Noria's insistence. This time, she'd only put a bit of water in the tub automatically.

When a male voice sounded through the bathroom door, my heart leaped, but then quickly sank when I realized it wasn't Ryvin. Closing my eyes and clenching my teeth, I cursed myself for getting so excited about seeing him.

I stepped out of the bathroom to greet Belan, and his cheeks flushed when he saw me in a towel. "I can come back."

"No, don't go." I turned to Noria. "Can you get me a dress?"

"Of course." She hurried to the wardrobe and grabbed something seemingly at random.

"I'll be right back," I told Belan before returning to the bathroom.

Noria followed me in, a gray peplos in her arms. "I don't think you should have him in your room like this."

"Based on the actions I've seen in this place, nobody seems to care who anyone is with," I said.

"You're not the same as them," she said. "I was tasked with keeping an eye on you."

"I'm not going to fuck him," I said.

She squeaked.

"He's a friend," I explained.

She helped me into the dress. "I really should do something about your hair."

"Leave it," I said, running my fingers through the wet, wavy tresses. "I'm not trying to impress him."

She nodded, then stepped aside as I walked back into the bedroom. Belan was seated at the vanity and stood quickly when he saw me. "You don't look hurt."

My brow furrowed. "Should I?"

"I heard you were attacked by a sea serpent," he said.

"I don't think attacked is the right word, but I did see one," I said.

"I heard it came for you," he said. "That it had you in its hold, then released you."

"Gossip gets around this place faster than it did in Athos," I said.

"There are no secrets here, your highness," Noria whispered. It was so quiet, I didn't think Belan could hear it. Laera's threats came to mind, and I nodded at Noria. She was warning me.

"I went to see a bit of the island, but my tour was cut short by the serpent," I said. "I hope your day has been less eventful."

His eyes darted to where Noria was standing before looking back to me. "I went for a walk down to the village. Did you know there's a village near here?"

"No. I thought it was just the city near the palace." I walked toward the couch and gestured for him to join me. "Noria, can you bring us some tea?"

She nodded, then exited quickly.

Belan settled in on the couch opposite the one I sat in. "Did you find anything?"

I shook my head. "Nothing yet. You?"

His jaw tensed, and a vein in his temple bulged. "The villagers weren't any help. They don't seem to hold any love for the king, but they were not interested in speaking with us."

"We need to be careful about what we say and where we say it," I reminded him. "I'm not even sure this is safe."

"I know. Half the servants seem like they can read minds, I swear. They bring things we want before we even ask."

"How are the others?" I asked.

"Nobody has been harmed that I know of," he began. "But most of them aren't really here, if you know what I mean."

"I saw the courtyard earlier today. Too much wine?"

"And other things. They have herbs and teas, and

certain foods that can alter how someone feels. You have to be careful, Princess," he said.

I sighed. This was going to be harder than I feared. "I know. So do you."

The door opened, and Noria strolled in, holding a tray with tea and a plate of pastries. After Belan's information, I was hesitant to even drink the tea.

She set it down on the small table between us, then handed me a folded piece of paper. My brow furrowed as I took it from her.

"What is it?" Belan asked.

"I'm not sure." I glanced at Noria, but her face didn't give any indication of what the paper contained. I opened it and read it quickly, then Noria snatched it from my hands and took it to the fireplace, where she promptly began building a fire.

"What just happened?" Belan asked.

"Nothing," I replied. "Tell me something about home. I don't want to talk about Konos. I want to imagine I'm far away. Back in Athos."

Belan's confusion was clear in his expression, but I was hoping he'd understand the sudden change in subject. I poured a cup of tea for each of us and took a sip of mine. After the note I'd just read, I had a feeling I could trust Noria. It had been a warning from her that there were guards at my door listening to every word.

We spent the next hour discussing memories from childhood. I discovered that his father had died when he was young and he'd joined the guard as a way to help his mother. It was a similar story to most of the guards I'd spoken with, and it made my stomach twist with guilt. I'd had so much handed to me.

"I don't want to let them down," I said suddenly. "Our people, I mean."

He seemed to know what I was saying. "You won't."

Someone knocked on my door, and I quickly set down my teacup. Noria answered and Vanth walked in, his face pale.

"The guards informed the king about the serpent," he said, then he glanced at Belan before looking back at me. "He's requested you join him for dinner."

"Alone?" Belan asked.

"I'm not sure who will be in attendance," Vanth said.

I swallowed. "Is this because of the serpent?"

Vanth's heavy stare felt like confirmation, but he cleared his throat before speaking. "I think it's because of your family ties to Athos."

"I see." I could practically feel the weight of the stares from the guards outside the door. Everything Vanth was saying was being monitored.

"I should get her ready," Noria said.

Belan set down his cup. "Come by after, if you want."

I nodded. "Thanks for the talk of home. It was nice to hear about Athos."

He gave me a weak smile, then left. The door was still open and I couldn't help but notice how the eyes of the guards kept darting toward me. I frowned, annoyed that such a close eye was being kept on me.

"Am I to help her dress while you all watch her?" Noria's hand was on her hip and she raised an annoyed brow while she glared at all the men staring at me.

"I'll return to escort her in an hour," Vanth said with a slight incline of his head.

As soon as the door was closed, Noria pressed her finger to her lips again. I nodded, grateful she was on my side.

"You'll want something more formal for a meal with the king, I think," she said a little too loudly. "What an honor to get to dine with him."

"Of course," I said, snapping back to reality. "I'm not familiar with traditions in Konos. Can you help me select the best option?"

Noria helped me dress in a pale gold silk peplos. "You should avoid red, since that's the color of the fae born in Konos, and blue is a reminder of your heritage. I'd avoid that until you know if the king is going to want to show off your ties to Athos or if he'll want to connect you more to Konos. Green is the color of the Court of Vipers, so that's out."

"That's a lot of rules," I said. "In Athos, it was about how expensive the dye was. If you could afford the more expensive colors, you'd wear them at formal events to show off. White was worn for mourning, but also acceptable any time."

"Every color here has meaning," she said. "The fae are easily offended, but they're the first to break their own rules."

"What other rules should I know?" I asked.

"Follow what the king does. After he sits, you can sit. After he takes a bite, you can eat. When he stands, everyone stands." Her fingers worked through my hair, twisting and weaving my tresses into an elaborate pile on top of my head.

"What about the food? I've seen what fae wine does to humans." My stomach lurched at the use of the word. Could I even claim that anymore?

"Even most fae are impacted by the wine, so I'd avoid that. But the other food should be safe. Especially what will be served to the king. Eat what he eats. He doesn't like to lose control, so he'll avoid anything that might impact him."

Her hands stilled for a moment, then she removed them from my scalp. "Just follow his lead and you'll be okay."

19

Ara

Vanth was silent on the carriage ride to the palace. My skin crawled at the realization that he was probably not speaking because it wasn't safe to talk to me. I hadn't been here long, but I was already starting to question the reality of finding any information about the king. If everything was so tightly monitored, how would I find any weakness? This dinner with the king might be my best chance. Maybe I could get closer to him, get him to drop his guard.

A chill ran down my spine. I didn't want to spend any more time with the king than necessary, but my options might be limited. Was there anyone here who would be willing to share information?

As I walked down the corridors with Vanth, I counted the number of guards, noting that most were in red, but some wore black. I wasn't sure yet if the guards in black were less of a threat to me or if they were still just as loyal to the king. Were the men Ryvin brought with him loyal to him or his father? Was Ryvin even loyal to his father?

Perhaps I wouldn't have to worry about getting closer to the king himself. Maybe it was Ryvin who would help me. I wondered where he was and what he was doing. I hoped he was safe. I shoved aside the alarming thought. Why couldn't I keep him out of my head?

Vanth stopped in front of an arched entryway. "I will wait here and escort you to your room after dinner."

"That won't be necessary." The princess stood in the doorway, a cruel smile on her lips. "It's been decided she will be moved to one of the palace guest rooms. I'm more than happy to escort her there myself."

"I was tasked with her protection by the prince," Vanth said flatly.

"Then you can wait at her room to stand guard overnight. Unless you feel she needs some kind of protection from the royal family?" Laera watched him, as if challenging him to say something.

"Of course not, Princess." Vanth inclined his head. "I'll inquire with the head servant to find her room."

Laera made a shooing motion with her hand, then gripped my elbow. "Come. Sit. I so look forward to learning about Athos."

My whole body tensed, but I walked with her, knowing I didn't have much of a choice. We were in a small dining room that reminded me of the breakfast room where I'd eaten most of my meals. It was missing the stunning view of the sea, but after my earlier adventure, I was a little grateful I didn't have to stare at it for once.

The king and queen were already seated, one at each end. The table was covered in food and flowers and shining gold plates and silverware.

"Please, take a seat," the king said, indicating a chair near him.

I swallowed hard and reminded myself that last time I'd dined with them, he and the queen had ignored me. With Laera moving to the opposite side of the table, it was possible I wouldn't have to endure too many of her threats.

A servant pulled the chair out for me and I sat, tensing as I was pushed in until my stomach nearly touched the table.

"It has been so long since we've had anyone interesting visit Konos," the king said as if I were a guest coming by who had the freedom to leave.

I glanced toward the queen, noting her sour expression. Her jaw was tight, her eyes focused on me. I turned away from her and watched as a servant piled food I didn't recognize on my plate.

The king stabbed what might be fish with a fork and popped it into his mouth. I noticed the queen and princess also began eating.

I picked up my fork, recalling Noria's words. If he ate, I probably should as well. I selected something that was probably a fruit and took a bite. Sweet liquid exploded on my tongue and I swallowed quickly, startled by the overwhelming flavor.

"Tell us, what is Athos like these days? I haven't visited myself in a century," the king said.

"It's difficult for me to know what you'd be interested in knowing. Athos isn't as impressive as Konos. Our palace isn't nearly as grand, our city is small and cramped, our food less flavorful."

"You have the practiced conversational skills of a courtier," he said.

I nearly spit out the food in my mouth, but made myself swallow. "I try, but I'm not as skilled as my sisters, since I was never in line for the throne." It might have been stupid to remind him of my lack of importance, but something about his tone made me defensive. Like I needed him to know I wasn't worth using as a bargaining chip. And that I wasn't a threat. I needed him to drop his guard, to allow me to wander, to ignore me because I wasn't important.

"I don't think that's true. You might not hold the same title, but the prince seemed to think you were your father's favorite. Why do you think that was?" he asked.

"Perhaps the prince was mistaken." I found myself wishing Ryvin was here. Whatever he was doing, I hoped he returned soon.

"He wasn't. My sources tell me she was favored," Laera said.

"Was it your mother, then? He must have truly loved her. Maybe that was it. Royals don't exactly get to marry for love." He glanced toward the queen and I nearly choked on the water I was drinking.

"That's an understatement," the queen replied coldly.

Doing my best to keep my coughing as quiet as possible, I cleared my throat a few times, then blotted my mouth with my napkin. The queen wasn't even hiding her dislike of the king. I wondered if I could use that somehow. Would she help me if it meant getting to cross him?

"Who was your mother?" The queen asked. "Was she someone of importance?"

"I honestly don't know," I replied.

"Whoever she was, they buried her name when she died," Laera said. "Even I couldn't find it."

It was odd hearing my mother spoken of this way. Sometimes, I could feel phantom sorrow about her passing, but it was an odd sensation. I'd never met her, so it was impossible to fully mourn her. I wondered if instead, I was mourning the loss of the relationship I could have had.

I was glad Laera didn't know. Glad none of them did. If anyone should know, it was me. And I didn't feel like sharing her with them.

"I heard the people turned on you," the king said. "And that you defended my son."

"I was doing my duty to uphold the treaty," I said.

"Too bad your father didn't do the same," Laera said.

"Come now, Laera. Perhaps it was for the best. Without his treachery, we'd never have met this lovely new guest," the king smiled at me, but the expression didn't reach his eyes. It was cold and cruel. Like a mask worn by someone who had read about what a smile looked like but had never actually seen one.

I made myself eat something, hoping it would slow the questions if they saw me chewing. After an awkward silence, the king cleared his throat. I looked up, knowing he was going to continue the barrage.

Setting down my silverware, I set my hands in my lap and stared at him. I refused to let him see how on edge I felt. In a way, all the backhanded comments and nasty glares from Ophelia prepared me for dealing with someone like him.

I had to refrain from smiling as I considered how strange it was that I was appreciating the struggles Ophelia had presented. Looking at the king the same way I handled her would make this so much easier.

The knots in my stomach loosened, and my gaze softened. I could see the king's brows furrow slightly as he noticed the change in my body language. He was good at reading people, but he wasn't going to get a read on me.

"Tell us about your adventures today with Vanth." The king maintained eye contact with me as a servant cleared his plate.

"I'm sure he already told you all about it," I hedged. Why was he so interested in this? The invitation for dinner came after the king found out about the sea serpent sighting. Somehow, it had to be connected.

"Why did you ask to go to the sea? Vanth told me you can't swim. And you know the waters are dangerous," the king said.

"I've always wondered what the water felt like, and I figured I'm already dead here, anyway." I shrugged. "It didn't feel like much of a risk."

"We would never harm such an interesting guest," Laera said with mock sweetness.

I turned my attention to her. "Guests are allowed to go home."

"I'm bored," the queen announced, standing suddenly. Everyone turned to watch her, but she was focused on her husband. "Do not come to my rooms tonight."

Without another word, she swept from the dining room, leaving me with the king and his snake of a daughter.

"You'll have to excuse my wife. They did things differently in the Court of Vipers," the king explained.

"Is that one of the kingdoms you took over?" I asked.

He grinned, an unsettling look on his handsome face. "It is. Perhaps I'll add Athos to the ever-expanding list soon."

"If you wanted to conquer Athos, you'd have done it already," I said. "I've seen what your men are capable of. I watched as hundreds of our people went down effortlessly."

He lifted a brow. "You were there? You watched my son kill them all."

"That's not the story I heard," Laera said. "The royal family was swept away and cloistered in the palace. She was there when Ryvin killed her father, though."

I tensed. Was there a reason Ryvin hadn't told the story accurately?

"Call in the shifter," the king declared. "I need to ask him a question."

"I sent him to her new rooms," Laera said.

The king scowled. "Then someone go retrieve him."

Laera motioned to a guard, and the man darted from the room.

"What is going on?" I demanded.

The king leaned back in his chair and took a long drink from his cup. When he set it down, he wore a different kind of smile. This one was satisfied and vicious. A chill ran down my spine. "My son hasn't used that kind of power in over a century. Very few are alive who've ever witnessed it. If he unleashed that kind of magic in front of you, and you lived..." he shook his head.

"She means more to him than we realized if he spared her," Laera said.

My heart thundered. They weren't supposed to know this. They shouldn't know this. I'd given something very important away, but I wasn't sure what it was. So what if Ryvin didn't kill me?

Vanth walked in, his posture straight, his chin high. He looked more like a soldier than I'd ever seen him. Gone was his casual, friendly nature. He was someone I hardly recognized.

With an elegant bow, he faced the king. "Your highness."

"General, tell me the events of the Tribute Ceremony," the king said.

Vanth came out of his bow and faced the king with stoic indifference. "The humans attacked before the names were called, just as we suspected. We'd already gathered the tributes so we could leave as soon as we had evidence of their treason."

"What of the royal family?" The king pressed. "How were they involved?"

Vanth's eyes never left the king. "Most of the royal family was ushered into the palace as soon as the attack began. They missed one princess in the chaos. I escorted her to the palace under the prince's orders. We were not to harm the royals, so we could leave them for you to punish."

"How much of the battle did she see?"

My jaw tensed and I waited, knowing that I was going to support whatever lies Vanth told. I knew it was dangerous to trust him, but I trusted him far more than the king.

"I'm not sure. I was in shifter form, guiding her through the fight to safety. I didn't watch what was going on around us," he said.

"I see." The king glanced toward me, then stood and walked toward Vanth.

The shifter tensed slightly, and I caught him swallowing hard. He seemed nervous. Even Vanth was afraid of the king.

20

Ara

THE KING CROSSED THE ROOM, and Vanth waited. Tension built until the air felt thick. Laera smirked, her gaze glued to her father. Whatever was coming was something she'd seen before.

The king reached for Vanth, his large hand over his eyes, fingers splayed so they were on his forehead and temples. Vanth grunted, then his eyes closed and he gritted his teeth. Sweat beaded along his forehead and his breathing grew rapid.

"What are you doing to him?" I stood, but Laera grabbed me. I didn't even see her move from her space across from me.

"Wait, the best part is coming," she hissed in my ear. Her fingers dug into my upper arm, and I tugged myself free, finally reaching Vanth just as the king lowered his hand.

Vanth collapsed to the ground, trembling and shaking. I dropped to my knees next to him, pulling him into my arms. "It's okay, I'm here." I glared up at the king. "What did you do?"

"It seems some of the details were left out of the report," the king said. "You were there. You were with this shifter, holding him much like you are now. Prepared to die to spare him."

The king clicked his tongue. "How very interesting."

I glared at him. "So? Why do you care? I could have told you all of that."

"But nobody did. Nobody told me that you were about to die and Ryvin unleashed magic he's refused to use for a century to save you." The king chuckled, then turned to his daughter. "I thought you said she was just a fling?"

"He was with several women while he was there. How am I supposed to predict he might have feelings for one of them?" Laera looked disgusted.

My chest tightened, and panic welled. Ryvin did all that for me? And he didn't want his father to know. Whatever was coming next couldn't be good.

Vanth stirred, groaning as he began to move. "Ara?"

"I'm right here," I said.

He sat upright on his own, gently lowering my arms before standing and facing the king.

"I know your loyalty is to my son, but next time you will give a full report or I'll go even deeper into your memories," the king warned.

"Of course, your highness. I'm sorry for letting you down." Vanth inclined his head, but I caught his fingers tensing, as if he was restraining himself from saying or doing more.

"What makes you so special?" Laera asked, turning her violet eyes on me.

"She's a fighter," the king said. "Probably had some training from the looks of it."

Laera hummed. "Then we will fight."

"What?" I stood, then turned to the Fae Princess. "I'm not fighting you."

"You'll meet me in the training courtyard tomorrow. Vanth, you'll bring her to me." Laera flipped her silver hair over her shoulder. "Sleep well, Princess." She walked out of the room and I took a step closer to Vanth, not liking the fact that I was left in here with the king.

"You might be even more useful than I imagined," the king said. "I've never seen a woman interest my son enough for him to make mistakes."

"Whatever feelings he had for me, they're gone now." I knew it wasn't true. I had tried to tell myself that everything that passed between us was a lie, but I was seeing it clearly for the first time. He'd killed all those people for me. I didn't want to see it then, but I knew it was the reason he'd used that magic.

Ryvin had always tried to protect me. Even now, wherever he was, it was for me. But he didn't want his father to know. He needed him to think I wasn't important. "I could never be with someone like him. He knows I have no interest in him."

The king smiled. "We'll see about that. General, please take her to her room. She's got a busy day ahead of her tomorrow."

WE WERE quiet on the long walk to my new room. The floor transitioned from marble to rough stone, the painted walls began to show signs of age. Cracks spiderwebbed across the ceiling. We passed empty rooms with fabric draped over the furniture. This part of the palace felt old and abandoned. I wondered if it was the original structure, a relic from a forgotten time. Just as the Tribute House was.

"Do you know where Ryvin really went?" I finally broke the silence, risking a glance at Vanth.

"No," he replied. "He wouldn't tell me."

"The king was right, wasn't he? About Ryvin? About the magic he used?" I didn't feel worthy of that kind of reaction. My life wasn't that important.

Vanth stopped walking, then looked around before turning his attention to me. "It was the first time I'd ever seen him lose control. And there's only one cause for that kind of lapse."

I swallowed hard, fighting the emotions making my chest swell with both fear and longing. I'd fought so hard against my feelings for him, but it seemed he wasn't fighting his. "You don't like him much."

"We have our differences," Vanth agreed.

"I never asked for this," I said.

"I know. But love is one of those strange things we can't control." He offered a small smile.

"I never said I love him."

"I never said you did." Vanth started walking again, motioning for me to follow. "But I should tell you, my disagreements with him have nothing to do with him directly. If things were different, I'd follow him by choice."

"Then how come you don't get along?" I asked.

"Because things aren't different. And shifters don't get a choice."

We stopped in front of a door and I peeked in to see a windowless room with a large canopied bed and simple wood furniture. It wasn't exactly a prison cell, but after the Tribute House, it felt like a dungeon.

"Are you feeling alright after what the king did?" I asked.

"I'll have a headache for a while," he said. "But it will fade."

"Can he do that to anyone? Read their thoughts like that?" I asked.

"Most anyone," he said. "There's a few he can't breech."

"Ryvin?"

He nodded.

"Why?"

"It's not my place." Vanth pushed the door open wider. "I summoned your maid from the Tribute House when they came to get me. She should be here soon."

"Can the princess do the same thing? Read minds?" I asked.

"Her power is different," Vanth said. "Not the same as her father's, but there are few secrets she can't crack. I'm amazed she didn't discover the reason Ryvin lost control during the battle."

"I don't want that responsibility. I didn't ask for that

kind of devotion. And I certainly didn't deserve that," I said.

"I know you don't want it, but you are worthy of it, Ara. Don't let anyone tell you otherwise." Vanth gave my upper arm a gentle squeeze. "You should get some rest. It'll either be me or Ahmet standing guard. We'll make sure you're safe."

My eyes widened a bit at the mention of another name. I trusted Vanth, but I didn't know about anyone else. Especially while Ryvin was away.

"Ahmet can't harm you. He gave you some of his blood when you were dying," Vanth said.

"What?"

"You didn't know." Vanth's face paled.

"No, I didn't know." I blinked a few times. "The injuries after the fight outside the Opal... I should have died. They gave me vampire blood, didn't they?"

"Vampire blood has healing properties. It's not enough to turn you, but it kept you alive. You would have died without it," Vanth explained.

I felt sick. Grateful that I was alive, but at what cost? After everything I'd been through, after all the years of being told how terrible vampires were, I'd ingested vampire blood? All my past bias was tugging at me, conflicting with the new things I was learning and mixing with the betrayal I'd faced from my own father.

"The blood leaves a bit of a trace," Vanth said. "It'll be part of you now, and that means he can't ever harm you."

"I'm guessing they don't give their blood often, then?" It seemed like a way to force loyalty, and suddenly the vampires joining with the fae made more sense.

"Most vampires would rather die than give some of their blood to another. It's used as punishment or to earn rank in the king's inner circle," Vanth explained.

"Ara, thank the gods," Noria's voice called down the long corridor, and she picked up her pace.

I turned and watched as the servant ran down the hall toward us.

"Ara, what happened? Why are they moving you here?" She was panting slightly when she stopped.

"The king was concerned about her safety," Vanth lied.

"Assassins?" Noria asked, her eyes wide, then she turned to me. "Or someone from Athos? Trying to find you?"

"The king didn't specify," Vanth said.

Despite myself, I stifled a yawn, the exhaustion of the last few days catching up to me.

"I think she's had enough excitement, General," Noria said.

"Good night, ladies." Vanth inclined his head, then Noria swept me into the room.

I turned, reaching for the door to prevent Vanth from closing it. "Can you find out how the tributes are doing for me?"

He nodded. "Get some sleep, Ara."

The new room felt claustrophobic. Balls of light hovered near the ceiling, glowing and flickering like flames, but too soft and full to be from fire. They were the only light in the windowless room.

I turned in a slow circle, taking in the space around me. Aside from the sparse furnishings, there was an arched doorway leading to a washroom. I walked toward it and looked at the basin on the counter and the small copper tub. The floor was scuffed and worn and the teal paint on the walls was peeling.

"Nobody's used this room in a while," I said, more to myself than Noria.

She joined me in the doorway. "It used to be the vampire wing of the palace. Back when they had more ruling power. There used to be a vampire governor who was ranked just below the king. But that was long ago."

"I guess that explains the lack of windows if the stories are true." I glanced behind me.

"Indeed. They used to be very sensitive to light. It's how we ended up with the cloud cover we have now."

I left the bathing chamber and sat down on the bed. "Can you tell me about what it used to be like?" I patted the space next to me.

Noria hesitated.

"You don't have to sit with me if you don't want, but I really don't mind," I said.

She moved slowly, then took a seat next to me. "Most of the people around here ignore us."

"I'm guilty of that, myself." I'd befriended Mila, but I rarely even looked at the other servants who'd worked in the palace. "But I'm trying to change."

"You're not what I expected when I was assigned to you," Noria replied.

"Did you expect Laera?"

She shrugged. "Maybe."

I laughed. "Well, I'll work on it."

Noria smiled. "Please don't."

"She's making me train with her," I said.

"You have to be careful around her," Noria warned. "She's never what she seems."

"I know." I took a deep breath. Laera had threatened me when we first met and her sudden interest in my combat abilities was concerning. It had to have a purpose, but I couldn't see it yet. I'd have to look out for any tells she offered when we fought tomorrow.

"What can you tell me about this place? The vampires, the clouds, any of it. What's the history of Konos?" Understanding the past might help me find a way to navigate the future. If I was able to get off this island, there had to be more weaknesses Athos could exploit. Aside from the monster in the maze, what else was there?

"The Fae King has always ruled from Konos. Past kings ruled from the island, holding summits every decade for all the rulers of the other Fae Courts. While they were under his influence, they ruled independently of his interference," she explained.

"Where do the vampires come in, then?"

"They were fae, once. A whole clan that used blood magic to gain more power with the goal of overthrowing the king," she said.

"What happened?"

"Their magic backfired, cursing their entire line. Anyone in the clan was struck with it, and they lost the ability to go out in the sunlight for a long while, forcing them to submit to the Fae King. They were weak without the ability to defend themselves during the day.

"The Fae King established an alliance with the wolf

shifters, sending them to patrol the vampire lands in the daytime. Under the alliance, their governor was housed here, and the king created the illusion of giving them some power, at least at first."

"How did the clouds come to be?" I asked.

"The short answer, a sorceress and a goddess. And a lot of favors and promises by the vampire clan," she said. "I don't know all the details, but the clan seemed to never get over their initial desire to overthrow the king."

"They tried, then? To kill him?"

She nodded. "And they failed. They were nearly wiped out and in a final turn, the king promised them he could grant them the secret to walking in the sun if they swore allegiance to him."

"How?"

"You know the answer already, I'm sure," she said.

"Humans." I shivered. "Human blood."

"Yes. It was the beginning of the end for humans. They had to have human blood regularly to retain the ability to walk in the sun. The part they didn't know was that some of the humans they fed from would become a version of them. Gaining their immortal life, but also gaining an unquenchable bloodlust. Original or born vampires can live without human blood. They can't walk in the light, but they'll live. The turned must have it or they'll die," she said.

"They fed their blood to the king, didn't they? Those early vampires?" I asked.

Noria nodded. "They're bonded to him forever. The rest won't rebel because they know they'll be forced to submit or they'll be dropped in the maze."

"He didn't stop with the vampires, though, did he?" I asked.

"No. The shifters rebelled next. Without the vampires to watch over, they wanted to leave, go to the mainland and form their own kingdom."

I thought about Vanth and his reluctance to serve the king, his dislike of Ryvin despite the fact that he served him, and his loyalty to his dead friend. The pieces were falling into place, painting a brutal king who was even worse than I imagined. It didn't seem it was Ryvin specifically he had a problem with. It was the system that forced him to serve.

"They didn't win," I said.

"They were nearly extinct," she said quietly, looking down at her entwined hands in her lap. "There's not many of them left now."

"With those allies, he took the rest of the fae?" I asked.

"After he betrayed Nyx," she whispered.

"Nyx?"

"Shhh." Noria's eyes widened. "Not too loud. We're not supposed to talk about her."

"Like the goddess of night and death?" I asked.

"And the Fae King's mate," she said.

"Mate?" My brow furrowed at the unfamiliar term.

She pressed her lips together as if steadying herself. "Supposedly, his true love. A match ordained by the fates themselves."

The story of the Tragic Lovers came to mind, the intertwined fates, love at first sight, a pull so intense that the couple would rather die than not be together.

"Did he kill her?" I asked quietly.

"Worse."

"What's worse than death?" I wasn't sure I wanted to know.

"When you meet your true mate, you can share magic. Use it to strengthen each other or help the other if needed. It only works between mates. The king knew this. He siphoned all her magic, then had her locked away somewhere," she said.

My jaw dropped. I knew the king was evil, I knew he was dangerous, but I couldn't imagine someone doing such a thing. Especially to someone they were supposed to love. "How could he do that?"

"He loved power more than he loved her," she said.

The story made something churn inside me as I considered the magic I'd summoned. I'd spent most of my time trying to ignore that it happened, trying to forget, but it was part of me. What would it be like to have it ripped away?

For me, it might be a relief. I didn't want this power. But for a goddess, that power was part of her. It would be like taking a limb. Or worse.

"What was her magic?"

"Her powers were vast. Death and destruction. Darkness. Control of the stars themselves." Noria's expression was full of sorrow. "They say she was radiant, even with such terrible magic at her disposal. She was loved. She deserved better."

The hair on my arms stood on edge and a shiver ran through me. Her powers were so similar to Ryvin. Wasn't that what I thought of him? His magic was like death itself. If the king had the same power, it would explain why nobody could challenge him.

"She's Ryvin's mother, isn't she?" I looked over at the woman sitting next to me.

She nodded. "He was there when it happened. Watched the magic stripped away from his own mother. His powers hadn't manifested yet, but he still tried to stop his father."

I covered my mouth with my hand, unable to stop myself from imagining Ryvin as a child trying to fight for his own mother.

"They say the king had him lashed for weeks. Every time the wounds healed, he was struck again so he'd scar." Noria stood abruptly, then walked away from me.

Tears slipped down my cheeks. I'd seen those scars and wondered how they'd occurred. His own father. His mother.

I balled my hands into fists, hating the king even more. He had to be stopped.

21

Ara

The training courtyard of Konos wasn't much different from what I was used to. Several rings of soft dirt for sparring, racks of weapons, piles of old armor, dummies in the distance for archery practice. The smell of dirt and sweat and even a lingering copper tang of blood tinged the air. It was almost comforting.

When possible, David and I had used the training grounds, but when it was busy, we'd had to go to the gardens, away from the prying eyes of the guards who didn't approve. I rubbed at the ache in my chest, the moment of comfort from the familiar environment gone in a flash as David's memory haunted me.

I was never going to forgive myself for what I did to him. I knew it was the only option. Had I killed Ryvin, the guards would have just killed both of us.

My thoughts wandered to the prince, and I wondered

where he was and when he was going to return. As much as I hated it, I'd feel better when he was back.

I dragged my fingers over the hilts of a barrel full of training swords, lost in my thoughts as we waited for the princess to arrive.

"Maybe something came up." Vanth's tone was hopeful.

"What's her specialty?" I asked, knowing I wasn't going to get that lucky. She seemed to want to fight me. If not now, it was a matter of time. "What did she train with?"

"Everything," the princess's cold voice cut in. "Wondering if your training is up to par? Why do they even bother to train humans in Athos? All your lot do is sacrifice yourselves at the wall."

Vanth's jaw tensed.

I spun to face her. "If you'd let us be, we wouldn't have to bother with training."

"Oh, that's not true. If we let you be, you'd eventually turn on us. It's in your nature. What all humans do."

Like me, she was dressed in trousers and a tunic. Her long silver hair was pulled back, tied with a leather cord at the base of her neck. Her violet eyes glittered. She looked wild, untamed.

I knew she wouldn't hold back or go easy on me. Maybe that was why I grabbed one of the swords and got into my fighting stance. I could use the workout, anyway. Maybe I'd even enjoy the pain. There was too much else in my head right now. If I hurt, maybe I could shut the rest of it off.

She moved with feline grace as she strode to the

barrel and selected a sword at random. With a grin, she passed it between her hands before gripping it with her left hand and settling into a fighting stance of her own. "This should be fun."

We circled, sizing each other up. Her movements were so fluid, each step was flawless. I knew she was going to be faster than me, and I also knew she wasn't about to underestimate me.

I struck first, lunging with my weapon, expecting her to dodge. She did, then I followed through with a spin, aiming my blade for her neck. It was a basic attack pattern I'd drilled a hundred times. One that had sometimes even worked against David. But she was faster, and I almost missed blocking her responding strike.

Our blades met, the steel singing through the courtyard as we worked through our attacks. I didn't hold back, coming at her aggressively. My blade always missing her as she dodged, or making contact with hers as she blocked.

I twisted and ducked; lunged and spun. Sweat rolled down my temple, the sword grew heavy in my grip. Twice, her blade drew across my stomach, the tip just barely brushing against my tunic. She'd smirked each time, as if I needed the reminder that she could have made more contact.

She was holding back.

With a scream, I charged her, nearly landing my blade in her chest, but she moved so fast that I got nothing more than the tip of my sword against the fabric of her tunic before she wasn't there anymore.

It was like fighting a phantom.

Suddenly, she spun, her blade coming toward me fast. I blocked, the vibrations of our steel making contact, setting my teeth on edge. Then her sword was pointed at my heart while mine was still extended from where we'd met.

Panting, I lowered my weapon. "How do you move like that?" The fear was gone. I was too impressed to worry. "Is that a fae thing?"

She lifted a brow. "I could kill you right now and you want to know how I move?"

"I don't like it when my enemy has skills I don't," I grit out.

She chuckled, then lowered her sword. "You're not a bad fighter. At least not for a human." She wasn't even winded.

"Who trained you?"

"I trained with some of my father's guards," I said.

"Sparring, nothing formal?" She shook her head. "Still that backward notion that women can't fight?"

"There's some who do," I said defensively, thinking of my aunt. Though she was very rare. Only a handful of women served at the wall. There wasn't exactly anything saying they couldn't fight, but it wasn't encouraged. None of the palace guards were women.

"You'd be better with some more advanced training," she said as she returned her sword to the barrel.

I held mine, not trusting that she wasn't going to do something terrible to me. It might be a training blade, but it made me feel a little better to hold on to it.

"I'll train you," she said.

"What?" Vanth said before I could get the word out.

"Yeah, what? I mean, why would you do that and why would I want you to?" I asked.

"Because as soon as the rest of the fae find out that you're important to Ryvin, you'll have a target on your back," she replied.

"And why would you care?" I snapped.

"That's not your concern. The smart thing would be to ask me what time we're meeting next," she said.

"I don't think the prince will approve of this," Vanth said.

"Well, it's a good thing that he's not around, then, isn't it?" She walked closer to me, and I gripped the sword tighter. Her eyes scanned me, dropping to my feet, then looking back up. "You'll need some decent boots."

I looked down at my sandals. I'd always fought in them, boots being something reserved for guards or soldiers.

"I'll take her to town," Vanth said.

"No. I'll send my cobbler to her room." Laera flipped her hair over her shoulder. "Be ready tomorrow. I won't go as easy on you and we'll not stop after one round."

22

Ara

The knock on my door made me jump, which meant I'd actually fallen asleep at some point. I'd tossed and turned for what felt like hours, and I groaned at the intrusion. With the lack of windows, the room was pitch black, but a crack of light split through the darkness as someone opened the door.

"Ara, you awake?" Vanth called.

"I am now," I said.

"Sorry. The princess wants to fit in a training session before breakfast."

I groaned again as I moved. My muscles were sore from yesterday's fight and the scab on my ribs felt tender, the skin still taught as it continued to heal. "Why is she doing this?"

"I'm not sure, honestly," he said.

I swung my feet over the edge of the bed, then rubbed my eyes. "Is Ryvin back yet?"

"Sorry, no," Vanth replied.

I sighed. Without him here, there was no chance for a reprieve from sparring with Laera.

Noria burst into the room, breathless. Her hair was a wild mess and her peplos was wrinkled. "I'm sorry I'm late. I didn't know you'd need up so early."

"None of us did, and it's okay, I can get ready myself," I said.

"Absolutely not. I have a job to do and I'm going to do it." She dragged her fingertips along the wall and the lights glowed to life. Then she noticed Vanth and her cheeks turned pink. "I didn't even see you there, General."

He ran a hand through his hair as he inclined his head at my maid. He almost looked a little flustered. "I'll leave you to it and I'll escort you to the training courtyard when you're dressed."

The shifter exited the room, closing the door behind him.

"What's his story?" I asked Noria. I wanted to ask her how long she'd been interested in him, but I thought that might be a little too forward. We'd need to get to know each other a bit more first.

"He's one of the good ones," she said. "I don't know all the details, but I know the prince claimed him for his personal guard after the shifter rebellion."

"He fought in the rebellion?" I was surprised.

"Most of the shifters you see did," she replied. "If they

didn't agree to serve the king, they were killed. There's too few of them to organize against him."

"Does anyone like the king?" I asked.

"I've said too much." Noria crossed the room to the wardrobe in the corner. She opened it, then frowned. "There are no more trousers in here."

I could fight in a peplos, I'd done it more times than I'd fought in trousers, but it wasn't my preference.

"There isn't time to get anything else," Noria said, sympathy in her tone. "I'll request some for you for tomorrow."

"Alright, whichever dress allows for the most movement in there," I said.

"They're mostly outdated." Noria wrinkled her nose. "In the Tribute House, everything is stocked and replaced before you all arrive. I don't think that was done here."

"I'll be fine. Unless Laera kills me during our training today," I deadpanned.

"Don't even joke about that," Noria warned.

"She's clearly trained to fight. And she's got magic." I had magic too, but I wasn't about to share that information and I had no idea how to use it. Unleashing something that could make a person explode probably wasn't a great way to survive here until I could find an escape.

"She's a rule follower, though," Noria said. "She'll follow protocols for training."

"That's good to know." I changed into the dress Noria handed me and my mind wandered to the Tributes. "How are things at the Tribute House?"

"I'm not sure," she said. "I'm back in the servant's quarters in the palace."

She quickly brushed my hair, then braided it so it was out of the way. Her fingers brushed against the serpent necklace around my neck. "This is pretty. Does it have any meaning?"

"Not really," I admitted. "Someone suggested I wear it when I came here. A piece of home, I supposed."

"It's an interesting choice. If I didn't know better, I'd say it more resembled a sea serpent than a snake," she said.

Before I could ask her to elaborate, another knock sounded on the door. "We need to get going, Princess."

Noria crossed the room and opened the door. "She's all yours, but please bring her back in one piece."

"I always do," he said.

As Vanth and I walked down the long abandoned hallway of the vampire wing, I tried to piece together all the information I was learning. There had to be a way off this island, but I was going to need to be able to explore more so I could learn. If I couldn't get to the king, escape was my best option.

"Can we go on another tour later?" I asked.

"I don't think the king will allow it after what happened last time," he said.

"How about a visit to the Tribute House? I'd like to check on the others," I said.

He sighed. "I was told to keep you in the palace."

"So I'm a prisoner."

He glanced over at me. "It seems that way."

"Why?"

"I'm not sure, but I guess it has something to do with the serpent," he confessed.

My brow furrowed. I'd suspected the same thing, but I wasn't sure how it was connected to me. "Why would a sea serpent sighting change anything?"

"I'm not sure yet." He paused right before the stone gave way to the marble floor of the main palace. "You need to stop worrying about the tributes."

"How am I supposed to stop worrying about them?" I asked.

"There's no way off this island," he said quietly. "The ships are heavily guarded and the ley lines are only strong enough in the labyrinth. The portal there is a natural occurrence where the lines converge. It can't be duplicated anywhere else."

"What if that's not my plan?" I asked.

"I told you, the king can't be killed," he said.

"You can't expect me to do nothing," I replied.

"I expect you to survive."

"Maybe simply surviving isn't enough for me anymore," I said defiantly.

He moved closer to me and gripped my upper arm gently. "Trust me on this, Ara. It feels like something is brewing and until we know what it is, we should use caution." He dropped his hand. "I hate that I'm saying this, but at least wait for Ryvin to return."

His eyes were wild, his expression determined and sincere. He was worried about me and if I was smart, I'd heed that warning. On instinct, I nodded. "Alright."

He let out a sigh of relief.

We walked the rest of the way to the training courtyard in silence. Princess Laera was already waiting for me. A bird made a forlorn cry in the distance, the sound jarring against the quiet.

"You can go," Laera said to Vanth.

"I was told to watch over her," Vanth replied.

"I'm not going to steal her away from you, shifter," Laera said.

"I'll be fine, Vanth." I set my hand on his arm briefly, trying to convey that I'd keep his words in mind.

Laera's eyes narrowed when they dropped to where I was touching the General. She smirked. "Wonder how my brother will feel about finding out his human is slumming it with a shifter."

My hands curled into fists by my side.

"Have a good session, your highness." Vanth's voice was tight, but there was a hit of a warning in his tone.

I unclenched my fists, realizing Laera was trying to rile me up. And it was working. A smirk crossed my own lips, and I looked over at her. "I must have rattled you if you're resorting to talking shit."

She smiled. "It's cute that you think you stand a chance against me."

"Why else would you make snide comments like that?" I lifted a brow. "You're trying to throw me off."

"Or maybe I simply tell it like it is. You're a bastard, why not sleep your way to power? My brother didn't fall for it, so now you go after one of our generals?"

"At dinner, you and your father seemed to think Ryvin was interested in me. Which is it? It seems you'll change your tune to whatever suits you in the moment," I sneered.

"You might be a pretty face, but you're fragile and you should remember that. In Konos, you're like a pet. A small creature we must look after so you don't get yourself eaten by larger predators." She walked to a wall of weapons and pulled two daggers from their pegs before casually tossing one toward me. It landed blade down in the dirt at my toes.

I didn't flinch.

The smile on my face hadn't faded because she was still trying to get in my head. I'd seen this tactic used by guards in the sparring ring. Generally the one talking the most was the underdog. I knew not to underestimate Laera. I knew she was powerful, and she'd bested me yesterday effortlessly. I knew I wasn't as strong or as skilled as her. Despite all that, I'd somehow gotten under her skin.

I yanked the blade out of the earth and adjusted my grip as I'd been taught. Laera held her own blade the same way I'd learned, gripping the hilt so the blade was perpendicular to her arm instead of an extension of it.

"These are not practice blades," she warned as she circled me.

"Good." I lunged forward, striking first.

She dodged, but I anticipated her movement and managed to graze her arm as she moved out of my way. Taking another step back, she glanced down at the blood seeping into the sleeve of her tunic. She grinned, then launched into an attack.

I spun away, then dropped low, missing her blade before sweeping my foot under hers, sending her down. Dust rose in a cloud around her, but she kicked her leg out, sending me to the ground before she jumped to her feet.

I rolled away, barely escaping the downward stab of her knife. One more roll, then I was on my feet, panting as I faced her. The smile was gone from her face and a little flicker of pride welled. I'd shaken her.

She came at me again, her teeth bared. I feigned, but she anticipated my movement and I ended up with a slice on my arm. Wincing, I sent the pain away, not letting myself look at the injury before spinning to face her again.

The princess paced, glaring at me as if seeing me for the first time. "You've had more training than I realized."

"Maybe your sources aren't as reliable as you hoped," I said.

"Perhaps." She charged, and I watched her movements, my body reacting to her. Then she kicked my knee instead of striking, and I went down with a surprised yell. My dagger fell from my grip and her foot landed on my wrist, pinning my arm.

She leaned down, then pressed her blade to my throat. "You're still not good enough. You have no sense of self preservation. If I didn't know better, I'd say you wanted me to kill you."

"That's not true," I grit out.

"Then why do you hold back?" she asked as she pressed the blade tighter to my throat.

The steel was cold against my skin and I realized she was holding the flat side of the blade to me. She wasn't going to kill me. At least not right this second.

"You won't improve if you're worrying about harming

your opponent. Even in training, you need to view your partner as the enemy. If you can't give it your all when you practice, you will never be able to win a real fight." She pulled the dagger from my throat, then took her foot off my wrist.

To my surprise, she offered her hand. I hesitated, and she lifted her brows. "If I was going to kill you, I'd have done it already."

I took her hand and stood, nearly going back down as soon as I put weight on my leg. Wincing, I shifted my weight to my left leg. My right knee was going to take some time to heal.

"I didn't want to hurt you, but I had to push you," she said.

"Why are you doing this?" I asked.

"I have my reasons," she said.

"How can I trust you if you won't tell me?" I pressed.

"You can't. And you shouldn't. Just know that for the time being, I think we have similar goals." She picked up my abandoned dagger.

"You want me off this island?" I asked before I could stop myself.

She chuckled. "You're not getting off this island. But I have a feeling you'll play into other things. Things that I've been waiting for."

I limped toward a tree stump and sat down. "You do realize that if you want my help for whatever your plan is, I'm going to ask for something in return."

"I'm already teaching you how to defend yourself," she said. "What more could you want?"

"I want the tributes unharmed. I want them sent home." And I wanted the king dead, but I wasn't about to say that part out loud.

She stared at me a moment, as if considering my words. "I shouldn't even be saying this, but if I get what I want, there won't be another Choosing."

My stomach twisted into knots. That was the same thing my father had said. Laera had no idea that the dragons were in Athos working on a way to take down the fae. If they won, whatever her plans were, I had a feeling they wouldn't matter.

"That's not good enough," I said.

She sighed.

"I want those who are already here cared for," I said. "I want them to make it back home."

"You do know how Ryvin had them chosen this year, right?" she asked. "Morta picked, which means their days are short already."

"What do you mean?" I asked.

Her brow furrowed. "You don't know?"

"What should I know?"

"Morta is one of the fates. My human-loving brother insisted on only choosing tributes who were already near death. Everyone selected will be dead long before the beast requires another meal."

I sucked in a breath, stunned by her words. Was she telling the truth? Were all the tributes running on borrowed time? Was that why Morta was involved? Why Ryvin had said she was the one who chose?

"She's a fate?" the question came out too quietly, and I

realized after I said it how dumb I sounded. She'd just told me that, why would she make it up? Laera had no reason to share that with me.

"She's the one who cuts the threads. She knows exactly when everyone's time is up," Laera said. "It's actually quite entertaining when you think about it. My father is counting on those humans to last nine years."

She handed me my abandoned dagger. "I'm tired of this conversation. Do you know how to throw a dagger?"

I accepted the blade then shook my head, still reeling from what she'd said, but shoved the questions aside. "I learned swords, daggers, and basic hand-to-hand combat."

"That knee of yours isn't going to hold your weight today, I'll send a healer later. I've got an hour before I have to get to my next meeting." She crossed the courtyard and grabbed one of the dummies, dragging it over to where we were. Then she pulled several knives and daggers from the wall before dropping them on the ground next to me.

"Throwing a blade lets you attack from a distance. And it's useful if you're injured and can't move from the location you're in." She causally threw a knife, and it landed in the dummy's head. "Your turn."

I picked up a knife and tossed it. It didn't even make it to the dummy. "Fuck."

"It gets easier." She walked me through the steps and after a few more failures, I finally got a knife to stick in the dummy's chest.

"Nice work," she said.

"I was aiming for its head," I admitted.

She laughed. "Alright. Go again."

By the time Vanth arrived to take me back to my rooms, I was sweaty and exhausted and I knew how to throw a knife at a target. I wasn't sure what had happened between us, but for some reason, Laera and I were on the same side. At least for now.

23

Lagina

My father's funeral had hurt more than I thought it would. Holding back tears as I watched the fire consume a stranger's body wasn't how I expected to say goodbye to him. Istvan had declared that the funeral rites would be for a select few, something about the will of the gods. Just enough witnesses to spread the news that the king's body had been sent with the full honors his role deserved. I shook the memory from my mind, refocusing on the meeting I was supposed to be listening to. My attention had wandered hours ago, but the ancient men who had served my father were still arguing about the same things they always did.

"That's enough for today." I stood, sending a clear message that the meeting was over. "We will resume our discussion tomorrow."

"Not tomorrow, your highness," Istvan said. "It's your coronation."

I'd been doing the job for a full week already, so the event had lost its luster. Most of my life, I'd imagined my coronation day the same way most girls pictured their weddings. Marriage was never in my mind, but ruling this kingdom was everything. I'd been trained as long as I could remember to take this role, but now that I was here, I'd give just about anything for things to go back to the way they were. "Of course. The day after, then. I'll see you all at the coronation."

The advisors filed out of the room, leaving me alone with Istvan. His lips were pressed into a tight line, and I could tell he was dying to say something. "What is it?"

"There's rumblings, your highness," he said. "News of people meeting to discuss rebellion."

"Do they know, or do they have other complaints?" I knew there were many in Athos who objected to my age or my sex. Earning their trust was going to take time, and I could deal with that. If they found out about my father, that was a different story.

"I'm not sure yet, but I've got some eyes on them," Istvan replied.

I'd always wondered why my parents had put up with the slimy priest all these years. His network and sources seemed to surpass that of our spymaster. Not that I could trust the spymaster anymore, anyway. I gave him the task of keeping me updated on the dragon's convoy and he hadn't given me news in days. Either the dragons were no longer coming, or his spies had been killed.

"And what of the other task?" I asked.

"There are few records of half-vampires who survived past infancy. My sources are checking some of the temples near the wall. They have tomes that are older than Athos," he replied.

I closed my eyes and took a deep breath through my nose. Sophia didn't know yet. Nobody aside from Istvan and I knew about that detail. And only the guards and my mother were aware of the half-vampire child she carried. For now, it had to remain that way. At least until we had more information.

"You should get some rest, your highness," Istvan said. "You have a big day tomorrow."

Sasha pushed another pin into my hair, the pointed end biting into my scalp. I winced, but didn't say anything. Usually, her touch was so gentle, but I knew she was feeling the pressure of today's event just as I was. Only yesterday, she'd tried to step down from her place as my lead maid. She'd been with me only a short time, but out of all my maids, I enjoyed her company the most.

"All finished," she said. "You ready for this?"

"No," I admitted. She was the only person I let my guard down around. "But I'll fake it until everyone believes I truly am the Queen of Athos."

"You're going to do great." She handed me a mirror and I held it up, peering at my reflection. It was almost as if my mother was looking back at me, rather than seeing myself. My hair was pinned in a series of intricate twists. Gone was my preferred style of letting my long gold tresses hang loose down my back. My eyes were lined with kohl, my cheeks rouged, my lips painted. A soft gold shimmer was dusted on my eyelids. It was a big change from the pink tint I applied to my lips for formal events.

"You look beautiful," Sophia gasped as she walked into the room. Her gold peplos flowed around her, making her look even more radiant than me. She never needed makeup or anything extra to make her glow. I'd always thought it was her natural personality shining through. For a brief moment, I wondered if it was the vampire blood.

I shoved the thought away. Even if it was, Sophia had never been a threat. Out of all of us, she was the only one I'd say would rather die than take a life. How could she be one of those bloodthirsty creatures we'd been warned about?

"Exactly like a queen," Cora added as she joined Sophia in my bedroom. Her matching gold gown was tighter than Sophia's, with a daring slit that showed most of her right thigh when she moved. I appreciated her little rebellion. There was no way mother approved that, but it was too late for her to change now.

"Thank you." I smiled at my sisters as I passed the mirror back to Sasha before rising from my chair. My blue dress created a strong contrast to my sisters. I suspected that was why Mother had insisted I be the only one in our family's color. She'd hesitated initially when I'd asked for my sisters to be by my side on the dais, but later backed down.

Now, with them on my sides, I'd be flanked by gold, drawing more attention to me. I swallowed against the lump in my throat. I could do this. I had been born for this. Trained my whole life. Even if I wasn't ready, I would pretend I was, if only to keep my family safe.

My mother was waiting outside the throne room door, ready to accompany us into the room. She smiled approvingly as we approached. "You look positively regal."

A guard flanked either side of the large wooden doors, and I tried not to think about how there used to be so many more of them around the palace. We'd called back most of the soldiers at the wall to increase our numbers in the city, but they wouldn't be here for a few more days at least.

The ceremony was small and somber. I was vaguely aware of my body going through the motions of kneeling and standing and reciting the words after Istvan. It didn't feel real. It was almost as if I was watching someone else be crowned Queen of Athos.

My sisters and my mother knelt before me; the nobles and elders following their example. I stood, Istvan setting the gold and sapphire crown on my head. "Long live the queen!"

A chorus rose up to greet him, chanting long live the queen. When I rose to my feet, my family stood, and the others joined them before erupting into cheers. I forced a smile on my face. It was all so surreal.

There were so many other, far more urgent matters to deal with. The fact that I was standing here, wasting time made me feel itchy. I wanted to flee back to the study to continue work on the dozens of other tasks I was torn between. Like how to prepare for when my youngest sister went into a bloodlust frenzy.

I glanced at Istvan, who gave me a knowing look that was part warning. He seemed to know how desperately I wanted to get away, but I knew I had to follow through with this. He, and the rest of my advisors, seemed to feel the coronation and party following it were too important to skimp. If we changed things, the people would be suspicious.

I walked down the steps and stood in front of the dais, waiting to greet each person one at a time before we retreated to the ballroom for the feast. Thankfully, I'd kept the numbers small so it wouldn't take as long.

The doors groaned and I tensed, turning to see who had arrived late. Guards marched forward, all wearing the colors of Athos, but they were worn down. Their faces were covered in dirt and some of them were injured.

"What is the meaning of this?" Istvan called.

That's when a familiar face swept into the room and I let out a relieved sound that was part laughter, part sob. My aunt Katerina was just as disheveled as the guards she traveled with, but I'd recognize those dark eyes and brown curls anywhere.

She froze a few steps into the throne room. "What's going on here? Where's my brother?"

"He's dead," I said, surprised by how steady my voice was.

"You're speaking to the new Queen of Athos," Istvan said smugly.

Her eyes widened, and her lips parted as if she was going to say something. Then she lowered her head and dropped to one knee. The soldiers around her did the same.

"Your Majesty," she said. "We are at your service."

"What is this about a new queen?" A deep voice called.

A man I'd never seen before strolled into the throne room, walking right past all the kneeling guards. He wore black, dragon scale armor and his dark red hair was pulled back into a braid at the base of his head. "I have been in discussion with a king. Who the fuck are you?"

"That is no way to speak–" Istvan started, but I lifted my hand, silencing him.

I strolled forward, keeping my gaze locked on the stranger. "I am the Queen of Athos and if you have a problem with it, you can turn around and go back to where you came from."

"Gina, that's the Dragon King," my mother hissed.

"I don't care who he is." I held his stare. "This is my kingdom."

The Dragon King grinned. "Well, nice to see the new queen has some fire to her. But what I want to know is if our original bargain stands."

Katerina stood, her soldiers rising with her. "The queen will honor her father's wishes, your highness."

"I'm aware of the arrangements you had with my father," I replied. "And we can discuss all the terms after you've recovered from your travels."

"I don't think so. I want to meet my bride," he said.

I balled my hands into fists. I thought we'd have more time. They must not have stopped to make camp as we'd anticipated. I hadn't even had time to have the conversation about this with her.

The Dragon King smirked. "She doesn't know. What an interesting twist."

I scowled at him. "Cora, come here."

My sister was pale, all the color drained from her face. None of her usual defiance or vitality was evident. She knew what I was going to say, and I hated that I hadn't told her sooner. She was never going to forgive me for this. "King Bahar, this is my sister Cora, your future bride."

24

Ara

The new boots and trousers made movement easier, but Laera was still faster than me. She ducked under my strike, then spun, her blade stopping just before making contact with my waist.

"Again." She lowered her blade and took a step back, waiting for me to get into my starting position.

I wiped the sweat from my brow and sucked in a few deep breaths before gripping the hilt and facing her.

We'd been repeating the same patterns for an hour already. Moves that were variations of what I'd learned in my training, but with a few modifications. According to Laera, they were to account for my lack of upper body strength. It sounded like an insult, but I wasn't as strong as many of my opponents, despite my years of training. If her methods would keep me from wearing out as quickly, I'd try.

She came at me, shifting her weight and staying low as she'd instructed. Even though I knew it was coming, I still wasn't fast enough. My jaw tensed as she held the point of her sword at my throat. "You're still defaulting to your old training. You have to let that go."

"I'm trying."

"You're not trying hard enough," she insisted.

"What exactly is going on here?" Ryvin's voice made my heart leap.

"I'm training your friend so she doesn't end up dead during whatever you have planned," Laera said. She returned her sword to the barrel and crossed her arms over her chest.

"Who says I have something planned?" Ryvin replied.

I returned my sword, then stepped closer to the prince, scanning him for any signs of injuries. He'd said he'd been away on his father's business, but I wasn't sure I believed that.

"You think you can keep something this big quiet from me?" Laera lifted a skeptical brow.

"Your spies must be feeding you incorrect information," he said.

"She summoned a sea serpent," Laera glanced at me, then looked back to Ryvin.

"I didn't summon anything," I said. "I'm lucky I'm alive."

Ryvin's brow furrowed. "Another one?"

"Another one?" I echoed. "Why or how could I…" The image of the dead vampire flooded my mind. Was this all connected? Did he think that whatever the magic I had was capable of bringing in a sea serpent? "That's impossible."

Laera glanced at me. "There have been no sea serpent sightings in hundreds of years. You arrive and we have two. That's not a coincidence."

She turned to Rvyin. "I know why you brought her here. I thought she was some fling, but it was never about that, was it? The least I can do is help her learn how to stay alive once everything goes down."

"Nothing is going down. And nothing is going to happen to Ara," Ryvin said.

"Someone needs to explain all this to me. Wouldn't I know if I summoned something?" I looked at the siblings, trying to understand what they were talking about. How was any of this possible? And had Ryvin known? Was that why he'd agreed to let me come here?

"You going to tell her your suspicions? I assume that's where you've been the last few days. Did you get confirmation?" Laera asked.

Ryvin scowled. "I'm not discussing anything with you. Especially not here."

Laera took a step closer to her brother. "If you think you can pull this off without my help, you're insane. I see everything and I'm the one who directs those eyes. I choose the information that gets to the king and which information gets lost. You can't afford me as your enemy."

"You're always playing for yourself," Ryvin said. "I can't trust you."

"You don't have a choice, Brother."

I waited, practically holding my breath as I watched the two of them. Ryvin seemed to be considering Laera's offer. If she was as connected as she claimed, I wasn't sure how anyone could get away with anything without her help. Not that I had any idea what was going on. Or how it related to me.

Laera started laughing. It was a slightly unhinged kind of laughter that made me take a step back from her.

"What's so funny?" Ryvin asked through gritted teeth.

"She's in Athos, isn't she? All this time. All these years. And she was right under our noses," Laera said.

"Our?" Ryvin arched a brow.

"You can't honestly think you were the only one looking for her," Laera said. "I thought we'd have to kill the beast to make any progress, but you found a loophole." Her eyes traveled to me, her lips curling into a smirk. "You're the key, aren't you? My brother actually found a way to bypass killing the creature."

"Can someone please explain what's going on here?" I demanded.

Ryvin narrowed his eyes at his sister. "Ara is not a part of this."

"I beg to differ. And I'm not the only one who suspects," Laera said. "Father isn't stupid."

"That's why he had me come to dinner..."

That finally got Ryvin's attention. "He invited you to dinner?"

I nodded. "Please, explain this to me. Don't leave me in the dark like my father did."

Ryvin sucked in a breath and he reached for me, but stopped suddenly, his expression growing hard. Someone was coming.

Approaching footsteps had us all turning at once.

Vanth paused when he reached the courtyard. "Why do I feel like I just walked in on something?"

"If you figure it out, will you tell me?" I asked.

"This isn't the place," Ryvin said.

"Midnight. Our old meeting place," Laera said.

Ryvin nodded, then Laera turned and left without another word.

I stared open-mouthed at Ryvin, not masking the confusion in my expression.

"What's going on?" Vanth asked cautiously.

"Not the time or place," Ryvin said, then he turned his attention to me, his eyes exploring me. He moved closer, then brushed his fingertips over a scrape on my upper arm. "Did she harm you? Did anyone harm you?"

"We were just sparring." Goosebumps trailed down my arms at his touch. "What is happening, Ryvin? Don't shut me out."

"It's not safe here," he said.

"Did you find what you were looking for?" Vanth asked.

Ryvin's jaw tensed, and he nodded.

"I'm sorry I didn't stop them from telling the king about the sea serpent. I didn't realize until he asked to see her." Vanth moved closer until he was right in front of Ryvin. "You can't cut me out if you want me to keep her alive. I owe her my life and she takes priority over you. Don't think I won't cross you if it means saving Ara."

My eyes widened. "Vanth, that's not..."

"I wasn't certain before," Ryvin said.

"But you are now?" Vanth asked.

Ryvin nodded.

Vanth ran a hand through his hair and glanced over at me before turning back to the prince. "This changes everything."

Frustrated, I balled my hands into fists. I wanted to know what they were talking about, but they were making it very clear they weren't going into details here. "I'm going to my room."

When I passed Ryvin, he grabbed my upper arm, then he leaned closer to me. His lips brushed against my ear. "I know who your mother is. And I'll tell you everything tonight."

I felt like I was drowning. As if I'd gone under, submerged in the churning, icy water of the sea. My breath stolen, my chest tight, my throat dry. Who my mother *is*, not who my mother *was*.

"I'll walk you to your room," Vanth offered.

I'm not sure how I made it back to that windowless, dusty room, or how long I sat on the bed in complete shock before Noria came in and insisted I change for dinner.

"You're quiet tonight. Did something happen with the princess?" Noria asked.

I realized I hadn't spoken to her, and she'd already finished my hair. I'd been staring at myself in the mirror, but wasn't even aware of what was going on around me. My mind was elsewhere, preoccupied by what I might learn tonight.

Forcing a smile to my lips, I looked up at Noria. "I'm fine. Just tired."

She hummed, then reached for the kohl to apply to my eyes. When she finished with the makeup, she looked at me with a solemn expression. "Whatever it is, I hope it goes in your favor."

"I'll be alright," I assured her.

The knock on the door broke the heavy silence between us and I was relieved that Vanth was here to take me to dinner. The king had ignored me the last two days, but it seemed now that Ryvin was back, my luck had changed. At this point, I wanted to get it over with so I could get to my meeting with Ryvin later tonight. I had to find out what was going on.

"Your highness, welcome back," Noria said.

I turned quickly, my heart racing at the sight of Ryvin in my doorway. I hadn't expected to see him here. I figured he'd be at dinner, but I thought he'd largely ignore me. He'd barely interacted with me earlier today and seemed eager to leave. Nothing between us was easy. I still couldn't figure out how I was supposed to act around him.

"Thank you for taking care of Ara for me while I was away." Ryvin's tone was sincere and Noria curtseyed in response.

I made my way to the door and his eyes found me, dropping lower, then rising up to my eyes after taking all of me in. "You look beautiful."

His formal tone and tense body language were making me uncomfortable. Was that how things would be between us now? He'd been so causal in our short conversation earlier.

"Thank you, your highness."

He offered his elbow and I accepted, feeling tingling up and down my arm in response to the contact. I hated this. I hated how I didn't know how to interact with him. And if I was being honest, I hated that I couldn't just drop my guard and let him in. It would be so easy, but would it be the right choice?

"I'm sorry I can't tell you more yet," he said.

"Can you tell me where you went?" I asked.

He shook his head.

"What should I expect tonight?" I asked. "Your father thinks you killed all those people for me."

He was silent for a moment, then stopped walking. He lowered his arm, then ran a hand through his hair.

"Ryvin, we can't keep doing this. Hot and cold, back and forth. It's too much." What was I saying? What was I asking? I wasn't even sure myself.

His eyes found mine. "I did kill all those people for you. And I'd do it again. Every time."

"Why?"

"It was the only way to ensure your survival. They were going to kill you. It was the only option." He brushed his knuckles along my cheek and I closed my eyes, leaning into his touch.

Why couldn't I stay away from him? He was dangerous, and we were on opposite sides. Even if I wanted to be with him, I couldn't. We could be allies, friends even, but I knew that wasn't possible. Because I would always want more from him. I would always feel that pull to him. There wasn't a way to keep him in my life without diving head first.

It was terrifying and exhilarating and dangerous. I couldn't be with him without losing myself.

I opened my eyes, then caught his hand, lowering it from my face. "Ryvin..."

"I know." He turned and took a deep breath before offering his elbow again. "My father is going to try to befriend you at dinner. That's how he tries to win people over. Play the game, but don't give him any details."

"I don't have any details to give," I countered.

"You have some things that need to remain hidden," he reminded me.

A rush of anxiety swirled in my gut. The magic I'd used. I'd been so good at shoving that away, at pretending it didn't happen. "I won't tell him."

"Thank you." He stopped at the end of the hallway, just before the floor transitioned back to marble. "You know I'd never do anything to hurt you, right?"

I nodded. At least that much I could let myself believe.

"Good. Because after tonight, everything is going to change." He didn't say another word as we walked the rest of the way to the dining hall.

25

Ara

Dinner wasn't in the same dining hall I'd visited before. Tonight, the entire courtyard was awash in red paper lanterns, flickering and swaying in the breeze. They bathed the attendees in ominous shadows that undulated and moved in an unnatural way.

Flowers and vines climbed up the columns that surrounded the courtyard, the color of their blooms impossible to determine in the eerie red glow.

Long tables were piled with food and servants carried bottles of wine, refilling any cup they crossed. There were so many different kinds of fae present, moving about the open space with smiles on their faces. I caught sight of fae who almost passed as human if not for their pointed ears. Then there were those with antlers or tails. Some had skin the color of sunsets or the sky on a clear day.

The only thing they had in common was that none of them were human.

I could feel Ryvin's tension, alerting me to the fact that this was not a typical dinner for the king. There was no sign of thrones, no guests bowing for their sovereign. Aside from Ryvin, there were no other members of the royal family. I wondered if the king was going to make a grand entrance. That seemed to be his style. Ophelia would love him.

"What's the occasion?" I asked over the din.

"I'm not sure," Ryvin replied.

A creature with furry goat legs and the body of a man stumbled past us, ruby liquid splashing from his cup. He wore a floral crown around his head, a pair of horns holding it in place.

I glanced around again and noticed that most of the guests were wearing floral crowns. The blossoms were familiar flowers I recognized in full bloom. There must have been an entire garden picked clean to allow for such an abundance of flowers here tonight.

A squat man with dark curls and a mischievous expression skipped toward us. He moved with the light-footed joy of a child, but there was a sense of power about him I couldn't place. Anyone in his path moved away quickly, inclining their heads in reverence as he passed them.

Ryvin straightened, his body even more tense. He moved slightly in front of me, a move that wasn't the least bit subtle. "What brings you to Konos, old friend?" Ryvin kept his attention on the newcomer despite the fact that we'd acquired an audience of fae.

The man didn't hide his interest in me, his eyes roaming my body in a way that made me want to retreat. Instead, I forced myself to meet his gaze, challenging him with a look of my own.

"I can see what all the fuss was about," the man said with a grin. "Princess Ara, you are as beautiful as the rumors said. Aren't you going to introduce us, Ryvin?"

"Keep your hands to yourself, Dion," Ryvin warned.

I took a step away from the safety of Ryvin before giving Dion one of the coldest smiles I could. I'd met men like this before. Men with power who think they can have anything they want. He wasn't even intimidated by Ryvin, which should make me worry. Instead, I was annoyed by his very presence. "It seems you already know who I am, but I don't know anything about you."

Dion extended his hand. "A dance?"

A vein bulged in Ryvin's temple as he tightened his jaw. I waited several heartbeats, leaving the man unanswered. When Ryvin didn't object, I set my palm in his and followed the stranger to the dance floor.

The crowd parted and I could feel the eyes of everyone on us as Dion swept me into the middle of the courtyard. Music started, a sorrowful, haunting tune that seemed to hover in the air before falling around us like raindrops.

After a few rotations, others joined in, though they kept their distance from the two of us. I watched for Ryvin every time we were near him. His eyes never left me, his posture was tense, as if he was ready to pounce at a second's notice. Somehow, that made me feel better about dancing with this stranger.

As the chatter around us grew to a soft din and the party-goers seemed to go back to whatever they wanted to do, effectively ignoring us, I finally turned my attention to Dion. "Who are you?"

He offered a crooked smile. "I have no idea what you mean by that question."

"Don't play with me. I watched how the guests reacted to you and how you addressed Ryvin. You're not afraid of him, and he seems to have some sort of misguided sense of respect for you." It was clear Ryvin didn't like this man, but he had all but encouraged me to dance with him.

"I thought the prince might try something if I stole you away from him, even if it was for a short time," Dion supplied.

"That doesn't answer my question," I pressed.

"No, I suppose it doesn't." He sighed. "How very unfortunate that you don't know who I am. You were raised so cloistered from the rest of the world."

"Yes, yes, the ignorant Athos princess. I get it. If you're just going to insult me, I'll be taking my leave." I stopped moving and stepped away from my partner.

Dion pulled me closer and swayed, making us return to motion. "Don't be so dramatic. I don't like to be outdone when it comes to drama. I prefer to be center stage."

"I can tell," I replied. "And I prefer not to be kept in the dark while everyone around me knows what's happening."

Dion looked around, flashing a bright smile at the other dancers. I watched as cheeks flushed, male and female dancers giggled, and a few even winked or batted their eyes. There was this odd mixture of adoration and fear. As if they wanted to bed him and flee from him at the same time.

"Are you from one of the other fae courts?" I guessed. "Or somewhere in Telos? A ruler before the Fae King took it all over?"

"Of course not, foolish girl. I may dabble in the politics and kingdoms of men and fae, but I don't stay beyond my own amusement."

Something hot and angry simmered. If he wasn't fae and he held this kind of power, there was only one other possibility. I didn't want to consider it. After all, they'd largely abandoned us. If the gods were still in this realm, why had they allowed the fae to dominate everyone? Why do nothing while humans were slaughtered and kingdoms were swallowed whole?

Dion's eyes found mine again and his brows lifted knowingly. "You figured it out." He stopped moving, then reached for my necklace, holding the tiny golden serpent in between his fingers. "Where did you get this?"

I batted his hand away. "It doesn't matter."

"So feisty. Despite the fact that you know what I could do to you." He lowered his hands to my hips and drew us back into the dance.

"I don't know anything because you won't tell me." This man very well could be a god, but he was infuriating.

He gave a tiny incline of his head. "Dionysus at your service."

I sucked in a surprised breath and stared wide-eyed at

the god. No wonder he'd done nothing to help us. He might have power, but if rumors were true, he was half human. He couldn't risk angering the other gods more than he had in the past. "What are you doing here in Konos?"

"I came for you."

"What?" That didn't make any sense. I stopped moving again. People continued to dance around us, but I wasn't seeing them. "Why would you come all the way here for me?"

"I think we should take this conversation somewhere more private." Dion offered his elbow.

Reluctantly, I gripped his upper arm and followed him through the crowd to where Ryvin was waiting for us.

"Are you ready to explain what you're doing here?" Ryvin asked, his tone an icy calm.

Dion gestured toward the entry and the three of us walked quietly forward, not stopping until we were in an empty room. I released Dion's arm and moved away from him, giving myself some space from the god while he closed the door behind us.

Several chairs were scattered around the space, but none of us sat. Ryvin came closer to me until our arms were touching. A little rush of tingles raced down my arm and I resisted the urge to clasp his hand.

"You've had your fun, Dion. Now, tell me what you're really doing here," Ryvin said.

"You once did me a favor, and I promised I'd return it in kind. Today is that day," Dion stated.

My brow furrowed as I watched their expressions.

Dion was smug, calculating, yet playful. Whatever information he was holding was important, and he was enjoying the weight he held over Ryvin despite the fact that it was him who was in the prince's debt.

On the other hand, Ryvin's face was a mask. Blank and devoid of emotion. I could usually sense how he was feeling at a rather annoying level of accuracy, but this was different. It was like he'd closed himself off.

A shiver ran down my spine. I'd seen that from him before. I'd even attempted the same. Shutting down emotions, going blank to avoid something uncomfortable to settle the building rage.

Ryvin was holding back with everything he had. Whatever Dion had brought up, it wasn't good.

"Isn't a favor owed meant to be asked for by the other person?" I asked, hoping to diffuse the situation. "What if he doesn't want the favor cashed in now?"

"He does."

"You seem very certain," Ryvin said. "And if I recall, you owe me a life."

"And that's what I'm giving you in return," Dion replied.

"Do I need to remind you of the magic I wield?" Ryvin's tone was deadly. "I don't care who your father is. If you are threatening—"

Dion held up his hand. "I'm trying to save a life, not take one."

"I think you need to leave," Ryvin said.

"The gods found out about Ceto's child. They aren't going to wait until you finish your business before they come for her," Dion said.

My heart pounded, responding to his words despite the fact that they didn't make sense. It was like some part of me, deep in my bones, knew what he was getting at. But it couldn't be true. I didn't want to hear it. I didn't want to know this.

"I have it under control," Ryvin hissed.

"Do you?" Dion cocked an amused brow. "Because last I checked, as long as she carries that magic with her, she's a target."

"Ceto?" I whispered the name of the goddess of monsters, the reason we couldn't go into the sea. She controlled the water itself and commanded every creature that lurked in its depths. Even the sirens listened to her.

"I was going to tell you tonight," Ryvin said.

"She didn't know?" Dion laughed, a boyish, musical sound that somehow made the gravity of the situation less intense. I almost wanted to join in, laughing at the absurdity of the fact that I thought I was human my whole life only to discover that all this time, something powerful lurked inside me.

"Ceto, the goddess?" I managed, not sure if I didn't believe it or if I was trying to get a different answer than the one I already knew.

Dion was in front of me before I saw him move and he touched the snake on my necklace with his index finger. "You wear one of her creatures around your neck."

I stepped back, then lifted the golden charm so I could see it better. Iris had said it was a snake. I thought it to be a snake. I'd largely ignored it, simply leaving it on because it came from home.

But he was right. It wasn't just a normal snake, it had the elongated body and larger head of a sea serpent. The very one I'd seen twice since arriving in Konos.

"Who gave you that?" Ryvin asked, also seeming to notice the details for the first time.

"A maid, the new one who was assigned to me right before I left," I said.

"How very interesting. A new maid who arrived the same time the prince from Konos did?" Dion asked.

"No, she came after." But his words made me question how Iris had reacted to me, how she'd said she volunteered after Mila's death.

"What was her name?" Ryvin asked.

"Iris."

Dion laughed again in that boyish chuckle. The one that made you feel like you were in on the joke. I had to force myself not to smile. "Oh, this is even bigger than I realized." He leaned forward and touched the necklace again, and I backed away.

"Stop touching me," I snapped.

"It's subtle, but I think I feel it," Dion said, ignoring my words.

Ryvin stepped between us, turning his back to the god. He reached for my necklace and I held my breath while his fingers brushed against my collarbone, sending delicious shivers through me. Hating that I still reacted so easily to him, especially in front of a god, I clenched my jaw tight and sent the feelings away.

"You're right," Ryvin said, releasing the necklace.

"What do you mean, he's right?" I asked, covering the charm with my palm.

Ryvin held up his arm, showing a gold bracelet wrapped around his wrist. "It's the same charm. Protection from the Queen of the Ocean. Someone went out of their way to make sure you'd be safe while crossing the sea. The queen can't touch you with that around your neck."

"That won't stop the others," Dion said.

"Hold on." I held my hands out in front of me, silencing both men. "Go back. Explain all of this so I know what's going on. You're saying someone is out to kill me and my mother is the goddess of fucking monsters?"

Ryvin ran his hand through his dark hair. "I made a deal with the Queen of the Ocean. That's where I was when I left."

"You knew this?" My chest felt tight. I was so tired of the secrets. Shaking my head, I turned away from him, taking a few deep breaths. I wasn't human. At least not all human. But I wasn't vampire or fae. If Ryvin was telling the truth, I was half god.

My breathing quickened as panic gripped me like a vise. I reached ahead, desperate for something to hold on to as my thoughts swirled. Ryvin caught me and I tensed in his grip but didn't fight him. He smoothed my hair. "Deep breaths. I'm sorry. I should have told you."

I wasn't sure how long I stood there, leaning against his firm chest, breathing in his scent, before I realized his touch was soothing even though I wanted to scream at him. Finally, I stepped out of his embrace, tears blurring my vision. I wiped them away. "Why did you keep that from me?"

"I swear I was going to tell you tonight. I just wanted to be sure before I said anything."

I nodded, recalling his comment when we'd been at the training grounds. "Who else knows?"

"Laera guessed and I'm sure Vanth figured it out," he replied.

"And Hera has to know if Iris was there," Dion said.

"Did you come here with something to offer or to simply warn us?" Ryvin asked. "Because if you're just here to tell me someone is hunting her, you should leave now before I test just how angry I'd make your father if I sent you to the Underworld."

Dion winced. "I'd rather not go back there again. It's not my favorite place to travel. Though, I doubt my father would care in the least." He waved a dismissive hand. "I told you, I'm here to return your favor. You helped me long ago. Now, it's my turn."

"And how exactly are you going to help us?" Ryvin asked.

"I'll marry Ara."

"What?" I exclaimed at the same time as Ryvin.

Dion chuckled. "It's not too much of an inconvenience for me. It's not like I expect you to stay loyal, but think of the fun we could have. You call the monsters to sink the ships and when the sailors beg for their lives, I'll turn them into dolphins. Think of the chaos we could create. The absolute terror we could cause."

"Ara is not one of your maenads." Dark shadows twisted around Ryvin's wrists.

"I didn't say she was. But if she's married to me, she's not a threat to the gods. She's one of them. One of us. She already is, they just don't want to acknowledge her. I suppose you two have that in common, don't you?" Dion leaned against the back of a chair and began to examine his fingernails.

"I am not marrying you." I didn't care if he was a god.

"Really, it's up to you, darling. I don't care if you live or die, but I saw my opportunity to repay a favor owed and I do rather hate being in debt. This clears me, and it gets the other gods off your scent."

"Are they really going to kill me?" I asked Ryvin.

"No. I have it all under control," he insisted. "You should go, Dion."

"How could you possibly have this under control? If you succeed in what I suspect you're after, the Ocean Queen will come after your princess. She can barely stand the fact that her sister can control the beings in her waters. You think she'll allow another? A weaker version?" Dion glanced at me. "Sorry, darling, but it's true. With that half human blood, you'll never be as strong as them. But you can still make their lives miserable. Look how well I do? I simply invented wine and now humans give me anything I want and the gods ignore me."

"I have it under control." Ryvin turned to me. "I swore to you I'd never let anyone hurt you. I have a plan."

Dion shrugged. "Suit yourself. The offer stands and you know where to find me."

"This party's your doing, isn't it?" Ryvin asked.

With a chuckle, Dion turned toward the door. "Of course it is. You should come join in. Things are about to get very interesting."

26

Ara

As soon as Dion was out of the room, I closed the door, then stood in front of it so Ryvin couldn't run off. "You have a lot of explaining to do."

"I know." He stepped closer until I could feel the heat of his body. "And I promised you that I'll answer any question you have."

"How are you going to keep the gods from killing me?" I asked.

He winced. "Except that one."

Giving him my best glare, I crossed my arms. "We are not going to play these games. I want to trust you, but you have to tell me things."

"Let's start with an easier question." He leaned so close I could feel his breath on my skin and I shuddered, my arms dropping to my side as my body reacted to him. Moving slowly, he closed the space until his lips were hovering above mine. He waited, achingly patient, as if certain I would push him away. I could hear my heart pounding, feel the anticipation winding like a spring tight and wanting low in my belly.

When his lips met mine, it was tentative. The ghost of a kiss, hesitant and questioning. Full of wonder and confusion and desire and anger and lust. It was all the uncertainty hanging between us, but my hesitation vanished the second I moved my lips and leaned into him.

This man had lied to me, but I'd been playing him just the same. He served a king who was after power at any cost; but so had I. Neither of us were who we said we were, or who we tried to be. I knew there was a great plan at play and, for some reason, the fates set him on my path.

I threw my arms around his shoulders and deepened the kiss. He pressed against me, my whole body flat against the door.

Somehow I was involved in a mess with gods and monsters and humans and fae. Who was I to question fate giving me this moment to feel something other than pure fucking terror at my situation?

I turned off my mind, closed out all the doubts and let myself truly feel the moment.

Ryvin's touch was like icy fire. Leaving heat that tingled like bursts of cold against my bare skin. His kiss was claiming and hungry and I welcomed every movement, every flick of his tongue, every feel of his stubble against my cheeks. We kissed like we were fighting a battle, only this time, we were on the same side. Working in unison, anticipating each other's movement, going deeper and faster together. Breathless, I devoured him, tasting wine on his tongue, and salt on his skin.

Panting, he broke away from the kiss and took a step back. His eyes were wild, his expression positively feral. I knew I looked the same. "Why'd you stop?"

"Because I don't know if this is what you want." He clenched his jaw and I could sense his frustration.

"What do you mean?" I kissed his jaw, but he turned away.

"Dion's magic makes it so it's almost impossible to resist, even if it's not what you want," he explained.

My skin felt like it was on fire. It was taking all my willpower not to lunge at him and tear his clothes off. I closed my eyes and took a few deep breaths. That was probably for the best. He hadn't even answered any of my questions yet. We'd gone from attempting our first actual conversation since arriving in Konos to blind lust. I had to be more careful around him. "Alright." I stepped back, wondering how much of what I was feeling was real.

"I really do want to tell you everything and we're meeting Laera and Vanth tonight. But for now, we should show my father that we're just a couple of spoiled royals. Can you do that with me?" He extended his hand.

I swallowed hard, then accepted. "What about his mind reading?"

"Vanth told me you had to watch that." He shook his head. "It's unpleasant, but he can't do it unless he's touching you. And as far as I know, he can't read the gods. He can't read me, and now that we know about your mother, he's probably unable to read you."

"That's helpful." At least there was one good thing about finding out your mother was the goddess of monsters. It still made my head spin. How was that even possible? If not for the accidental magic I'd used to destroy that vampire, I'd tell both Dion and Ryvin that they were insane.

I sucked in a breath as we left the privacy of the room, nearly laughing out loud at the fact that I had just had a conversation with an actual god.

And a marriage proposal.

I thought things had been difficult to figure out when I first arrived, but they seemed to be getting more complicated by the day.

The party was in full swing, servants wandered with casks of wine, filling every glass. Guests weaved and bobbed, sloshing the crimson liquid from their cups with careless abandon, only to have a servant immediately top it off.

Music played, lively and loud, and the center of the courtyard was full of dancing couples and groups. Most of them had discarded their clothing at some point, the floral crowns the only thing they wore.

We passed several couples and groups who'd taken their dancing to new levels, exploring each other's bodies in carnal ways without any concern for their surroundings. Newcomers joined in, satyrs and fae entwined without care. I slowed when I caught sight of a tribute tangled in the mess.

Ryvin gripped my hand tighter. "After we find the king, we can leave."

I nodded, then made myself move, hating that the

tributes had been sucked into another party where they were supplied with fae wine. How many of them would choose this if they weren't here?

We walked near the colonnade, avoiding the groups of people hiding in the shadows and the dancers in the center of the courtyard. A long table was piled with food, but nobody was interested in eating. They only seemed to gravitate toward the wine, draining their cups, only to be topped off by servants. I wondered how much of this was Dion's influence. I hadn't been allowed to hear most of the stories involving him and his cult, but the pieces I had heard involved parties with activities that were considered unacceptable for mine and my sisters' ears.

The crowd parted and the king and queen appeared, walking toward us with an entire entourage in their wake. I stopped, frozen in place when I caught sight of a naked human with his arm casually slung over the shoulder of a beautiful fae male with jagged features and pale blue skin that reminded me of ice. Belan was barely able to walk straight, his eyes were glazed and his smile was goofy and lopsided.

"Belan? What have they done to you?" I found my voice and quickly released Ryvin's hand to rush to my friend's side.

The former guard hiccupped, then his unfocused gaze found me. "It's the princess, everyone! Quick, hide! I don't wanna get caught for drinking."

The king and the gathered crowd laughed, making Belan's face flush deep crimson. He joined in the laughter, sending blood-red wine splashing from his cup. A servant immediately refilled it and Belan put the cup to his lips, drinking deeply.

"It looks like you're the last hold-out," the king said. "Enjoy your time here, Princess. Konos can be a lovely place if you allow yourself to relax."

The queen stepped next to the king and he scowled, his nostrils flaring as if he might scream at her. Before he could get a word out, she set her hand on his upper arm. "I think she has relaxed some, my king. Did you not notice that she was elsewhere with your son?" Her eyes scanned me, then she smirked. "And her smeared makeup isn't exactly hiding what they were doing."

My cheeks heated, and I had to fight to keep myself from denying everything outright. It wasn't like it was a secret that Ryvin and I had been together in the past, but this was new. Different. And all we'd done was kiss.

The king chuckled, then nodded at his son. "Enjoy her while you can. Humans live a surprisingly short life on this island."

I recognized the threat for what it was, but held my ground. There would be a time I'd face off against the king, but this wasn't it.

"Enjoy the party," the king said before walking past us, his group of followers trailing behind him. I turned, watching as Belan stumbled along with his partner for the evening. I wasn't sure if I was hoping that he'd chosen to drink the wine or if he'd been forced. I hated the idea of him being forced, but I also hated that he might have given up.

With a quick glance around the room, I found more

tributes. All of them intoxicated and blending right into the debauchery around us.

They were all lost. None of them were going to be able to fight with me or help find a way off this island. I was going to have to figure out how to take down the king, then hope they were still alive to get a ride back to Athos.

"It's time," Ryvin said suddenly. "The king returned to his private chambers, and with all that wine from Dion, they'll be occupied until dawn."

I caught a glimpse of silver hair as Laera stepped through a side door. I wasn't sure where he was, but I knew Vanth was around here somewhere. Finally, it was time for some answers.

27

Cora

The Dragon King was a massive beast of a man. His sleeveless tunic showed off bulging biceps zig-zagged with black tattoos. I'd never seen anyone with tattoos before, and I found myself staring at the intricate designs. Bands of black ink circled his forearms in patterns of various widths and sizes. Higher up on his arms there were shapes that resembled animals, probably dragons, though there could be some other beasts mixed in there. I forced myself to look away before I got caught staring. The last thing I needed was for him to think I was interested in him.

"Shouldn't you be speaking to your betrothed?" Sophia asked, her tone innocent and a little dreamy. Leave it to Sophia to find an arranged marriage with a brute as something romantic.

"Lagina is insane if she thinks I'll actually go through with this," I told her.

She hid her smile behind her glass as she sipped, giving me a knowing look.

"What is that look for?"

She shrugged. "I'm going to dance. You should talk to him at least."

That was not going to happen. I watched as Ara was thrust toward the Ambassador from Konos and saw how that turned out for all of us. Most of our kingdom was dead, Ara was gone, and our entire life was in shambles.

I knocked back the rest of my wine in a single gulp. I missed my sister, but I knew she would want me to learn from her. I knew she'd encourage me not to follow her lead. She'd want me to fight this.

Istvan followed Lagina, his turquoise robes standing out against the sea of white peplos. It was the color of mourning in Athos and only the priests would bypass the tradition of wearing only white for the next few weeks in honor of the dead king. My jaw tightened as I shoved aside the conflicting thoughts surrounding my father's death. I'd hardly had time to mourn when Lagina threw this betrothal at me.

My gaze returned to the visitor, and I squeezed the glass in my hand tightly as my anger deepened. How could they expect this of me? I was in love with Tomas. Everyone knew. How could they expect me to abandon him for this?

The Dragon King's men mingled through the courtyard, outnumbering the members of the court and our dwindled household numbers. Without Father or Ara, everything felt so empty. Many of the surviving nobles were too terrified to attend a reception for the Dragon King and we were left with the smallest party I'd ever attended. Then there was the fact that some of the usual attendees had been burned in the funeral pyres.

My throat felt thick as I shoved the memory of the smoke filled air and cries of the onlookers from my mind. I turned toward Sophia, who was looking at me as if I were about to combust. It made everything inside me tense. She was going to hate me for what I was about to do.

"Can you tell Lagina and Mother that I'm not feeling well?" I handed her my empty glass, and she took it without hesitation.

"What are you up to, Cora?"

"Nothing." I leaned over and kissed her cheek. "I'll see you later."

She nodded tensely, and I could feel her eyes on me as I left the party. She'd forgive me, eventually. Mother would too. And hopefully, one day, Lagina would welcome me back to the palace so I could visit them.

Aside from the occasional servant, the palace was empty. Everyone was gathered at the party, distracted by the visitors. It still didn't sit right with me that we'd welcomed the kingdom who'd been at war with us for so long.

Making my way down the familiar halls, a pang of sorrow made my chest tight. As much as I hoped Lagina would forgive me, part of me worried this would be the last time I saw the inside of the palace. How had Ara felt when she left? I really hoped she was still alive. I hoped she was making the fae miserable however she could.

Slowing down, I turned down the darkened corridor, my footsteps the only sound. Carefully, I pushed open the seldom used door that was closest to the stables. Before the Choosing, this door would have a guard. Now, it was simply locked from the inside, but Tomas left it unlocked for me.

Goosebumps spread down my arms as I stepped into the breeze. It wasn't cold, but the twisting anxiety was making me on edge and my body reacted.

The scent of horses filled my nose and the pebbles of the makeshift path bit into my slipper covered feet. Good thing there would be boots and riding clothes waiting for me.

A single lamp glowed from within the stables and I couldn't see any signs of the servants who were usually here through the night. I smiled, knowing the bribes Tomas paid had worked. We were actually going to pull this off.

My pulse kicked up and the nervous anticipation grew to something more optimistic.

"Tomas?" I whispered as I stepped into the stables. "Where are you?"

A figure emerged from the shadows, and I gasped. Taking a step back, I stared wide-eyed at the Dragon King. "What are you doing here?"

"Imagine what my people will say when they find out my bride-to-be tried to run off with another man. That's not going to help my reputation." He studied me, as if expecting he'd see something on me that would give him a response.

I crossed my arms over my chest, suddenly feeling far too exposed. "What did you do to Tomas?"

He lifted an amused brow. "That little boy you were going to run away with?"

"Where is he?" I said through gritted teeth. "If you hurt him, I swear to the gods I will end you."

His lips curved into a smile. "I was so pissed the fates threw us together, but maybe they knew what they were doing."

Dropping my arms to my side, I marched toward him. "Where the fuck is Tomas?"

He shrugged. "I'm not sure. Where would he go with two bags of gold?"

I flinched, my expression showing my shock for a moment before I gathered myself. "He wouldn't."

"I would have paid a lot more. He didn't even ask for a higher amount. Agreed to never speak to you again for two bags of gold. Can you imagine? As if you were worth so little."

It wasn't possible. Tomas loved me. He'd come back to Athos for me. We were going to start a life together. We made plans.

I was breathing too fast, but I couldn't stop it. My knees buckled, and I fell, but before I hit the ground, the Dragon King caught me, then lowered me to the floor. I didn't have the energy to push him away because my whole body was shaking. It couldn't be real. After a few heaving breaths, I regained enough composure to push

Court of Vice and Death

the king away, then glared up at him. "You're lying. What did you do to him?"

This couldn't be true. Tomas couldn't have walked away from me for money. "He wouldn't. He loves me."

The king's smile faded, his lips tightening into a line. His forehead creased in concern. His look told me everything I needed to know.

Something shattered inside me and tears streamed down my cheeks. Leaning forward, I set my forehead on my knees, sobbing into my lap. Just like that, it was over. He hadn't even tried to fight for me. He'd taken gold over me. I was going to give up everything. Walk away from my family, my home, my kingdom, everything.

"I'm sorry, Cora," the king whispered.

I looked up at him through blurry vision. "How could you?"

"He gave you up for two bags of gold. You deserve better," he said.

"Like you?" I spat. "How much did you pay my sister for me? What was my price? I know you don't need an alliance with us. What did she promise you?"

"There was no dowry," he replied.

"You're a liar." I pushed myself off the ground, sniffing and wiping the tears from my face. I hated that he was seeing me like this. Forcing myself to stand with my chin high, I shot him my best judgmental glare. "You came after my people for generations and suddenly you want to play nice? And throw in one of the princesses for good measure? What is it? Famine? Drought? Why now?"

"You speak like I wanted this. Like I have some plan

that brought me here." He barked a laugh, then shook his head.

I balled my hands into fists. "Then leave. Take whatever they're going to pay you and go home. You don't need me."

"That's where you're wrong. There's no money, no resources. I didn't come here to make an alliance with your people. I came here for you. If the price of bringing you back to Drakous with me is helping them take down the fae, even better."

"That makes no sense," I countered.

"Trust me, if there was an alternative, I'd take it. But a dragon can only create offspring with their true mate and according to the fates, you're mine. So you will be my wife. You will bear my child. Then you can hunt down that worthless human trash who gave you up for money if you want. I don't care what you do with your life once I have an heir." He moved closer to me, then leaned down so his face was level with mine. "So clean yourself up and get yourself together. You show weakness like this in Drakous and my court will eat you alive."

28

Ara

The wood creaked as we crept up the plank toward the darkened ship. A warm light glowed below, inviting us to the depths. A chill ran through me as I followed Ryvin. It didn't feel like a very safe meeting space considering there'd be only one exit, but I didn't have much of a choice.

The ship swayed and rocked as we made our descent and I gripped the rails, moving slowly so I didn't fall. The scent of salt and damp wood was thick in the air, an improvement over the smell of too many people in too small of quarters last time I'd been below decks.

Vanth was already waiting for us when we arrived, illuminated by the light of a single lamp. The interior looked ominous and small with the limited light.

"Nobody saw you come out here, right?" Ryvin asked.

"No, the king and most of the court seem rather occupied," Vanth replied.

"What the fuck is Dion doing here, anyway?" Laera said as she jumped from the ladder onto the wood floor. "Not that I'm complaining about the endless supply of wine that'll make nobody recall what they did tonight. But honestly, why do I get the sense that this has something to do with you?" She pointed at me.

"I didn't ask him here," I said. "I've never even met a god before tonight."

"Aside from my brother," she sighed, "though he refuses to use the term."

"I'm not a god. I'm the child of a goddess, but that's not the same," he said.

It was the first time I'd heard it confirmed and it should have terrified me, but after finding out about my own mother tonight, it was oddly reassuring to know I wasn't alone.

"Dion is only half god," Laera pointed out.

"He was reborn from Zeus's thigh," Ryvin reminded her.

"You can't honestly believe that story." Laera rolled her eyes. "Even if it was true, it doesn't change the fact that his mother was mortal and your other half is fae. You have far more power than him."

"I don't want the title," Ryvin said through gritted teeth. "And that's not what I'm here to discuss."

"Why is he here, Ryvin?" Laera demanded. "Tell me this isn't going to throw off whatever insanity you have planned. I've waited too long for this."

"For what, exactly?" I asked.

Her gaze snapped to me. "To see my father dead."

"Well, then I guess we are on the same side after all," I replied.

"The god already left the island," Vanth added. "He was only here long enough to rile everyone up and deliver more wine than this court can drink in a year."

"You underestimate the court," Laera said darkly.

"He was here for me," I confirmed, hoping to speed things up. "But I'm guessing the rest of you already knew that I was in danger?"

Vanth looked down, suddenly very interested in the hem of his tunic. Laera smirked. "So you do have power. Enough to make the other gods envious. You exploded that vampire, didn't you?"

I glanced at Vanth, noting his unsurprised expression before turning to Ryvin. He nodded. "Go ahead."

With a sigh, I looked at the princess. "It wasn't on purpose."

Laera dropped her arms to her side. "Well, that's not going to help us. That kind of magic should have been honed from childhood. I thought she knew what she was doing and now we have gods on our trail. What was Dion here for? To collect a bounty on her? To find where she was so he could tell his brothers and sisters?"

"He offered to marry me," I blurted out.

Ryvin threw me a look that made it clear I should have kept that to myself.

"That's great!" Laera said. "When's the wedding?"

"She's not doing it," Ryvin snapped.

"She's not going to last long if he's already found her,"

Laera said. "How long until the Queen of the Ocean realizes she's here?"

"I have a deal with the Queen of the Ocean. She wants Nyx out as much as I do," he said.

"Stop. Back up and explain this from the beginning," I pleaded. "I still have no idea what you're talking about. So the Queen of the Ocean wants me dead because of who my mother is? And other gods do as well? I get that Ceto's dangerous, but I've never done anything. I didn't even know I had any kind of magic until I arrived in Konos. How did I never figure this out before?"

"I think being around magic helped awaken yours. If you'd stayed in Athos, you might have never known," Ryvin explained. "It's why your mother hid you there and left you."

I rubbed at a dull ache in my chest. I'd often wondered who my mother was. Imagined that she'd loved me and that she'd whispered tearful goodbyes from her deathbed. But she wasn't dead. And she wasn't even human. It felt like I'd been abandoned all over again. At least when I thought my mother was dead, I'd never thought I'd been left behind.

"Ceto is forbidden from having children," Laera said. "She's too powerful, and her offspring have a history of causing wars and wreaking general havoc."

"This explains the sea serpent, but doesn't explain the vampire," Vanth said quietly.

"Ceto hides her most destructive power. Simply controlling monsters isn't a concern for the gods. They could care less if someone sends creatures after anyone else," Laera said. "In fact, they'd probably enjoy the chaos."

"Dion wanted me to summon monsters to destroy ships so he could turn the dying sailors into dolphins," I murmured.

Vanth shook his head. "He thrives on chaos and insanity. I can't imagine the destruction he'd cause with you at his side."

"That's not going to happen," Ryvin said.

"So what is it that makes her their concern?" Vanth asked.

"She can control water. Well, any liquid. Including the blood inside a person." Ryvin said. "It was how I knew, but I couldn't tell you until I was sure."

"That's what I did to the vampire?" I asked.

Ryvin nodded. "Yes. You manipulated the blood in his body."

"That's the power the gods don't want passed along," Laera said. "With practice, you could wipe out hundreds at once. And you could even eliminate a god. It's one of the few powers strong enough to take them out."

It felt like my heart fell to my stomach. "I don't want that kind of power. I never asked for that."

"Nobody asks for their gifts," Laera snapped. "And you don't hear the rest of us complaining. You find a way to use it and you find a way to make yourself important enough that keeping you alive is worth the risk."

I glanced at Ryvin, seeking assurance, but his expression was unreadable. "Is that the point of all this? Have me do something so they won't kill me?"

"Nobody is going to kill you," he said.

"How does she fit into all this?" Vanth asked. "How does Ara's magic help you release Nyx?"

"That's what you're after?" My chest tightened. "You're trying to free your mother?"

"She's the only one who can take out our father," Laera said.

"How is Ara supposed to help with this? There's no way she can get past anything your father set up to guard Nyx. Otherwise you would have found her years ago," Vanth said.

Ryvin's jaw tensed. "She's in Athos."

"What?" It didn't make sense. Why would one of the most powerful goddesses ever be in a human city? How could our kingdom possibly restrain her? "Where?"

"She's in a prison in a cavern below the Black Opal. There's an entire network of caves under the city," Ryvin explained. "Selena Vastos is the proprietor."

Vanth let out a growl and Laera couldn't hide her surprise.

"She's supposed to be dead," Laera hissed. Ryvin seemed to have struck a nerve by knowing something she missed.

"I watched that woman die," Vanth bit out.

"She's very much alive, and she still hates you."

"Are you saying Selena is fae? I had no idea." The woman who ran the Black Opal was known for her discretion, she couldn't be bought by anyone in Athos. She was also known for enforcing the rules with the cruelest strokes. She was not someone to cross, but every time I'd seen her or interacted with her, she'd been kind to me. Polite and elegant, yet stern and cold. She never crossed the lines with patrons, none of them were friends, but I knew if I had a problem in the Opal, she'd take care of it.

"She's fae. Worked as the assassin to the Court of Vipers before they fell," Ryvin explained.

"Selena and my mother were very close," Laera added.

"I never had any problems with her in the Opal. She seemed nice," I offered.

"She's one of the fiercest warriors I've ever fought," Vanth said. "Don't let that pretty face fool you. Her magic makes her impossible to defeat, apparently. Even when you think she's dead."

"That's why we have to be careful about how we do this," Ryvin said. "She must be guarding the entrance to where they're keeping Nyx."

"Why would she do that? She fought against the king during the rebellion," Laera said.

"I don't think she's guarding my mother because she wants to help the Fae King," Ryvin pointed out.

Laera pressed her lips into a tight line, and she shook her head. "If Selena is in on it, there's a good chance my mother knows."

"So the queen wants him dead as much as the rest of us do," Vanth said. "Why not ask her to let Nyx out?"

"We can't ask that of my mother," Laera explained. "She's only out for her kingdom. If she could barter Nyx for The Court of Vipers, she'd give her right back to my father. He'd keep his power, and she'd move home. She's too short-sided to realize it would never last."

"Why hasn't she made a move then?" I asked.

"For whatever reason, she's decided it's not yet time," Laera replied.

"She'll know everything that Athos is planning," I realized. "I'm sure she hears everything inside the Opal. She'd know all the details. She'd know about the dragons."

Three heads turned to me and I felt my face heat. I forgot I hadn't told them yet.

"My father already knows about the dragons. They're already in Athos," Ryvin said.

Vanth shook his head. "I fucking hate fighting dragons."

"Maybe this is good," Ryvin supplied.

"How could that possibly be good, Brother? They're going to come for us and we're currently planning a coup. We don't have time to deal with them," Laera snapped.

"They want the king gone. Our goals are aligned," Ryvin said. "It might even help. Taking out our father is still a challenge without Nyx's magic. With a dragon attack as a distraction, I can get close to him. We could end this."

"You think they're going to let us walk right up to them and plead our case?" Laera shook her head. "They'll burn you alive before they let you speak."

"They'll let her speak." Ryvin was looking at me. "Her sisters will listen to her."

I turned to the princess. "He's right. If you can get me to Athos, they'll listen to me. We might be able to work together. They want Athos free of the grip of the Fae King, and you want the king dead."

I looked at the group around me, feeling more confident in what we were going to do. "No more secrets or lies. We have to trust each other."

Ryvin was watching his sister. "You're really in on this? I know things haven't been great between us, and I want to trust you, but you haven't made it easy."

Her eyes snapped over to her brother. "You stopped trusting me after the Shifter Wars and never gave me a second chance."

"You told him where they'd hidden their children," Ryvin bit out.

Vanth growled, the sound low and ominous. It was clear there was so much history between these three.

"I have never let him in my head again," Laera snapped. "It was one slip. One time I dropped my guard. I learned my lesson and I have the weight of all the dead on my soul. When they cut my thread, I'll have to answer for that day."

"I didn't know he read your thoughts," Vanth said. "I thought you were immune."

"Not when I'm depleted of power and bleeding to death," she hissed.

"You never told us that was how he found out," Ryvin said.

"You never asked. You assumed I changed sides. You assumed I wanted him to kill all those babies. You looked at me like I was a monster without giving me a second thought." The hurt in her voice made my chest ache.

"I'm sorry," Ryvin said.

"I'm sorry, too," Vanth said.

Laera flipped her silver hair over her shoulder and lifted her chin, giving the males her most defiant stare. "I know where my loyalty stands and I've been waiting too long to watch my father pay for what he's done."

"And he will," Ryvin assured her. "Jason and his crew will be stopping here in two weeks. He owes me a favor. We can ride to Athos with them. That gives Ara some time to practice."

"Jason doesn't do favors," Laera said.

"He will when two of the four passengers wear protective magic from the Ocean Queen and Ceto."

My fingers brushed over the necklace, wondering if it really would help me long enough for us to survive this.

"What about the sky or ground? The other gods aren't going to be happy about a child of Ceto's with magic. Once Ara starts using it, she'll attract attention," Laera said.

"The Ocean Queen will keep the other gods away until Nyx is free." Ryvin sounded confident. "But we have to make sure our father doesn't know what we're doing. I can't be away all day training her without drawing suspicion."

"I'll train her," Laera offered.

Ryvin looked unsure.

"It'll be fine." I touched his arm. "You help keep your father from finding out what we're doing. She can teach me."

"Do you think we're going to make it two weeks without him catching on?" Vanth asked.

"We don't have a choice," Ryvin said. "So it has to work."

29

ARA

VANTH KNOCKED ON THE DOOR, then stepped back as if it might turn into something that would bite him. I was already on edge enough being outside Laera's rooms, but his tense behavior was making me more nervous. I wished Ryvin could be here but he'd had to return to his duties to avoid suspicion.

"You're sure you can't come in with me?" I asked again.

"It's better if I wait out here."

The door swung open, and the princess grinned at us. "Don't worry, shifter, I'll return her in one piece." She gestured for me to enter. I knew we were on the same side and we'd trained together before, but this was different. We were going to be tapping into my magic.

Part of me was afraid I'd never be able to do it again, while the other part of me was concerned I'd hurt her. Or maybe I'd be terrible and I wouldn't be able to help anyone or use it effectively. There were so many scenarios playing in my mind it was difficult to find one to focus on.

Laera closed the door behind us, and I looked around her rather plain room. After everything I'd seen in the palace, I was surprised by the simple designs and minimal furniture. The room was large, with a small sitting area on one half and a bed on the other. Aside from that, there was a wardrobe and a doorway that led to a bathing room. She didn't even have a table or a desk. It gave the impression of being a temporary place, or a place someone spent little time inside.

"Nice room," I commented, desperate to break the silence. When we'd sparred, I'd felt confident by being in my element. And I'd wanted to show her up a little. Now that we were on the same side, things felt awkward.

"Belonged to my father's old spymaster. The wards are better than any I've ever seen." She pointed to each corner. "Excellent spell work at all angles so even I can't penetrate it from the outside."

"That explains why we're here instead of the training grounds." I glanced around, wondering if I could see the signs of the magic used.

"Anything that happens in this room will be between the two of us. Unless you share or let my father into your head, assuming it would work for you."

"I keep my word," I said. "And I am doing my best to avoid your father."

She sat down on one of the two small chairs near the large fireplace and nodded to the open chair. I sat, noting that it was just as uncomfortable as it appeared. Nothing in this room was designed for guest comfort.

"I need to know about your magic if I'm going to help you. What have you done with it, and how did you summon it? How often have you used it? When was the first time you realized you were different?"

"You're going to be disappointed if you think I can answer all those," I said. "It was the night I arrived here. With the vampire. That's it. I never had any sign before then and I'm still not sure I believe it."

"Nothing before that? Not even a hint of magic?"

I shook my head. "Nothing."

"We've got our work cut out for us," she said.

"What about you?"

She lifted a brow, staring at me as if my question was insane. "What do you mean?"

"You have to remember that I grew up thinking I was human." I winced as soon as the words were out. I still hadn't given myself time to really think about all of the new things I'd discovered in the last few days. "I haven't been around magic, at all. It's rare in Athos and aside from making our water warm, it's frowned upon."

"I keep forgetting you were so cut off. Your kingdom did everything it could to stay isolated from the rest of the world."

"We can critique Athos later. Tell me about your magic. I don't even know what you can do." I adjusted on the uncomfortable chair, wondering if it would be better to move to the marble floor.

"For future reference, it's generally poor manners to ask someone to tell you what their magic can do. We don't go around sharing the details because it eliminates some of the benefits. If others know what we can do, they can prepare to stand against us or find a way to stop our powers. I'm only asking you so I can help train you."

My cheeks heated. "That makes sense."

"But since I'll be seeing all of your magic and expecting you to be open with me, I'll share some of mine with you."

I didn't push despite the fact that I knew she'd still be holding back. Anticipation grew as I waited for her to continue. Now that I was in a safe space, the fact that we were talking about actual magic was really sinking in.

"My father can read minds, among other things. You've seen that. My mother can shape shift."

"What?" My jaw dropped open. "Like Vanth?"

She scoffed. "No, please. She's not limited to one shape, and she's got other gifts as well. But that one is widely known, so it's not a secret."

"Does that mean you can do those things as well?"

"We get variations of gifts based on our parents. Sometimes they're duplicates. Sometimes it's something new. But there's always a connection."

"What is it exactly that you can do, then?" I scooted to the edge of my chair and leaned forward, waiting for her to finally spill.

"I deal in emotions," she said.

My brow furrowed.

"Reading them, controlling them, changing them," she said.

I blinked as I considered what someone could do with that kind of power.

"I can't read minds exactly, but I can make people want to tell me everything. Or I can make them want to hurt someone so badly that they'll give away every secret. I can destroy relationships and treaties in seconds. I can create new friendships or bonds between enemies. I can break someone by making them relive their worst experiences over and over until they crack."

My mouth hung open, and I sat in stunned silence. No wonder everyone was terrified of her. "What do people think you can do?"

"They know I get information. I figure they assume I'm like my father." She shrugged. "Honestly, you know more about my powers now than even he does."

I wondered what else she could do that she wasn't willing to share with me. The magic she disclosed was dangerous enough. "Have you used it on me?"

"Unfortunately, anything you're feeling for my brother has nothing to do with me." She smiled in a way that felt a lot like a peace offering.

My cheeks heated. "I wasn't asking about Ryvin."

She laughed. "The fact that you walk around here calling the most deadly member of the court by his first name tells me everything I need to know."

"I didn't know who he was or what he could do when we met," I replied.

"Yet, you've seen his destructive power first hand and you aren't afraid of him. If you were, I'd know. Fear is the most difficult emotion to mask and the one that's the easiest for me to read. Even when I'm trying not to dig into people's feelings."

How many times had I told myself that I *should* be

afraid of him? "I don't think we're at the stage in our relationship where we discuss our feelings for men. Especially not your brother."

"Good. I would rather not know, anyway." She stood. "Though, if you asked me how he really felt about you, I'd tell you it's all genuine. Even if I don't believe it myself. You're a liability. You are a weakness. And as soon as everyone else finds that out, you'll be a target. So even if this magic training is focused on getting Nyx out, consider that it might also be about your own survival."

She didn't wait for me to respond before walking toward the bathing chamber. I sat there, feeling numb and overwhelmed while also fighting the urge to squeal in girlish delight. Ryvin was everything I should run from, but I didn't think either of us was going to be able to fight our attraction to the other for much longer.

"Are you coming?" Laera snapped.

Shoving the memory of Ryvin and I tangled in the sheets aside, I made myself focus. Laera was right about one thing for sure: if the prince felt for me the way I felt for him, I was absolutely a distraction because he was going to be the death of me.

When I joined Laera in the bathing chamber, my whole body tensed at the sight of the full bathtub.

"You're afraid," Laera commented, turning her violet eyes on me. "But you weren't before."

"I had an incident in a bathtub." It felt odd to share that with her. I hadn't even told my own family.

Her brows furrowed. "You realize we're going to be manipulating water, right?"

"I know. It's just been difficult."

"What happened?" she asked, her tone more patient than I expected.

"A maid poisoned me while I was in the tub. I let myself go right under the water without a fight. If Ryvin hadn't arrived in time..."

"He saved you?"

I nodded.

"I was lucky he came to my room when he did."

"Yes, I'm sure it was luck." She sighed. "Once you master this power, I'm not sure you'll have to worry about drowning ever again. The water will be your friend and you'll be its master. Besides, I'm sure you won't allow yourself to be tricked by anyone into ingesting poison again?"

"I'm eating the food in an enemy court," I pointed out. "I'm not sure I have that luxury."

"In this court, we don't use such subtle methods. If anyone here wanted you dead, they'd want witnesses and they'd want you to suffer."

"Is that supposed to make me feel better?" I asked.

She chuckled. "It's supposed to make you train harder."

I approached the tub, reminding myself I didn't have to climb inside. For a long moment, I stared at the clear water's unbroken surface. It shimmered like glass. When I looked up I saw Laera watching me, her patience surprising me.

"You ready?" she asked.

I nodded.

"I don't know anything about water magic, so we'll be seeing if your magic responds to you the same way mine does to me." She knelt in front of the tub and nodded, indicating I should do the same.

I knelt, my heart kicking against my ribs as I stared at the now rippling water that was so close to me. I told myself it wasn't any threat. The sea didn't make me nervous, and I wasn't inside the tub. My pulse slowed, and I regained control of my rapid breathing. Even my hands stopped shaking. I was safe. This was fine. I was in control.

"When I first started training, I had to work to find the magic. Concentrate, feel it inside me, force it forward to do my bidding. Now, it comes without effort. It's harder to turn it off than it is to summon it. But you're not there yet. You'll have to work to use it and you'll feel it. Just like any kind of skill, it takes practice and energy."

"Am I going to be able to master enough to accomplish what we need?" I asked.

"For all our sakes, I hope so." She gripped the edges of the tub. "We'll need you to move the water for us, to clear a path when needed. If you can't hold it, we're all going under."

My pulse kicked up. "I don't need that kind of pressure."

"It's true, though. There's no room for error and no time for you to struggle with this. You have to go from beginner to master in a matter of weeks. Less if my father finds out the truth about you sooner."

I reached toward the water, brushing my fingers across the surface. A chill ran down my spine and my chest tightened. I couldn't afford to fear the water here if I had to master this magic quickly.

"If it helps, you should know that for the time being, you and I are allies. Which means if anyone tries to harm you, they have to go through me."

It actually did help a bit. Even Vanth was wary of the princess. "Thanks."

She lifted an eyebrow. "Don't get soft on me. This doesn't mean we're friends. It means our goals temporarily align."

"I'll keep that in mind." My brow furrowed and I turned from her, suddenly feeling something odd in my fingertips. It was almost as if they were vibrating. Like the water itself was pulsing and buzzing under my touch.

"What is it?" Laera asked.

"I'm not sure."

"You're feeling something?" she inquired.

"Yes. The water feels…different."

"Don't fight it. Lean into it. Let yourself flow with it. When I use my magic, my emotions feel like they meld with the people around me. For a long time, it was difficult for me to find where my feelings ended and theirs began. They flowed together as one, like a stream meeting a river. Find that intersection and ask the water to move."

My brow furrowed and I eyed her skeptically. "Ask the water?"

"Just try it."

I blew a breath out of my nose, then gazed into the tub. I felt ridiculous, but there was no denying I was feeling something different than usual. Leaning into the sensation, I commanded the water to move.

Nothing happened.

Pressing my lips together I shoved down the humiliation I was feeling toward my task. I was supposed to be able to do this, but it also felt foolish to tell water what to do. Water was a force, I'd watched it churn in the sea, unyielding and powerful. It moved to its own rhythm, cut its own path, made its own choices.

Making myself steady my breathing, I closed my eyes and thought about the movement of water. I imagined myself making it flow and churn the way the sea did. It still felt impossible, but I needed to imagine what it might look like before I tried again.

The room suddenly felt charged, the hair on my arms standing on edge. It was as if we were too close to a storm. I could almost feel the lighting nearby but we were indoors, away from any threats.

"Ara, open your eyes."

I opened my eyes then pulled my hand away from the tub quickly. The water was rippling and splashing lightly against the sides of the tub as if someone had tipped the whole thing up and down, making it slosh back and forth in tiny waves.

The movement slowed until it finally stopped and the clear surface returned to its original form.

"How did I do that?" I turned to Laera.

"You connected with it. Commanded it as if you're part of it. Try again."

Feeling invigorated, I eagerly set my hand into the water again, and let myself move my fingers along the surface, pretending I was the waves as I stared into the cool liquid.

The water responded, moving with me, creating tiny

waves as my hand moved back and forth. I lifted my hand higher, drawing out larger waves, changing direction, and eventually creating a tiny vortex right in the center.

Laughing, I pulled my hand away and looked over at the princess. She was actually smiling. "That's a good start. But we're going to need more than party tricks to pull this off."

I stood, then stepped into the tub. Laera silently studied me, her expression curious. Squatting lower but not sitting in the water, I placed my hands on either side of me, palms resting on the surface.

Closing my eyes, I let my love of the sea fill my mind. I focused on the way it called to me, how it calmed me, the feeling I got from simply staring at its blue waters. Slowly, I pushed my hands away from me. I could feel the water leave from around my ankles, moving to the sides of the tub as I'd commanded.

I opened my eyes and smiled. The water sloshed over the sides of the tub as it moved away from me, leaving me in a space with a wall of water on each side of me. I'd cleared a path, held the water away while I stood in the center of the tub, my body untouched by the water around me.

I released it, dropping my arms to my side, panting from the effort of keeping the water away.

"It's a start," Laera said. "Keep going. We don't stop until you feel like the water is an extension of you."

Swallowing hard, I nodded. My body was already feeling the exhaustion of using my newfound skill, but I was determined. For the next six hours, I worked until I became part of the water.

When I finally gave in, my limbs shaking, my muscles aching, I felt confident that with more practice, I would be able to help us get Nyx out of her prison.

"You can add more water." Every muscle ached, and I had never felt more drained in my life.

Noria hesitated, then turned the faucet back on, adding more steaming water to the copper tub. I watched, fighting against the fear squeezing my insides. It was just water. I could control water. I shouldn't be afraid. I couldn't be afraid if I was going to have to pass through tunnels of the stuff to get out of Nyx's prison once the goddess was free. I'd just spent the whole day working with water, but taking an actual bath still made me hesitate. I had to get over that fear.

Noria turned off the water. "Is that enough?"

I looked at the half-full tub. It was slightly shallower than I used to use, but not by much. "It's great, thank you."

"Call for me if you need anything," Noria offered as she left the room.

"Thank you." I removed my clothes and stared at the water, wondering how this magic had been inside me all this time and I'd never noticed. Brushing my fingertips over the surface, I concentrated on how the water practically sang to me, how I could feel its rhythm, its churning, flowing energy. How had I missed that all my life?

Carefully, I stepped into the bath, holding my breath as I sat, letting the water cover my legs and stomach.

Biting back at the little flickers of fear, I called on the magic, making the water part until it formed a wall on either side of me, extending beyond the copper of the tub, leaving me surrounded by water but no longer covered in it.

With subtle movements of my fingers, I directed the water until it formed an arch over my head, encasing me in a water cocoon. This was what it would be like in the caves, keeping the water at bay while we walked through.

My hands trembled and my pulse raced. Even this small amount of water was causing me to tire but I had been using magic all day. Reluctantly, I sent the water back into the tub, some of it sloshing over the side as it ungracefully returned to where it started. Leaning back, I let my arms drop to my sides, and I took a few breaths. Closing my eyes, I let myself feel the way the liquid moved around me. How it seemed to call to me, how I could feel it flowing around me.

There was no reason to fear the water. Opening my eyes I realized that I'd always felt a connection to water. It had always been there, tucked away from me. While everyone around me feared the sea, I'd felt a call to its depths.

Skimming my fingertips over the surface, I smiled as I realized I could do this. I was meant to do this.

30

Ara

A knock sounded on my door.

"That must be Felicity with the salve." Noria wrapped the towel around me and I held on to it, grateful for her gentle touch.

Everything hurt. Who knew using magic was even harder on the body than combat training?

I slowly dried myself while Noria's footsteps faded. Moving so I was more concealed from the door, I hung up the towel and pulled on the soft nightgown Noria had left for me.

Footsteps sounded and Noria peeked into the washroom. "You have a visitor." The smirk on her lips told me it was someone I'd want to see.

I'd been forcing myself to push any thoughts of Ryvin away all day, knowing he had to be away from me to keep his father from discovering what I was doing with Laera.

Trying not to seem too eager, I stepped through the archway to find my suspicions were correct. The prince stood silently near my door, his posture rigid and his expression giving nothing away. He was playing up his title, not showing that casual familiarity we'd given each other so often.

Just like yesterday, I got the sense that he wasn't quite sure how to interact with me. It made something tight and uncomfortable squirm inside me.

"Are you up for some company?" he asked.

Another knock sent him behind the door, then nodding at Noria. The maid understood the silent instruction and quickly answered, accepting the jar of salve from a confused woman who was sent away with a rushed, thank you.

Noria closed the door, and we all stood there in awkward silence for a moment. Finally, I cleared my throat, then spoke, "Noria, I think I'm good for the evening."

"Do you want me to apply the salve?" Her eyes darted to Ryvin briefly before looking to me.

"I think I've got it under control," I replied.

Ryvin took the jar from her. "I can help the princess."

Noria's lips were pressed together, making her look like she was trying not to squeal. She nodded, then quickly left the room, closing the door behind her.

Ryvin lifted the jar. "Would you like some help?"

I nodded, then turned so my back was to him. After moving my hair aside, I slid the straps of my nightgown off my shoulders. "It's mostly my neck and shoulders that hurt."

I heard him unscrewing the lid from the jar. "It gets easier when your body learns to channel the magic. Eventually, it's like breathing."

"Even when it's something bigger?" All I'd done today was play with water in a bathtub. How was I supposed to manage moving water inside tunnels?

"You'll find magic is a strange skill. Once you figure it out, the scale doesn't even matter. It's more about realizing you can than the actual act you're performing."

"How long did it take you to get it?" I asked.

"Once I stopped doubting myself?"

"I suppose." Goosebumps spread along my skin as I felt his presence behind me.

"It was years of fighting myself before I realized I was sabotaging myself because I didn't want to be like my father. Once I accepted that, it came quickly."

"I'm sorry for everything you've had to endure. I heard that you were there when your mother's magic was taken," I said.

"That was a long time ago. This is going to be cold," he warned.

I sucked in a breath as he began to rub the chilly salve onto my shoulders. It didn't stay cold for long. His touch was gentle and soothing. I felt myself melting into it, the tension leaving me.

With a movement so tender it took my breath away, he slid the straps of my nightgown back onto my shoulders. I turned to face him. "Thank you."

"Any time."

My heart raced and I found myself forcing myself to maintain my distance.

"How was training today?" he asked.

"Good." I tried to recall some specific details, anything to encourage the conversation so he'd stay longer, but my mind was foggy. Any thought that passed through slipped away like water pouring through my fingers.

"You know, if you don't want to help with this, I'll find another way," he said.

"I want to help. I already told you that." I took the salve from his hands and reapplied the lid before setting it down on the small table.

"I never wanted this for you. I should have made you stay behind," he said.

I walked toward him. "And you think I'd have listened?" Stopping in front of him, I placed my palm on the center of his chest. "I'm glad I'm here. I'm glad I can help."

He tucked a strand of damp hair behind my ear. "As much as I hate that you're here, I'm wondering if I really could have left you behind. There's so much I need to tell you—"

I pressed my fingertip to his lips. "You're talking too much."

He grinned.

"There's no god here now to influence my feelings." I pulled my finger away and he caught my wrist, lifting it back to his lips. He kissed the pulse point, then moved higher, kissing his way up my arm and sending shivers through me that made me moan.

When he got to my shoulder, he moved to my neck, then grabbed me around the waist and pulled me in tight, his lips finally finding mine. The kiss was tenuous as if we were trying to remember how we fit together. It didn't take long before we increased the intensity, our kiss turning frantic as Ryvin quickly tugged at those straps he'd so gently returned to my shoulders moments ago.

My nightgown was in a puddle around my ankles and I pulled away from him, breathless and desperate. I had never felt this kind of need for a man before. Ryvin brought out a different part of me. A side I didn't even know existed. I was driven by instinct when I was with him; blinded by lust. And I didn't care. I just knew I needed him.

Before he could question my sudden movements, I lifted his tunic. Ryvin took over and pulled the fabric over his head, tossing it aside. Stepping over my nightgown, I unlaced his trousers and yanked them down.

As soon as he kicked them aside, he grabbed me with a growl, then threw me onto the bed. He was on top of me in a heartbeat, his hips between my thighs. I wrapped my legs around his waist and clawed at his back, desperate to feel him closer to me, to feel him inside me.

He thrust into me with a groan and I gasped, reveling in the fullness of him. My fingernails dug into his back as he pushed deeper. My hips moved with him, the two of us working in tandem as we chased release.

It was as if all the denial I'd worked so hard to force was being tested. My resistance crumbling with each movement. I couldn't deny how much I needed him or how desperate I'd been for his touch.

For his everything.

His lips brushed against my earlobe. He kissed and

licked and teased my ears and neck, sending delicious shivers down my spine. I ran my fingers through his hair and trailed them down his back, my fingers gliding over the scars as I reached lower.

"I hate that I'm glad that you're here," he whispered before silencing my reply with his lips.

His movements slowed, the rhythm less frantic. Our tongues met, the kiss growing slower, less intense but more sensual. More intimate. I froze, sucking in a sharp breath. This was different. It wasn't the same as what we'd done before. It was personal. It wasn't just sex.

"Do you want me to stop?" he asked, ceasing movement. He studied me, brow furrowed.

I shook my head, fighting against the part of me that was terrified about the increased intimacy. "I don't want you to stop."

He kissed my forehead and I closed my eyes. "Please don't shut down on me again. Let me in."

Last time I let someone in, he betrayed me. But Ryvin had shown that he'd put me first. I was hesitant, but at least I could be open to letting him in more.

I opened my eyes, then lifted my chin so I could kiss him again. Our lips moved in a gentle motion, then Ryvin's tongue flicked into my mouth, testing. I met it with mine then deepened the kiss.

He thrust into me again, slowly at first, before picking up the speed and pushing deeper. My back arched and I moaned. Suddenly, Ryvin's hand dipped low, his fingers finding my sensitive nub. He teased as he increased pressure with his thrusts.

Tossing my head back, I broke from our kiss. The

pleasure built and I grabbed at the bedding, needing something to hold onto as my hips bucked and my moaning increased. Wave after wave of pleasure built in a crescendo until I couldn't hold back. I cried out, the explosion of pleasure too great to contain. Ryvin groaned a heartbeat later as he found his own release.

He leaned down, resting his head on my chest. I ran my fingers through his hair while we caught our breath together.

When we nestled under the blankets, I rested my head on his chest, listening to his heartbeat. It didn't take long for him to fall asleep, and I stared at his handsome face. He was so at ease, his body relaxed, his expression peaceful. I wasn't sure I'd ever seen him truly drop his guard. With a sigh, I let myself melt into his warmth, I let myself enjoy the moment.

I let myself imagine what it might be like to fall asleep in his arms every night. The thought didn't terrify me. Instead, it made me settle more into my own body, finding a peace I didn't know resided within me. Closing my eyes, I allowed the sensation to wash over me.

For the first time in a long time, I was truly happy.

31

Ryvin

"The dragons are in Athos." The king's voice echoed through the marble hall, making all his advisors cease their conversations.

He swept into the room, the fabric of his long crimson robe flowing behind him like a river of blood. We all fell into place, following him before waiting at our assigned places at the long table.

Once the king was seated in his large golden chair at the head of the table, the rest of us took our seats. Though my father couldn't read my thoughts, I still worked to empty my mind. I already knew the dragons were on the move. I knew where they were and why they were there. And I planned to join them. I couldn't allow my expressions to change or react in any way different than he expected. It was a game I'd been playing longer than I could remember.

"Do they mean to claim Athos for their own? They know it's our territory. This is an act of war!" Keron, the only vampire in my father's innermost circle, looked too eager. He was one of the first vampires and didn't require blood to survive, but I knew he enjoyed battle, simply because he could drain as many victims as he wanted. Then he'd return after the fight to kill any who may have turned from his bite.

"I think they mean to ally with the Athonians against us," my father explained. "The Dragon King himself is in their city, meeting with their new queen."

Conversation erupted around the table, the advisors talking over one another and arguing. My father watched, his gaze moving around the table until he stopped on me. "Ryvin, you're rather quiet about this." The room quieted and I could feel all the eyes on me.

"Tell us, what exactly did you discover while you were warming the Athonian princess's bed?" My father demanded.

"We saw them together last night. Everyone saw them," Keron hissed.

I glanced at the ancient vampire, taking in his paper-thin, translucent skin and the way his claw-like fingers tensed as he realized he might have pushed too far. I offered a bored smile before returning my attention to my father.

"As you already know, I was unaware of their plans to meet with the dragons. I agree, I was distracted." I shrugged as if it was common for me to abandon my tasks for a pretty face. My father knew I was too focused to make that kind of mistake, but the gathered advisors chuckled and commented as if it was something they could relate to.

"I did discover that their king was a vampire and found out the queen is pregnant, meaning they'll have a half-vampire growing up there if the baby survives."

"Is that why you killed him?" Francesca, one of my father's oldest advisors, asked. She locked her bright green eyes on me, her unrelenting stare adding weight to her question.

"I killed him because he was dangerous and he was plotting against us. He wanted us to break the treaty on our end so he would have reason to rebel. It makes more sense with the dragons on their way." I shrugged, as if it wasn't a big deal.

Francesca narrowed her eyes. "You're slipping. I've never seen you so cavalier in your duties. I've never seen you make mistakes like you did in Athos."

"It's the girl," Keron said. "She's still a distraction."

The door swung open and everyone turned to see who would be foolish enough to enter the hall. Morta glided in and the room seemed to take a collective breath and tension rose. Nobody crossed the fates, especially not Morta.

My father rose, then inclined his head in greeting. "To what do we owe this pleasure?"

"I was sent by my sisters," Morta's deceptively sweet, strange voice floated around us, filling the marble hall as if she was many instead of one.

"How can we be of service to you and your dear sisters?" My father asked.

I fought against a scowl. Only he was conceited

enough to think that by showing reverence to the fates he could gain their favor. It didn't work that way. Everyone knew that your time came when it was your time. It didn't matter if you were good or evil. It didn't matter if you were a king or a slave. Nobody outsmarted the fates.

"There's been a change in the stars," Morta explained. "A great sacrifice must be made. A demonstration of power and might. Konos must tip the scales in her favor or the entire city will burn."

Gasps and whispered prayers to the gods sounded around me. My father's face paled. "Is it the dragons?"

"The cause isn't clear. But you must send eleven into the labyrinth. The gods demand the sacrifice in blood. It's the only way," she said.

"When?" I asked.

"At the full moon," Morta replied.

"We have exactly eleven tributes still alive," Francesca said.

"We have ten," I spat. "Ara is not a tribute."

"She came with the tributes, so she is one of them," Morta said.

"The gods demanded eleven?" My father asked.

Morta nodded, her empty eyes not leaving my father.

"That must be what the gods want," another advisor said. "Why else demand that number when that's what we have left of them since they arrived?"

"Not Ara. We can use her against her sister," I reminded them.

"She's already cost us too much. It's better if she's not here to distract you," the king said. "Enjoy your time with her while you can. In two days, she goes into the labyrinth with her people."

32

Ara

The bed was empty when I woke and an unquenchable sense of loneliness sprawled wide inside me. Like a void that only Ryvin's presence could fulfill.

I was in so much trouble. I'd tried to keep our relationship casual, but it was impossible to deny it any longer. Maybe it wouldn't be as complicated since we were going to ask to join Athos and the dragons when they took down the fae. It was possible we could be together.

An entirely different feeling replaced the void. Fear and hope. I wasn't sure what to do with the fact that I was considering thinking of Ryvin as my forever.

I turned so I was face down in the pillows and screamed, letting out the giddy energy.

I was in love with him.

It was so impossible and yet, it was incredible. I'd

never hoped for a husband. I'd never seen myself getting married or even staying with one man. But this was right. I didn't understand it, yet I knew I needed to stop fighting it. Ryvin was where my path was supposed to lead me.

With a giggle, an honest-to-gods giggle that made me feel like an idiot, I wondered if I could get Morta to confirm it for me.

Maybe I didn't want to know.

I rolled over and stared at the ceiling, wondering if letting my hopes rise was just tempting the gods to strike me down. Especially now that I knew they were possibly hunting me.

Sitting up, I went through the motions of getting ready for training while considering how odd it was that I'd always thought the gods didn't notice us. All this time, I was part of them. Even if I didn't want to be.

I was already dressed when a gentle knock sounded on my door. "Come in."

"I was worried you'd sleep the day away," Noria said. "It's after lunch already."

Without windows, it was impossible to tell. "Why did nobody wake me?"

"They told me you might need some extra rest."

I pressed my lips together as I thought about yesterday's training. Using magic had been exhausting. If I was going to sleep through lunch after doing basic exercises, how was I going to be ready to take on something larger so quickly?

Noria set a tray on the bed. "You should eat."

"Join me?" I suggested, gesturing to the tray.

"Oh, that's not necessary," Noria said.

"Please." I moved the tray to the center of the bed so there was more room for both of us. "Sit."

She hesitated, but after I patted the empty place on the bed, she finally agreed.

I grabbed a bowl of fruit and held it up, offering it to her. She took a bunch of grapes. "The general is outside your room. He said he'll escort you to your meeting when you're ready."

"I've kept him waiting all morning?" I leaped off the bed. "I should go. I can't believe I slept so late."

"Sit." Noria's tone was firm. "You must eat. Sleep isn't the only thing that helps nourish and replenish strength."

I wondered how much Noria knew about what we were doing. "I am supposed to meet the princess. I'm not sure it's a good idea to keep her waiting."

"If it was urgent, they'd summon you." Now she was the one patting the bed. "Eat."

I complied and reached for a piece of flatbread. It was still warm.

"It's nice to see you getting along with the princess. I've never really seen her with friends. You must have done something special." Noria popped a grape into her mouth.

"She's not as bad as I thought." It was all I could say to try to appease some of the obvious concern in Noria's tone.

After some awkward silence, Noria began to tell me stories about Laera as a child. She told me how she'd sneak into the kitchen and steal sugared dates, then blame the cats that lived around the palace grounds. She also told me how she and Ryvin had been inseparable as children, constantly causing trouble and getting into things they shouldn't. Once they'd even run away, managing to evade all the soldiers looking for them for an entire week.

"Where did they go?" I asked.

"They found them in Drakous," she said.

"How did they get there?"

She shook her head. "I'm not sure. But it was shortly after Ryvin's mother disappeared."

I could tell she was choosing her words carefully. "It sounds like they were so close when they were young."

"They were. Until the prince came into his magic. As soon as that happens, childhood is over and training begins." She cleared her throat. "But that's not my story to tell."

We made small-talk for a bit while we nibbled on the food, but I could tell she was nervous. Like she wanted to say something else. Was it more about Ryvin or Laera? Did she want to tell me something about the princess?

"You know, if there's something wrong, you can tell me," I offered. "I won't share."

Her eyes darted to the door, then back to me. "Nothing's wrong."

"Noria." I lifted my brows, giving her a look that told her I was on to her. "What is it?"

She abruptly got off the bed, walked to the door, then opened it. She peeked outside, then came back into my room and closed the door behind her. Her hands were shaking slightly as she rushed back to where I was sitting.

Getting close, she spoke in such a low whisper that I

struggled to hear what she was saying. "They're going to sacrifice all the tributes."

"What?" I tensed, sitting straighter. "When?"

"On the full moon," she said.

I dropped the orange slice that was in my hand and looked up at her. "Are you certain? I thought they had to volunteer."

She nodded. "Something's changed. And it gets worse."

"How could there be something worse?"

"You're considered one of the tributes," she said.

Her lips were moving, but I couldn't hear another word she said. We were so close to getting off this island and freeing Nyx. I was going to help end the Fae King and save all my people.

"Ara?"

I blinked, then forced my eyes to refocus so I could pay attention to Noria. "I'm sorry, what were you saying?"

"I was saying that you need to go. Now." She glanced toward the door again. "There's a ship at the docks called the Eleftheria. My cousin is the captain. Tell him I sent you and he'll take you with him. They can hide you and you can get off this island." She was clasping my hands in hers, the desperate tone making my own throat thick with unshed tears.

"I can't do that." I shook my head, so honored that she was willing to risk so much for me. "Thank you, really. But I can't."

"They're going to feed you all to the beast. You can't stay. Nobody can defeat that monster." Her voice was pleading, tears streamed down her cheeks.

I stood, then squeezed her hands. "I have to go. We'll figure something out."

She wiped at her cheeks. "Please, don't try to be the hero. The last time a hero went into that maze, he never found his way out."

I nodded. "Thank you for telling me." When I opened my door, Vanth was waiting in the hall, the tense set of his jaw alerting me to the fact that he knew what Noria had just told me.

"You heard," I said as I closed the door.

"I think the whole palace knows by now," he said.

"Where's Ryvin?"

"Still with the king," Vanth replied. "But I'll take you to Laera."

We walked silently to the princesses chambers, and I was surprised to see two guards standing outside her rooms.

"Step aside," Vanth ordered them.

"We don't answer to you, Skylos," one of them said, a sharp bite in his tone.

I flinched slightly at the guard calling Vanth a dog. That had to be an insult to a wolf shifter.

Vanth tensed, his fingers moving to his weapon. "You will step aside and allow the princess entry."

"Was this cleared by the king?" The guard asked.

"I cleared it. So step aside, Opados," Vanth said as he took a step forward. "Or do I need to move you myself?"

The guard, the one Vanth had called a follower, bared his teeth and for a moment, I thought he was going to charge the wolf shifter. But then he lowered his hands and stepped to the side. "We can take it from here. Your services are not needed. I'm sure you have more pressing matters than to play babysitter to a human."

"I'll be accompanying her," he said, his hand still resting on the hilt.

"The king will not approve of a guard inside his daughter's room," the guard replied. "Even if you are a general."

Vanth growled and the door opened, an irritated Laera staring out at the scene, her hands on her hips. "What is going on out here? Why are there so many guards at my door when there are people around this kingdom who need actual protection?"

The two guards inclined their heads. "Sorry, your highness. Your father sent us to watch over you."

"That's insane. Find something worth your time to do. I can take care of myself," she hissed.

"The king required us to stand guard," one of them said apologetically.

Laera rolled her eyes. "Well, at least you can leave, General."

Vanth tensed, but inclined his head. "As you wish, Princess."

With a saccharine smile, Laera waved him away, then pulled me into her room and closed the door.

"Can we talk?" I asked, hoping her room was still a private place to speak.

"Yes, they can't hear us."

"Is this because of the sacrifice? The tributes? Did they know I'd come here? Do they think you'll help me escape?" The questions tumbled out so quickly that Laera had to grab me to get me to stop talking.

"Panicking isn't going to help," she said.

"We're nowhere near the two week mark. I haven't had enough time to practice. And I can't leave the tributes behind even if we could get out. What are we going to do?"

My eyes widened as my concern about our plan faded and terror gripped me, making my insides feel like they were being crushed. "Oh gods, did something happen to Ryvin?" How had that not been my first thought? What if his father found out and had him killed?

"Nothing happened to Ryvin," she assured me. "And we're going to figure this out."

"The full moon is in two days." I stared at her, wondering how she could look so calm.

"And you'll be ready," she said.

"For what?" I demanded. "To die?"

"To kill the minotaur."

33

RYVIN

THE KING KEPT me busy all morning. His advisors practically salivating over the war planning. It was like watching them play a game. We all knew if we wanted Athos, we simply had to sail there and take it. The humans were no match for the fae, especially as weak as I'd left them after the destruction I caused.

But the dragons were an actual threat. And instead of finding fear or respect at their forces and abilities, the members of the council couldn't hold back their grins as they moved stone figures around on a massive map.

"We call in the Court of Vipers tomorrow," my father said. "The other courts will be summoned by the end of the week. With all of Telos's forces at our disposal, we're unstoppable."

My warning about holding Drakous had gone unheeded, and I didn't bring it up again. I knew that look in my father's eyes. Pure determination driven by insane lust for power. The same look he'd had when he nearly killed my mother by taking her magic.

Forcing that memory away, I glanced around the table, hoping for some kind of distraction. I caught sight of a slack-jawed guard near the door, his vacant eyes stared into the room without any hint of awareness. That meant Laera knew what was happening, though if she hadn't gone into the man's mind herself, one of the several servants who'd brought food and drink to the council would have already told her.

My father never considered the people who worked for him as a threat. It was one of his greatest weaknesses, but he felt invincible with the power he held. The worst part was, he nearly was.

The doors behind us swung open and Evyon, my father's oldest servant, stepped inside the room. "Lunch is ready in the great hall."

Appreciative sounds and general chatter sounded around the table and the advisors all rose, following my father toward the doors. The king paused, reminding the guards to keep everyone out.

"Your highness," I walked alongside my father, "Unless you need me in the war room, I should see to the updated training for our soldiers and ensure that the tributes are being kept alive."

He nodded, then patted me on the shoulder, a rare sign of affection likely applied for the sake of his trailing advisors. He liked to pretend that he was a good father when other people were watching. "Very well. I expect a report in the morning."

I nodded, then stepped away so the group could pass me. Once they were out of sight, I turned and hurried down the hall until I reached the lavish rooms where we housed visiting dignitaries. I didn't bother to knock, and I slammed the door behind me before the guards could say a word.

"Morta, I know you're in here." My hands were balled into fists as I glanced around the sprawling, ornate space. I was standing in a formal sitting room dotted with gold painted chairs, elegant rugs, and silk pillows. Three doorways led to other rooms: a bedroom, a dining space, and a private sitting room.

I walked deeper into the room, considering which door to enter, when the ethereal form of Morta floated from the dining room. She smiled that unsettling, childish grin and blinked, drawing attention to her vacant eyes. "I was expecting you." She gestured to the dining room, then turned and walked into it.

I followed. "You should have told me."

"You would have tried to stop me if I did," she replied.

"Of course I would have," I agreed. "This wasn't the plan."

"It's the only way," she said as she settled into a bright white chair. Wind from the open air colonnade behind her whipped her hair around her face. A fountain bubbled in the small private courtyard. A group of doves were eating crumbs someone had thrown, their happy coos making me want to throw something at all of them.

"You should have said something to me," I snapped.

"You know it's the only way. We discussed this," she reminded me.

"And we agreed it was too dangerous," I said.

"The stars have changed," she said.

"Don't give me your lines. I am not my father. We have always been clear with each other."

"Sit. Eat." It was a command, a tone I hadn't heard from her since we'd built a strange friendship during the Shifter Wars.

Reluctantly, I took the seat opposite her. "What is this really about?"

She placed two figs on her plate, then slid the bowl of figs across the table to me. With a sigh, I added a fig to my plate. Silently, we filled our plates and then she began to eat.

After what felt like an eternity, she pushed her empty dish away and lifted her empty eyes to me. "My sister was here."

I swallowed the bite of food in my mouth without chewing, wincing slightly as it went down. "Which one?"

"Nona," she replied.

I waited silently. While Morta ended lives by cutting the thread, she did so at Nona's command. Much of the time, Morta had the ability to choose how to deliver death; but Nona dictated life. She determined how much time any of us had.

"She told me there's been some changes now that there's word of a new Demi-god."

I clenched my teeth. I hated that term. Half-god, Demi-god, none of it mattered. You weren't welcome by the gods and you were often hunted by them. I didn't want any association with the gods. If they noticed you, it was usually the end of the line. "You're talking about Ara."

She nodded.

"You better not tell me she's slated to die by that monster. You told me she had more time, Morta. You swore it to me." I was gripping the armrests so tight my fingers were aching.

"The gods are watching her now. It changes her path," Morta said.

I stood so quickly the chair toppled to the ground. Morta didn't even flinch at the sound. "I will not lose her. I will follow her to the Underworld if I have to."

"If you go by sea, she will die and none of your plans will come to pass. Your father will rule until the fae are nothing but ashes," Morta said.

"What?" My shoulders eased a bit, in both defeat and relief at her words. Ara didn't have to die. But then the meaning crashed in. "You're saying she has to fight the minotaur?"

"I'm saying she can't leave this island by sea," Morta replied.

"What if she doesn't? What if she stays in Konos?" It would mean allowing my father to reign unchallenged, but would it keep Ara alive?

"Then perhaps the two of you could be happy, for a time. But it would be gone in a blink and when her family is destroyed by your father's war, she will lose all her light and you'll be forced to watch her descent into madness." Morta's expression fell, the sorrow of a life like that for Ara practically radiating from her, making the room feel darker than it had been.

"Will she survive the labyrinth?" I asked quietly.

"You know I can't answer that. The monster is a being made of magic. It corrupts mine and prevents my sight. But that portal is her only chance of leaving this island," she said.

"You didn't even give me a choice," I accused. "You made the decision for me."

"I made the decision the princess would want, and you know it. Had you been given the choice, tell me, would you let her fight for her own life? Would you let her have a chance at seeing her sisters and finding happiness? Or would your selfish desire to keep her for yourself make you choose to keep her a prisoner here for the rest of her life?" Morta was standing now, the fabric of her dress whipping around her as if she was in the middle of a windstorm.

I pulled out the chair next to me, ignoring the one I'd knocked to the ground, then sat, feeling defeated. "You're right. I would have kept her here. I would have watched her descent and it would have been my doing."

Morta sat, the chaos that had been stirring around her growing calm. She passed a ball of red thread across the table. "This will give her a chance. It will give all of you a chance."

I reached for the thread, feeling the sizzle of magic as soon as I touched it. "Last time a hero used this thread inside the labyrinth, it didn't matter." Theseus had left a trail to follow, but he'd been unsuccessful in slaying the beast. Even with the help of an enchanted weapon that Laera had gifted him.

"This isn't for finding her way out of the maze," Morta

explained. "It's to find her way back through the portal. As long as this thread connects the labyrinth to the other side of the portal, it will remain open. A gateway between the two destinations that anyone can pass through until the thread is cut."

"I thought you said the portal was her way off the island?"

"She can use the portal to go to the palace at Athos, to her home, or she can use it for your other plan," Morta said. "The choice must be hers."

"Will the portal open into the prison?" I asked.

Morta nodded. "But don't ask me to tell you what will happen. When it comes to Nyx, not even Nona can see the future."

34

Ara

I blinked, wondering if I'd heard her correctly. "What did you say?"

She grinned and her eyes gleamed with that hint of insanity that always seemed to accompany any of her smiles. "It's brilliant, honestly. I'm upset we didn't think of it ourselves."

"What are you talking about? Nobody survives that monster." I'd seen what that thing could do. Even with all of the tributes at once we didn't stand a chance. Especially now that they were all lost to the fae wine.

"You do realize what's at the center of the labyrinth," she said.

"You're insane. We'd never make it before being ripped to shreds."

She walked away from me and picked up a huge melon that was sitting on the ground next to one of the chairs. Wordlessly, she set it down in front of me, then stepped back a few paces. Her eyes moved down to the melon, then up to me.

I understood what she was saying, but it seemed insane. Even if I did make a melon explode, it wasn't the same as doing it with a giant half-man, half-bull monster. "It's not going to work."

"Humor me."

I stared at the melon. I should be focusing on the fruit, trying to control its water to make it explode. I should be worrying about the tributes or myself. Instead, the only thing filling my mind was worry about Ryvin.

It was ridiculous. I'd seen the magic he could wield. I knew he could take care of himself. But he'd been in my bed last night and he wasn't there this morning. The only thing I could think of was how badly I wanted to see him.

"Your concern is clouding your abilities," Laera warned. "You have to clear your thoughts so you can focus. You're not going to be accurate with all that stress. If you can do this, the tributes will be spared. You'll live. You get to avoid the caves and go straight to Nyx. It's so much easier."

I looked up at her, hating how happy she seemed at the fact that I was going to have to face the monster. "Then you do it."

"If I could have killed that beast myself, I'd have done it already. I know my limits," she said. "It has no emotions, no desires, no wants other than destruction. I can't influence it in any way. Believe me, I've tried."

After a deep breath, I returned my gaze to the stupid melon. If this was my only option, I should be focusing.

I'd spent so much time training over the years, single-minded on my goals.

"You're a mess, Ara. Get yourself together," she chided.

"You're certain Ryvin is fine?" I asked.

"That's what you're worried about?" Her brow furrowed.

"Yes, I'm worried about him even though I know I shouldn't be." I turned away from her, embarrassed that I was so distracted by one person.

"You actually have feelings for him, don't you?" She asked.

I didn't turn to face her and I kept quiet. It felt like weakness to admit it out loud. Thinking it to myself this morning was difficult enough as it was.

"If it helps, I sent Vanth away for a reason. If he's not with you, there's only one other place he'll go and that's to Ryvin's side. The two of them are like oil and water, but they'd die for each other. I don't get it, but that's how they've always been," she said.

It actually did make me feel a little better. Thinking about Vanth and Ryvin together, and knowing how formidable that duo would be, I turned back around and squared my shoulders.

After a long moment of staring at the fruit I looked up at Laera. "I feel like an idiot facing down a melon."

She smirked. "Well, blow it up and then you won't have to look at it anymore."

Recalling everything we'd practiced yesterday, I shoved all other thoughts from my mind. My vision tunneled in on the melon and I let the darkness tumble through me in a bundle of chaos. It was just a melon, it hadn't done anything to me, but it represented something greater. A threat against me and all of the remaining tributes. It was standing in our way of returning to Athos. I let it become a representation of everything I wanted to destroy. The fae king and the minotaur; the lies and deceit; the gods themselves.

The melon exploded, the liquid hitting me snapping me out of the dark thoughts I'd relied on to create the energy for my magic to rise to the surface. I stumbled back, startled and panting. Pulp and juice ran down my face and coated my arms.

Laera was laughing and cheering. I offered a weak smile, then I collapsed and everything went black.

There was a sweet smell that stirred me from sleep. Something familiar that should be welcome but somehow made me wrinkle my nose with disgust. My eyes fluttered against the bright light and I grunted, feeling light headed and a little nauseous.

"Well, this is not going to do at all," Laera scolded.

I glanced around and noticed I was on the floor in her room, the splattered remains of the melon still around us. That explained the smell.

She helped me to sitting, her expression annoyed. "Magic takes a lot from someone and it takes practice to be able to withstand it. Unfortunately, we don't have time for you to build up your strength."

"I passed out." It all came crashing back to my mind

and my shoulders slumped. She was right. I couldn't afford to go down from using my magic on the water of a melon. How was I going to do this to a minotaur? "I didn't pass out with the vampire."

"Ryvin told me what happened. He'd nearly killed him already. You simply finished him off. We won't have that head start with the monster."

"What am I going to do?" Panic seized my insides. "Is there any way we can get out of this? Is he really going to dump us into the labyrinth?"

Laera stood, then offered her hand to help me rise. "We can probably sneak you off the island, but it's going to be impossible to get the other tributes off and it will put a target on your back for the gods. Even with that necklace, you won't be able to avoid them all. You're safe in the sea, but not on land. And only until the Queen of the Ocean decides she's done waiting for us to release Nyx."

I closed my eyes and pressed my palms to my eyelids then quickly removed them when I realized how sticky my hands were. The magic I held was dangerous and I wasn't sure I even wanted it. It was a cruel twist of fate that I had the opportunity to use it to help people with it, but only if I could figure it out fast enough.

The door swung open and Ryvin walked in with Vanth at his heels. They closed the door quickly before stepping into the room. Both males looked confused for a moment as they took in the mess around us. Laera and I were both covered in melon remains and the floor and furniture were coated in sticky residue. The confusion melted into amusement.

"So you were eavesdropping," Ryvin said. "And you've already decided we're sending her in."

Laera shrugged. "It's easier than expecting her to empty tunnels of water for us to pass through."

"Easier for who?" I asked. "You're not going into the labyrinth."

"What's that?" Laera pointed to a bundle in Ryvin's hands.

He looked down as if he was surprised he was holding something. "A gift from a friend. It's a tether."

"You have friends with that kind of magic?" Laera sounded both annoyed and impressed.

"What do you mean a tether? It looks like sewing thread," I said skeptically.

"You can tie it around you before you go through the portal. As long as it's still on the other side, you'll be able to cross back through the portal without concern of it closing or blocking you out."

"I wouldn't have to go through the caves?" Relief made me let out a long sigh. Exploding the monster was one thing, having enough reserve magic left to create a path through tunnels full of water was another.

"It has to be your choice how you do this. If you want to do it at all. Noria told me about her cousin and I had his ship held until sunset. There's time for you to change your mind," Ryvin said.

My brow furrowed. "Do you want me to leave?"

"It's not about what I want," he said.

"She can destroy the creature," Laera said. "And with that tether, getting Nyx back here is so much easier. That was some gift you got, Brother."

I looked at the spool of thread in Ryvin's hands then took the rest of him in. His shoulders were slightly slumped and he had dark circles under his eyes. He didn't look like he'd slept in weeks.

"This is the only way," I said firmly. "I think it's why I ended up here."

"Whatever choice you make, we'll support," Ryvin said.

"I've made it," I assured him. "I can do this."

"She can practice the rest of the day and she'll be ready," Laera said.

"Your doing?" Vanth gestured to the mess around the room.

I couldn't help but smile. I might have passed out, but I had made a melon explode. "Yeah."

"Well, I would like to see that monster get what it deserves," Vanth said.

"It will," Laera confirmed.

I wished I felt as confident as she sounded. I'd agreed to do this, even knowing there was a way out.

"We need to train more and the two of you in here is going to draw suspicion," Laera had her hands on her hips, "time to go."

I wanted to run to Ryvin, to feel his arms around me, to have him stroke my hair and tell me everything was going to be alright. But I knew once I let myself melt into his embrace, I was going to let all my frustration and fear free and I was going to be a mess.

"Can you check on the tributes for me?" I asked. "Especially Belan? He was a mess at the party. I want to know if they're alright."

Ryvin retrieved the thread he'd set down. "Of course. I'll come see you tonight."

My insides felt like goo and I knew I was wearing a smile that gave all of my feelings away. Ryvin's cheeks flushed and he bowed in the most formal gesture I'd ever seen him give anyone, then he winked. "My lady."

My knees felt weak and I wasn't sure how I remained standing as I watched him and Vanth leave the room.

"You do realize the more you let him in, the worse it'll be when the fates tear you apart," Laera said the second they closed the door.

David's face found its way into my mind and I shoved it away. She was probably right, I'd never met anyone who was with the person they truly loved. Especially not a royal. But I was determined to let myself have this. Even if was only for a couple of days. "Who broke your heart?"

"I'll tell you a story sometime," she said. "But right now, we have a lot more work to do."

We spent the next several hours practicing on the dozens of melons Laera had brought to her room. Over and over I called to the magic until I made the fruit explode. Each time, I had to sit and rest, but I wouldn't let myself pass out again.

By evening, I was sweating and covered in sticky fruit juice. As I stared down the final fruit, all I could get it to do was shake. "There's nothing left."

Laera nodded. "You did better than I expected. The magic of the gods is supposed to come on more quickly than fae magic. Let's hope that's true."

I sat on the ground, not really caring that it was in a

pile of fruit pulp. Everything was coated in the stuff. "What now?"

"Tomorrow you should rest. Eat well, regain your energy. You know the concepts. It's going to be up to you to apply them in the labyrinth," she said.

"Then what? Assuming I succeed. I go right to Nyx. You think I'll really have the skills to get a goddess out on my own?"

"We'll be right behind you." Laera said. "As soon as that beast goes down, it'll be pure chaos. The king won't even notice if Ryvin and I jump into the labyrinth after you. As soon as you step back through that portal, we've got it from there."

35

Lagina

My head throbbed, and I rubbed my temples before standing and facing my advisors. "Enough arguing. This plan was set in motion before I claimed the throne and I will not act on outdated information. Our forces are depleted and until we know what the fae are planning, I will not start a war. My sister is in Konos. Have you forgotten that? Have you forgotten that if we attack them, they could kill her in retaliation?"

"There is always a cost to war, your highness," Gustav, the youngest of my father's advisors, said quietly.

I glared at him. "I understand that. I'm not saying we won't fight. I'm saying I need updated intelligence. We lost hundreds during the Choosing ceremony. I will not sign off on a war when I don't have all the pieces in place."

A knock sounded, and I nodded to the guard standing

near the door. When he opened it, I saw the Dragon King framed by the opening, my aunt Katerina next to him.

With an exasperated sigh, I walked away from the table to greet our guests. We were supposed to reach an agreement on what we were going to say to the king prior to him joining the meeting, but all we'd done was argue.

My advisors all wanted me to charge in with all the dragons and wipe Konos off the map. Meanwhile, we had no intelligence about their numbers in Telos. Nobody could tell me how many wolf shifters there were or what the vampires were up to. I had no information about the other fae courts that answered to the king.

While Konos was our primary target, it was simply the capital of a much larger civilization. My advisors seemed to live in a bubble where they thought they were just like us. A small city isolated from the outside world. I knew that wasn't the case. How could they not see the bigger picture? They were so focused on the plan my father created that they couldn't ask any other questions.

"Thank you for joining us." My tone was forced, the frustration I was feeling still seeping into my words. "Please, take a seat." I gestured toward the table where my advisors were gathered.

The Dragon King inclined his head and Aunt Katerina followed behind. She paused in front of me and gave my hand a quick squeeze before proceeding to the table.

"Your palace is beautiful," the king said as he settled into his chair. "But I was hoping to see the rest of the city. My tour felt rather confined."

"After the fae attack, the city is still in mourning. I

don't think having a foreign king riding through the streets is best for my people," I said abruptly.

A few of my advisors sucked in sharp breaths and I could feel the tension around us. They wanted me to play nice with the Dragon King. No, not nice, subservient. Like I was the desperate one here. Maybe we were. We were outnumbered and didn't have the magic or strength the dragons or the fae held, but I was tired of being pushed around. My father wasn't here to hold my reins. This was my kingdom, and I was going to do what I thought was best.

"Are we not allies?" he asked.

"We thought the fae delegation was friendly," I pointed out.

"They came to steal away your people. They were never friendly," he countered.

"You still haven't explained why you're here." I ignored his very obvious point about the fae.

"We desire peace and we feel that Athos can help us gain that peace." He flashed a dazzling smile that was more flirting courtier than diplomat.

I bristled, not hiding the expression of mistrust and disgust on my face. His smile faded, then he glanced at all the men sitting around me, then turned his attention toward me. "I believe we need to have a discussion privately. Ruler to ruler."

"That's out of the question," Istvan hissed. "We will not allow anything to happen to our queen."

"Throw your bones, old man. You know I won't harm her. You know what's coming. And I'm guessing you know what Athos guards." The king stared at Istvan and the priest's face went pale.

"What is he talking about?" I asked.

Istvan stood suddenly. "The guards will stand outside the doors."

"You can't possibly think leaving her in here with him is a good idea," Gustav said. The other advisors began talking over each other, arguing about my safety.

I slammed my hand on the table. "Enough. All of you, out. If he kills me, our deal is off. And he wouldn't be here if we didn't have something he wanted."

The room quieted, and all of the men around the table gaped at me in surprise.

The king lifted a brow, and I swore I saw the faintest hint of a smirk. I turned away from him, then looked to my aunt. "You traveled here with him. What of his character?"

"He'll keep his word," she said.

"Good. You stay with me. Istvan, keep everyone else out."

My aunt inclined her head, and the priest rose from his seat, giving me a nod before walking to the door. The others grumbled in protest on their way out, but none of them said anything to my face.

As soon as the door was closed, I turned my chair so I was facing the Dragon King. "Tell me what's really going on."

"The only thing I want from Athos is my bride. But seeing as how we'll be connected through marriage, you should probably know that a war with the fae might cost you more than you're willing to sacrifice," the king said.

"What do you mean?"

"You've been sold lies your whole life," he said.

"Excuse me?" This king was not doing any favors to win my approval. I was starting to wonder why my father ever invited him in the first place.

"For starters, we've never been at war with you."

I glanced over at my aunt. "What is he talking about?"

"We were lied to, Gina."

"We're happy in Drakous. We don't need Athos. The only attacks at your wall were stupid young dragons who wanted to rile up your soldiers," he explained.

"That's impossible." How could we be in a one-sided centuries long war?

"I believe him. I've seen his army. If they really attacked us, none of us would stand a chance," Aunt Katerina said.

I rubbed my temples. There had been too much information. Too many lies. Dropping my hands into my lap, I looked at the three remaining people in the room. My father's sister, my father's most trusted priest, and our enemy. How did it come to this?

"There's more," Aunt Katerina said quietly.

I laughed, it came out slightly unhinged. "Of course, there is." Shaking my head, I let out a sigh. "Just tell me."

"The fae protected Athos because we have something of theirs they don't want anyone else to get their hands on. The tributes were a ruse. A way to keep you all fearful of them and to justify their protection," Aunt Katerina said. "I found out when I was around your age, so my father had me sent to the wall. He told me if I ever said anything to anyone, he'd have one of his guards push me from the top."

My throat burned, and I had to fight against the rising emotion. How could someone treat her like that? "I thought you were there because you chose to be."

"It was the wall or a temple," she said.

"He was going to send Ara to a temple." I had heard him say it so many times, but I never thought he'd really follow through until I watched him betray her in the worst possible way.

"It's Athos best kept secret," Istvan cut in. "Many have been killed to keep it."

"So what was so important that it caused this much suffering?" I demanded.

"A prison below the city in the underwater caverns," Istvan said. "Designed by the Fae King himself."

"Who would need such a prison?" My palms felt damp, my heart racing. There was someone that dangerous below us?

"Nyx. Goddess of Night and Death," the Dragon King answered.

I swallowed hard. I knew who Nyx was. I'd heard the stories of her terrible power. Centuries of eternal night just because someone insulted her. Cities full of dead babies for no reason. Whole civilizations wiped from the map at her whim. Out of the goddesses who controlled the sea and the sky, she was the most dangerous and the most volatile. "How?"

"She was the Fae King's mate," he explained.

My brow furrowed.

"A mate is a bond between two beings, deeper than

love, a need to be together ordained by the stars themselves," Aunt Katerina explained.

"I don't understand. Why would he lock her up if she's his mate?" It seemed tragic and senseless even for someone so dangerous.

"Nyx is the only one who can bring down the Fae King," the Dragon King said. "But she's too dangerous. She can't be tamed."

"Why are you telling me all this? Are you saying we must adhere to the Fae King's demands?" I asked. "I thought you were here to help us defeat them and gain our freedom from the Choosing."

"It means that if you choose to go to war against the fae, you must decide if you're trading one evil for something worse," the king said.

The door opened, and I turned to see who was stupid enough to come in without knocking. The breathless, pale guard stole the anger from me, replacing it instantly with concern. "What is it?"

"It's Sophia. The healer says you need to come now." The guard stepped back out into the hall, still catching his breath.

My chair tumbled to the ground, but I didn't stop to fix it as I ran from the room.

36

Ara

Despite the fact that I'd drained the water and washed a second time, I still felt a little sticky. I wasn't sure I'd ever feel clean again. Not with all the things I'd done in the last few weeks. I was pretty sure the stain wasn't on my skin, it was on my soul.

Noria was waiting with a nightgown and a cup of tea. My arms hurt to lift, so I was grateful that she was there to help me dress. She went through the motions of brushing my hair and I found myself staring at nothing, my mind blank and overwhelmed.

When I caught myself disconnecting from the world, I took a deep breath and turned so I could see Noria.

She lowered the hairbrush and waited.

"Is Vanth outside?" He hadn't been there when I returned this afternoon, but I had a feeling I wasn't unguarded for long.

"He was there when I arrived," she replied.

"Can you get him for me?" I asked, feeling too tired to move.

She walked to the door, then returned with the shifter.

"Is everything alright?" Vanth moved quickly to my side.

"I'm fine. I wanted to ask if you saw the tributes."

He nodded.

"How were they?"

He sighed. "Much the same as when you last saw them."

"But they're safe?" I asked.

"They are."

"Do they know about what's coming?" I asked.

"No. The king didn't want to risk any of them running since all are required to appease the fates," he said.

"Do you think I have a chance at surviving this?" I asked.

Vanth looked a little green. "I hope so."

Morta had told me she couldn't see my fate. I wondered if it was because I was going to be torn to pieces by the minotaur. If it ended that way, I hoped it was quicker than Clayton's death.

"You should get some rest," Noria said. "The princess insisted you spend the remaining time building up your strength."

Remaining time. As if the countdown was on already and I was nearing my end. I stood, wincing a bit against the discomfort of moving my body in the most simple ways. I really did need the rest, but if this was it, I wasn't going to spend the last of my time alone in a windowless room.

"Take me to Ryvin," I ordered. I never gave commands, and I was startled at how the words came out.

Vanth raised his brows, telling me I wasn't the only one surprised by my tone.

"Please," I added.

Vanth inclined his head. "As you wish, your highness."

"I'll be in the servant's quarters if you need me," Noria said.

"Thank you. For everything," I said.

She shushed me. "That sounds far too much like a goodbye. I will not have it."

"See you soon," I replied tentatively, hoping I really would see her again.

She nodded. "I'll see you soon. If I don't see you before... well, good luck."

As I followed Vanth down the now familiar hallway, I was a little hurt that Ryvin wasn't at my room already. Doubt needled into my mind. What if I'd waited too long to tell him how I felt? What if he'd dismissed me as already dead? What if I was reading everything wrong?

"Vanth?"

He stopped walking and turned to me. "Yes?"

"If I don't make it..."

"Don't talk like that. You're going to make it," he said.

"If I don't," I pressed. "Please promise me you'll try to

help my sisters. Somehow. Even if it means giving them a quick death, if that's the only option."

"You'll help them yourself when this is over," he said. "In two days, you'll be meeting with them, making plans for the future."

It was a lovely picture, reuniting with them to plan the overthrowing of the Fae King. I couldn't help but smile at the thought. All I ever wanted was to help my kingdom and protect my people. This was so much greater than that. I had the chance to change the world.

"Alright." I started walking, slowly so Vanth could lead since I didn't know where Ryvin's rooms were.

We stopped in front of a door identical to several others we'd passed along the way. Despite all we'd been through, my insides twisted as nervous flutters filled my stomach. What if I found him with someone else? What if he sent me away? What if he wasn't here?

Before I could even knock, the door swung open and Ryvin nearly collided with me. His initial surprise quickly turned to elation, the smile on his lips quite possibly the first truly genuine one I'd ever seen.

"I was just on my way to your room," he said.

"You took too long," I replied.

"Noria was to inform me if you were up for company." He rubbed the back of his neck and his expression seemed a bit boyish. He was nervous. Was it possible he'd had the same concerns about me that I'd had about him?

He moved to the side and gestured for me to enter. I glanced behind me, remembering that I never thanked Vanth for the escort. The shifter was already gone. I supposed I didn't need additional protection while I was with the prince. Even with magic of my own now, I knew his was on another level. He was a threat, whereas I still felt like I was a few weeks into training to use a sword all over again.

The difference was that I wasn't thrown into combat so early in my training. This time, the few skills I learned were going to have to destroy a creature that nobody had ever survived.

The door clicked behind me and I turned to face Ryvin. He was studying me, his eyes scanning me, taking me in as if memorizing every detail. I found myself doing the same thing, my throat tightening as I reminded myself that this could be the last time I saw him. Would I remember what he looked like from my place in the Underworld? What would happen once I met my death? Would I even exist in any form anymore or would I simply fade, my bones turning to dirt?

Ryvin silently closed the distance between us and his large hand reached for my face, cupping my cheek. I closed my eyes, leaning into the touch, breathing in his scent. When I opened my eyes, I realized tears had worked their way out, rolling down my cheeks unbidden.

He wiped them away, then traced his thumb over my bottom lip. "No more tears, this isn't goodbye."

"It feels like it," I confessed. "Nobody has returned from that maze."

"You will." His thumb brushed across my jaw.

"I'm sorry, Ryvin." I could feel the walls crumbling, my resistance melting away. I'd fought so hard against my feelings for him. There was so much complication. So many reasons I shouldn't allow myself to fall, but if I was facing death, why not give myself this? "I should have told you, I should have..."

His lips crashed into mine with an intensity that nearly knocked me to the ground. I wrapped my arms around him to steady myself and kissed him back, hungry and desperate, and for the first time since we'd met, without holding anything back. "None of that tonight," he managed between kisses. "No regrets, no goodbyes."

"The things I've said to you...the things I haven't..." I was panting and unwilling to stop kissing him to get the whole sentence out.

He bit down on my lower lip and I moaned, tilting my head back. His lips moved down my chin to my neck, trailing kisses and nips of his teeth along the sensitive skin.

"I never told you...I should have told you," I was breathing too hard and my mind was a fog of lust. Conversation wasn't possible.

He pulled away, cupping my cheeks between his large hands. His dark eyes stared into mine with an intensity I'd never seen. There was danger in that look, but I wasn't afraid of him. I wasn't sure I could ever be afraid of him. "You don't need to say anything."

I set my hands on top of his. "You tried to tell me, and I refused to admit it to myself."

"I know, Ara. Trust me, I know." His mouth was on mine again and all reason and thought dissipated. I was completely lost in him, unable to consider anything beyond the way his lips felt on mine, the way his hands grabbed at the fabric of my nightgown, and my rising need.

It was like burning alive but not feeling any pain. Instead, the fire between us was a dizzying, delicious sensation that sent tingles to every part of me. Warmth grew between my thighs and I pressed against him, feeling like I couldn't get close enough.

Tangling my fingers into his hair, I claimed him with my mouth, matching the hungry strokes of his tongue with my own. His hands moved down my back, to my hips, then back up again. He touched me everywhere, never stopping in one place too long. It was as if he had to touch every part of me, explore all of me. Every time his hands moved, I was left with a phantom longing for his touch, desperate for that contact. I needed him like I needed to breathe.

I pulled away and stared intently at him. "You need to know that I'm not going to fight it anymore. I don't want to fight it anymore. I just want to be with you."

For a moment, his expression almost looked pained, but he covered it with a smile. "You have no idea how long I've waited to hear that, Astari."

He lifted me, carrying me to his bed. After setting me down gently with my legs hanging over the edge, he pulled up my nightgown so it was around my waist, then he dropped to his knees. His lips trailed up my inner thigh, and I fell back into the bed, already gasping from his touch.

By the time his mouth found my center, I was already soaking wet. His tongue moved in expert strokes, making my hips buck. Then he added two fingers, moving them in time to the strokes of his tongue. I moaned, not able to spare any thoughts about who might hear me. With each stroke and each thrust of his fingers, I lost more control until I was crying out, pleasure rolling through me in a series of explosions.

Panting, I sat up and grabbed Ryvin's tunic. "Your turn."

He didn't fight me when I shoved him to the bed. When I finally got the trousers off, his full length sprung free, the tip already glistening. Now it was my turn to drop to my knees for him.

Positioning myself between his feet, I started at the base, licking and kissing my way up the shaft. He groaned as he leaned back on his elbows. When I closed my mouth around the head, he fell to his back and gripped the sheets.

Working slowly at first, I built speed. Adding my tongue and changing my positions, I continued until he was panting. I could tell he was close to release, so I moved faster, taking him as deep as I could.

He sat up suddenly, then pulled himself away. "I'm not done with you yet. Stand up."

I obliged, eager for more.

He moved in front of me, then began to explore my body with his tongue and teeth and lips. He kissed along my collarbone, down to my breasts. His hands caressed each one before taking my nipples into his mouth. I ran my fingers through his hair, my knees getting shakier as he continued to lavish attention on my skin.

Just when I was worried I might faint from the sensations, he picked me up so I was facing him, my legs wrapped around his waist. He walked toward his desk, then pulled a chair out.

Carefully, he sat down, still holding me. I shifted my hips so as he sat, he could enter me. With my feet on the ground now, I was able to ease into it, having him enter me slowly. I watched his expression as I teased him, raising and lowering myself little by little, drawing it out. When I finally lowered my hips completely, he groaned, then gripped my hips tightly. His fingers dug into the soft flesh and I rocked forward and backward, finding an angle and rhythm that made me moan.

We moved together, our hips rocking, our breathing as one. I leaned down and kissed him, pressing my breasts against his chest. The intensity grew with the closeness of our bodies and he wrapped his arms around my back, holding me tight.

Panting and moaning, I chased release, rocking and moving until both of us were gasping for breath. Pleasure rolled through me, escalating until my back arched and my fingers dug into his shoulders to keep myself from toppling over. He leaned into my chest, groaning as he came. Wrapped together, I breathed through the little aftershocks of my climax, reveling in the feel of the two of us so close we were almost as one.

Shaking and spent, I stayed in his arms for a long while before climbing off. He instantly grabbed hold of my hand, as if he couldn't stand the thought of not touching me. I was glad it wasn't just me.

"My bathtub is large enough for two," he offered.

For the first time since I arrived in Konos, I didn't even

feel the slightest fear about getting in the bath. With a grin, I followed him to his bathing chamber.

For the next day and night, we stayed in his room. It became our private world. Food was dropped at the door, though we ate little as we were too distracted by each other.

When Vanth knocked on the door on the morning of the full moon, the haze of lust was rudely stripped away, reality finding us again.

"Time moved too quickly in your room," I teased.

"When this is over, I'm taking you somewhere far away and we're not leaving our room for a month," he promised.

"Then you better not let me die in that maze," I warned.

He squeezed my hand. "I won't let anyone harm you."

In that moment, I knew Ryvin was my future. I wasn't sure what it meant for my status in Athos, or what it meant for us after we eliminated the Fae King. Whatever came next, I knew we would be by each other's side.

37

Ara

Ryvin's grip on my hand was so tight I was losing feeling in my fingers, but I was squeezing him just as hard. I'd skipped breakfast in favor of more time with Ryvin in bed, but even if I'd had food set in front of me, I wasn't going to be able to eat.

"Shouldn't you stay away from me so your father doesn't suspect anything?" I asked quietly as we neared the palace's grand entrance.

"Everyone knows what we've been doing in my room."

My cheeks heated. "But they don't have to know it meant anything." I loosened my grip so I could pull my hand away.

He clasped it tighter. "They know."

It was almost worse knowing how deeply he cared for me. It was definitely worse now that I'd allowed myself to admit how much I cared for him. Losing him just when I dropped my guard and let him in was almost more painful than when I walked away from my sisters. It shouldn't be that way, but when I let myself feel everything, it was too intense.

The wind whipped my hair and sent my white peplos twisting around my ankles. Dark clouds loomed, denser and more ominous than usual. It was as if the sky itself was warning me about what was coming.

I wished I could turn around, run back inside to the refuge of Ryvin's room. Stay there, just the two of us, hidden away from the world while the fae and the gods tore each other apart. Why did they have to involve us?

Shoving those thoughts aside, I focused on my sisters. My people. The other tributes. I might not be fully human, but I was of Athos and even if it couldn't be my home again after all this, I knew the world would be a better place without the Fae King.

The rumbling of a carriage sent my heart hammering against my ribs. Ryvin moved even closer to me, leaning down so he could whisper, "You can do this. Taking out the monster is no different than a melon."

I had to laugh, even though he wasn't trying to be humorous. "It doesn't feel the same."

"All you're doing is controlling the water. You can do that." He sounded confident.

"Your highness." Vanth was standing next to us and I startled, not realizing he'd approached.

"Sorry, Princess. I didn't mean to sneak up on you."

"It's fine." My pulse was racing, but I wasn't sure how much of it was from Vanth and how much of it was in anticipation of what was coming. With that carriage parked in front of the palace, I knew my time was up.

Ryvin kissed my cheek. "I'll see you soon."

"This way," Vanth instructed, sweeping his arm toward the carriage.

I glanced at Rvyin, then let my hand drop from his. The only thing that helped me to move forward was the reminder that when this was over, we could find a way to see where everything between us could lead. There was hope in that thought. Hope that my actions could bring me joy while also helping to protect those I cared about. For once, I wasn't only thinking about my family or my people. I was also thinking about myself. It should have felt wrong, it went against everything I'd been taught, but if I learned anything while on Konos it was that life was short. Even if you were part god. I deserved at least a little happiness.

"See you soon," I said before making my way to the carriage.

"I'll be watching you the whole time," Ryvin promised. "You can do this."

When Vanth closed the door of the carriage behind me, I gave myself a moment to let all the fear in. My breathing quickened and tears streamed down my cheeks. I dug my fingernails into my palms and clenched my jaw so tightly my head ached.

Then, I blew out a breath and shook out my hands, forcing myself to shove it all away. It was a lie to tell myself it was going to be fine, but I needed that lie right now. I needed to believe I could do this. And mostly, I needed to survive this so I could see my sisters and Ryvin again. There was no way that creature was going to be the last thing I saw.

Holding onto that hope, I stared out the window, watching as we drew closer to the amphitheater.

I brushed against the hidden pockets Noria had sewn inside my peplos, feeling the spool of thread and the fae light. There was so much at stake today and so many ways it could go wrong. Knowing those items were there helped center me, remind me that I wasn't exactly alone.

The carriage shook as it came to a halt and I tensed to brace myself. The door opened too quickly, Vanth greeting me with a stoic expression. We were outside the amphitheater, but I could already hear the roar of the crowd. The bloodthirsty fae gathered here wanted a show. They wanted to see us all torn to pieces and eaten alive.

I balled my hands into fists, my anger at them for their callous ways overcoming my fear and concern. They were exactly why I had to succeed today. The Fae King had gathered the most vicious around him, teaching them by example that destruction and death were how they should live. Showing them that brutality was not only allowed, but something to celebrate.

It had to stop.

"You ready?" Vanth asked as we slowly walked toward the gate where I saw the other tributes waiting.

"Yes." It was the only word I could manage. I was too distracted by the sight of the humans. They'd looked so healthy and well-cared for last time I saw them. Now, they were disheveled and dirty. They were bound together by their wrists in a line, each tribute shuffling along in the dirt. Most of them were without shoes.

"How can they run like that?" I hissed.

"They shouldn't be bound." Vanth's brow furrowed.

"Nice of you to finally join us, Princess," a large guard with a ruddy red face sneered. "Wouldn't you like to join your companions?"

"You don't need to bind me, I'll go of my own free will," I said with false confidence. Seeing the tributes in this state shook me more than I wanted to admit.

"The king said to get you all into the labyrinth by any means necessary." He stalked forward with a rope in his hands.

"If she's not resisting, you have no reason to tie her up." Vanth moved in front of me.

"She's not your concern anymore, Skylos," the guard spat.

"Then you can explain to the prince after he sees her hauled into the arena like a criminal," Vanth said with a shrug.

The guard flinched, then retreated. "Fine. But if she tries to run, I'll make sure getting her back is painful."

I resisted the urge to roll my eyes. He was hoping I'd run, and I wasn't going to give him the satisfaction. "Lead the way."

He grunted toward the other guards waiting with the tributes and they lurched forward. My chest tightened, hating seeing them like that, but if I was successful, I was going to get us all home.

We stepped in through the archway, right into the center of the amphitheater. The crowd intensified, their cries and hollers even louder at our entrance. I gritted my teeth, letting myself hold on to the anger at all of them.

Some of the members of this crowd had danced with or fucked the tributes at parties without any care. Now, they were here, calling for their deaths. I wished I could throw them into the pit and watch the color leech from their faces as they stared down the monster.

The small hole in the center of the oval was already open, and I knew the labyrinth was waiting below our feet. Was the creature already awake, waiting for us? Or would it stalk us slowly the way we'd observed with Clayton in the maze?

My mouth went dry, and I licked my lips before trying to swallow down some of the fear. Shoving it away, I glared at the stands, making myself focus on the anger I felt toward all the fae. Turning slightly, I faced the royal box, finding the king and queen already seated in their thrones. There wasn't any sign of Ryvin or Laera, but I knew they were here somewhere, waiting for me to play my part so they could help. That thought helped return my pulse to a more steady rhythm.

The guards hauling the line of bound tributes paused at the entry to the labyrinth, then looked up to the king.

"Good luck," Vanth whispered, leaving me next to them before he retreated from the space.

I was surrounded by screaming fae and standing next to ten humans and several guards, but I suddenly felt more alone than I ever had.

The king stood and raised his arms, the cheering fae quieted. When he spoke, his voice was amplified, booming through the amphitheater for everyone to hear. "The gods have spoken and they have demanded an offering of eleven humans this day."

The crowd responded with approving cheers. I glared at them, despising all of them more than I had just a moment ago.

"Your sacrifices today will earn you a place of honor in the Underworld." The king nodded, and the guards shoved the first tribute down the hole, the others trailing behind, the rope tying them all together dragging each of them in after the other.

Fear flared, and I raced forward. "What are you doing?" They were going to land on each other, possibly harm one another, and they couldn't run like that.

I was next to the hole before I realized I'd made a mistake. Someone shoved me and I tumbled in, right after all the other tributes.

38

Ara

We were a tangle of bodies, all of us grunting and moving and apologizing as we tried to get off and away from each other. The air was stale and damp, with a hint of rot. Glancing up, I noted that everything around us was dark. There was no sign of the crowd, no sign of the top of the labyrinth, nothing but the void.

Several of the tributes were screaming or crying, some sat on the ground, refusing to move. I tried calming them as I moved, reaching through the darkness around me as I distanced myself from the others.

Once I thought I had moved enough so I wasn't blocking anyone's progress, I found the fae light in my pocket and squeezed it as Noria had shown me. I knew there was a chance the people above watching us would do something to quash the light, but I had to get the tributes unbound if they were to have any hope of survival. A few people shrieked at the light and some made relieved sounds.

"Stay calm, everyone. We need to get those ropes off," I said.

"What's the point?" someone asked.

"That beast can't eat all of us," another responded. "There's a chance some of us could make it to the portal."

Another tribute punched someone in the face. "Not if I make it there first."

"Stop it!" I screamed. "None of you are getting eaten."

"What are you even doing down here?" someone asked.

"Stop talking and listen to her," Belan's familiar voice cut in.

I turned to see him, looking ragged and worn down, but relatively unscathed. "It's nice to see you again."

"I lost myself for a bit," he admitted.

"You're here now," I replied.

"As nice as your reunion is, we're all fucked, so why would we listen to you?" a man with a black eye asked.

"Because I can kill the monster," I said.

The group went quiet.

"Nobody can kill that creature," someone said.

I turned so the light I was holding was illuminating the tangle of tributes. "Isn't it worth letting me try?"

Nobody responded for a long time. Finally, Belan broke the silence, "We can die fighting each other, or we can try to survive by working together."

"Listen, I know you don't trust me and I don't blame you." I fished the spool of thread from my pocket and held it up. "This will allow me to go through the portal and return."

"She's going to leave us behind!" A woman called.

I shook my head. "We're wasting time. Listen. Then decide if you want to believe me."

I was itching to start making progress toward the portal, but I couldn't have one of these tributes stab me in the back. I wanted to help them, but at the very least, I couldn't have them disrupt my mission.

"The goddess of night is trapped under Athos. I'm going to kill the minotaur, then go through the portal and release her. Then we can all watch as she helps us take down the Fae King." I looked around, watching my words sink into the tributes.

"She's crazy," a man said quietly. He looked at the man he was still tied to. "Isn't she?"

"So what if she is?" Belan added, before giving me a guilty shrug of his shoulders. "What harm is it in letting her try? If she's right, we don't get eaten. If she's wrong, it's every tribute for themselves to get through that portal."

"What would we have to do?" A woman stepped forward. She'd already removed her bindings, and I could see the glimmer of defiance in her eyes. I instantly liked her.

"We stay together and we make our way toward the center. When we find the monster, you all stay out of the way so I can destroy it. Then you wait while I use the portal. When I return, you can stay and watch or you can go through to Athos," I said quickly.

The air seemed to shift, and I caught the scent of

death. We were out of time. "I think the monster has entered the maze."

There were whispers and whimpers. These people had been so broken with all they'd done under the influence of the Fae wine. I hated asking more of them but we were already on borrowed time. "Get out of those bindings. We're out of time."

They actually snapped into action, those who were already out helping those who were still bound. While everyone worked to quickly free their bindings, I pulled Belan aside. "I need your help with something."

"Anything."

"I need you to hold the thread on this end for me. No matter what, you have to keep it on this side of the portal or I won't be able to get back," I explained.

He nodded. "You can count on me."

Some of the tributes were still complaining or crying as we moved through the neglected, ancient maze. The damp stone was crumbling, and the dirt was full of holes from the various vermin and insects who called this place their home. I wondered if that was what the monster ate when it wasn't consuming humans.

"Can you really kill this thing?" Belan asked in a whisper.

"Yes," I said, surprising myself with the confidence in my tone. It was true, in theory, I could kill the monster. And if what Ryvin had said was true about size not being an issue, I could do it. The problem was going to be keeping it distracted enough for me to focus.

"I'll be using magic," I admitted, glancing at the former guard to see his reaction.

"Thank the gods. I thought you were going to try to fight it like Clayton." He offered a weak smile.

"That doesn't scare you?" I asked.

"I don't care what you need to do if it gets us out of here," he said.

Each step was cautious, avoiding the divots and holes in the ground. The tributes behind me quieted, their cries less frequent and their footsteps slow. We could all feel the rising tension, even though we couldn't yet see the monster or the portal.

I wondered how long we'd be wandering, taking turn after turn, sometimes into dead ends, before we met the beast. And once I did destroy him, how would we find our way to the center where the portal was? I felt a little foolish that I'd never asked about that. It was a labyrinth after all, designed to make one feel lost.

"This way," someone behind us called.

We all stopped, and I turned to see a tribute pointing to a fork in the path we'd walked by.

"How do you know?" another tribute challenged.

"Because there's a glow."

I walked back, the tributes moving aside for Belan and me to pass through. Sure enough, there was a faint blue glow coming from that path. "Good catch."

Cautiously, I took a few steps on our new route, holding my breath. It felt like any second, the minotaur was going to leap from the shadows and devour us all.

Turn after turn, we moved in the direction of the faint glow. It didn't work like light should and I was starting to get nervous that we were making the wrong choices until the next turn revealed the portal.

We were there, right in the center of the maze, the portal in front of us. "I don't understand."

"Where's the monster?" Belan asked.

"Maybe it wasn't hungry?" someone said hopefully.

Every hair on my body stood on edge. This wasn't right. Something was very off. It had been too easy.

"You should go," Belan said. "I'll hold the thread."

"What if it comes as soon as I'm through?" I asked.

"I'll hold it off," he said.

Something bellowed, so loud the walls rattled and dirt and rocks crumbled from them, making a cloud of dust around us.

One of the tributes screamed and ran for the portal, diving toward it. The blue glow sizzled and with a burst of light, the tribute was sent flying backward, smoke rising from their charred form.

"The portal doesn't work," Belan said. "It's a trap. The whole thing was a trap."

I couldn't worry about the portal right now, I was too busy worrying about the massive creature glaring down at me. He was twice my size. His huge bull's head was topped with massive horns that came to sharp points. Yellow eyes glared at me and hot, putrid breath came from his nostrils, making me want to gag.

The creature's body was covered in thick fur, but was shaped like a man's. The biggest difference was the size. His limbs were like trees, his chest larger than a barrel of wine. My hands shook. How was exploding a melon supposed to prepare me for this?

Without taking my eyes off the beast, I yelled to the tributes, "Run!"

The scrambling and screaming behind me told me they were likely trying for escape but the monster was faster. The beast moved, charging after the tributes, far more interested in the chase than in the people who were standing still in front of it.

It was now or never.

I spun, focusing on the lumbering monster chasing the tributes. For once, I wondered if the gods were giving me a push. The creature was fleeing from me, and it moved slowly. As if it enjoyed the chase. Or it knew there was a dead end ahead.

Panic welled as the realization that the tributes would soon be trapped. Taking a deep breath, I shoved it down, finding my outrage at the fact that they were even down here in the first place. Tapping into that anger, that dark energy that seemed to swirl and rise up at the injustice before me, I stepped forward.

My whole body felt like it was on fire, heat rising, limbs tingling. This wasn't supposed to be any different than a melon. Or a vampire. I could do this.

The minotaur stopped, caging in the tributes. His massive bull's head swiveled back and forth, as if trying to decide where to start. The monster roared and screams filled the air, but they sounded so far away.

Everything tunneled in on the beast. All I had, everything inside me raced forth. I let it all out. The anger at my father, the frustration toward the Choosing, the injustice at the way humans were treated by the fae, the crowd who was here to see a bloodbath, the lies I'd been told my whole life.

And the gods for their desire to end my life simply because they didn't want my mother to sire a child.

All of it left me in a screaming rage and excruciating pain exploded from my chest, racing down my arms. A flash of light filled the dark walkway and spots exploded before my vision. As the light receded, I lowered my arms, panting and sweating. Angry tears streaked down my cheeks.

Shaking, I looked down at myself and noted that I was covered in blood and bits of flesh. The smell made me retch and I turned, emptying my stomach on the dirt next to me.

Sounds reemerged, cries and cheers. When I regained control, I looked to where the minotaur had been. There were bloodied tributes and pieces of the monster littering the ground.

"You did it," Belan said in awe.

I looked over at the guard who'd never left my side. He was also covered in the monster's remains, but he wore a smile I would never forget as long as I lived. The pure joy was obvious, and I found myself smiling despite the exhaustion.

Suddenly, deafening sound erupted around us, and I looked up. The amphitheater was now visible, the crowd screaming at us from their seats. There was no time to linger in victory or to catch my breath.

"We have to get you to that portal," Belan said. "If you think it'll work."

After watching another tribute die trying, I was hesitant, but I didn't think the Fae King was going to let me live if I decided to skip that part and somehow climb free of the labyrinth. There wasn't another option. Hoping it worked only if the monster was defeated, I charged forward. I had to try. "Let's go."

Belan followed me back to the portal, and I noticed the other tributes had followed at a distance.

"There's someone coming," one of the tributes called.

They must have already sent guards in after us.

"Now or never," Belan said, extending his hand for the thread.

Quickly, I tied the thread around my waist, then handed him the spool. Before I could talk myself out of it, I raced toward the glowing blue oval.

39

Lagina

The entire room was splashed with crimson. Pale, wide-eyed guards were shaking near the door, afraid to step deeper into the room. Terror gripped my chest, making it difficult to breathe. I stepped onto the bloody floor, my slippers sticking to the ground as I walked.

My stomach churned, and I frantically scanned the bodies around the room seeking Sophia. When I found her, breathing and alive, only part of my tension eased.

She was the only one alive in the room.

We were surrounded by death, and Sophia was the murderer.

"Get them out of here," Istvan hissed, waving his hands at the terrified men standing near the door.

My gaze was fixed on my sister, her huddled form in the corner shaking with sobs. She was drenched in blood.

Her gold locks hung in red strings, her pale skin was smeared scarlet.

"Wait." As the pieces came crashing together, I realized the danger we were in. I forced myself to turn away from her and locked eyes with Istvan. "Make them wait in the hall. Nobody leaves. Nobody speaks."

He inclined his head, an unspoken understanding passing between us. These men would have to prove they could maintain their silence or we would have to force their silence. Nobody could know what was going on here.

"You shouldn't be alone in here," Argus said quietly.

I glanced at him, then nodded once, indicating he could stay. My newly appointed head guard had seen too much already. He was just as condemned as I was if word got out.

"Soph?" I called gently, using the same tone I'd used with her when she was young. How was this cowering, bloody mess huddled in the corner the same girl I'd helped ride her first pony? The same girl I'd picked oranges with and taught how to sneak honey cakes from the kitchen between meals?

Her head snapped up at my voice. "Don't come near me. Get out of here before I hurt you, too."

"You'd never hurt me," I assured her.

She shook her head and tears left trails in the blood smeared on her cheeks. "Please, kill me quickly. Do it quickly, even though I don't deserve it. And don't tell Ara. Please, don't tell her what I became."

I took a step closer, my heart shattering at her words. "I'm going to help you get through this."

"There's no helping me!" she yelled, then wailed, burying her face in her knees as she cried. I froze. It was the first time I'd ever heard her raise her voice.

"Your highness?" Argus's soft words were a contrast to Sophia's cries.

I looked over at the guard, then followed the direction of his stare. My knees buckled and if not for the chair near enough for me to grab, I'd have fallen to the ground.

She was nearly unrecognizable in her bloody peplos. Her golden hair, the same color as mine, the same as Sophia's, was matted and soaking up the crimson puddle under her head. Lifeless blue eyes stared up at the ceiling. A chill ran down my spine and I made a choked sound of pain.

My mother was dead.

Argus grabbed hold of me seconds before I'd have gone down. Even the chair wasn't enough to hold me. I'd lost my father, then Ara, and now this. Sophia was a monster and my mother was dead. Cora was being sent to Drakous. I was losing everything and everyone I loved. I couldn't lose anyone else.

"I didn't mean to. I don't know what happened," Sophia was looking at me now, having regained some control. "Please, kill me. I can't. I won't. I didn't mean to. I don't know what happened but I can't be allowed to live. I'm a monster. I'm a monster."

I turned at the sound of the door opening and saw Istvan slip into the room. "What should I do with the other guards?"

"Will she lose control again?" I asked.

"I don't know. I'm still awaiting the information I requested," Istvan said.

"You knew?" Argus asked.

"We suspected," Istvan replied.

"I won't kill my sister," I said.

"You must!" Sophia was standing now. Her slim frame looked even more frail and small covered in blood. "I killed her. I killed them all. Don't let me hurt anyone else."

She should look terrifying; I should be terrified, but she was my sister. "You'll go to your room and you will not leave. We're going to figure this out."

"The guards will talk," Istvan warned.

"What if she needs to eat again?" Argus asked.

"Bring her sheep, pigs, goats, anything to appease her," I ordered. "I will not have her punished for our father's choices."

"We can't house a vampire here," Istvan said.

I shot a glare at him. What I wouldn't give for my mother's advice right now. My chest felt like it might cave in with grief, but I knew the only way I could honor her was to save Sophia. That's what my mother would beg for. She'd have died for any of us. I just never knew she would have to. The things I would have asked her had I known how limited our time together was...

Swallowing hard, I shoved the grief away. That was for private moments. I could lose it all when I was back in my room alone. "You tell them one of the Konos delegates bit her and we didn't know. You tell them we're going to make Konos pay."

"They won't be satisfied with that," Istvan warned.

"They will be if it means war with Konos." I balled my hands into fists. Wasn't that what they all wanted from me? "Tell them I'll agree to attack Konos."

Sophia was crying again, and all I wanted to do was hold her and comfort her, even if she'd just killed five people. I knew it wasn't her fault. This was on my father's shoulders. If he even made it to the Underworld, I hoped he was paying for all his mistakes.

"Keeping her alive is a mistake," Argus muttered.

I shot a glare at the guard next to me. "If you want to keep your position and your head, you'll keep those opinions to yourself."

"My apologies, your highness." The guard dipped into a bow, showing his submission. "I am at your service."

I pressed my lips together, alarmed at my own threats against the guard who'd already helped me cover up so much. Pinching the bridge of my nose, I allowed myself a moment to take a deep breath, then I faced Argus. "If she kills anyone or turns anyone, we'll discuss next steps. Until that time, she is to remain alive and well cared for." I glanced at Istvan. "We'll have more information on what she needs and how half-vampires can survive soon, correct?"

Istvan nodded. "I expect delivery of several important volumes by the end of the week."

Argus opened his mouth but none of us got to hear what he was going to say because suddenly, everything went dark.

Sophia's chambers had been illuminated with bright midday sunlight, no flames were needed. But now it was as night. The windows showing nothing but deep midnight.

"There is no record of an eclipse coming today," Istvan said.

All of us stumbled forward, drawn to the windows. Even Sophia stood and joined us, her cries silenced by the surprise of day turning to night.

40

ARA

WATER COVERED my feet and dripped down the walls. The fae light in my hand reflected off the surfaces, making the cave walls shimmer. It wasn't enough to eliminate the eeriness of the small, wet space. Nearby, water dripped, the sound echoing through the enclosed space. On one end, I saw a wall of water. Not a waterfall, exactly, but water covering the space, sealing us in. That had to be the tunnel out that we'd initially planned to use. I was grateful there was a better option for escape.

"Hello?" I risked a step forward, my movement making the water around me slosh, creating more noise. I winced, wondering if I should have been trying a more stealthy approach. Too late for that now. "Nyx? Are you here?"

"How do you know my name?" The voice was snakelike, hissing, cold, and low. As if she'd forgotten how to speak. Maybe she had.

"I was sent to get you out. I came through a portal in Konos," I said.

"Unless you have a way to move stone and water, you'll be trapped here the same as me," she warned.

"I have a tether," I replied, checking that the thread was still tied around my waist. It was there. Hopefully Belan was still holding his end. "But we should go quickly in case anything happens to the other end."

Drip. Drip. Drip.

I waited, my breathing too loud in the lingering silence between us.

Shadows moved across the wall, and the fae light flickered. I put my hand in front of it on instinct, as if it were a candle, before remembering it was working by magic. Feeling a bit foolish, I lowered my hand.

Glancing back, I looked at the glowing blue oval sputtering and flashing behind me. The thread was the only thing keeping it here. I wondered how long I should wait before I returned. If the guards cut the thread or tossed it into the portal, I'd be stuck here and that was not in my plans. Even if I could potentially use my magic to escape.

"Nyx? We really should go," I said.

A female form emerged from behind a rock. She was more skeleton than person and I sucked in a breath, startled by her appearance. Her eyes were hollow, her cheekbones protruded at sharp angles. Her skin was ashen, though I think it might have once been the same beautiful golden tan color as Ryvin's.

"You fear me, girl?" she hissed.

"I'd be insane not to," I replied. "I know of your power."

She smirked. "I used to have power. Now, it's only my immortality that keeps me from being a corpse."

I felt a tug on the thread and my pulse raced. We had to get out of here, but Nyx didn't look like she was in a hurry. "This portal takes us to the labyrinth in Konos. The king is there."

"How do I know this isn't a trick?" she asked.

Honestly, that was a valid question. "Ryvin sent me. He's waiting for us."

She lifted a thin eyebrow. "He's alive?"

I nodded.

"Is he powerful?"

"Almost more powerful than his father," I replied. "Even with your stolen magic."

She smiled again, the expression a bit ghastly on her emaciated face. "He'll be more powerful than the king after I claim what's mine."

The thread tightened around my waist, harder this time. Belan was signaling me. "We have to go or we'll lose the portal."

"How do I know I can trust you?" she asked. "Why did he not come himself?"

"Because I killed the minotaur."

"That explains the blood. I thought maybe you were one of those followers of Mithra." She laughed, a huffing, dry sound. "I suppose I won't kill you when we return. Your skills might be helpful."

I pressed my lips together, biting back the response I wanted to give her. We were running out of time. "Please, we need to go."

She strode forward, her skeletal form clothed in rags that barely covered her. I wondered if they'd given her anything when they trapped her here. It didn't seem so, or if they had, she'd gone through it quickly. It wasn't like they could send things to her in this prison.

I found myself hating the Fae King even more, something I didn't know was possible.

She stretched out a bony hand, and I clasped it, trying not to react at how cold it was and how frail it felt in my grasp. Without a word, we stepped forward, entering the portal.

We were greeted by chaos. Guards clashed with tributes, fae of all kinds raced by, shrieking in feral debauchery. I couldn't tell if they were enjoying themselves or fleeing for their lives. The spool of thread was tied around a rock and I couldn't find any sign of Belan. Where had he gone? I glanced around, hoping to find him, but there were so many people racing by.

We took a few tentative steps away from the portal and I peered down the bend, trying to gain my bearings. A pack of satyrs charged through and I shoved Nyx, moving her just in time. Any exhaustion I'd had from using my magic was gone, replaced by a surge of energy urging me to keep the goddess alive.

"This way," I steered her away from the loudest part of the labyrinth, wondering where Ryvin and Laera were. Looking up, I could see everything. The shroud over the labyrinth was gone, allowing anyone down here to see up into the amphitheater. I could tell that the stands had emptied. The crowds were gone. From the mass of people we had to dodge as we weaved our way through, it appeared they'd mostly poured into the labyrinth.

This was not how things were supposed to go.

While making progress toward what I hoped was the end of the labyrinth, I caught sight of the thrones in the royal box. They were all empty. Had the king fled?

Nyx stopped suddenly, grasping my arm with her bony fingers. "I need to get my magic back."

"I'm trying to find the king," I said.

"You killed the creature. His shield is gone," she said.

"What?"

"The beast in the labyrinth. It was created to protect him. A buffer that sealed my magic inside him. With it gone, I don't need him. But I do need something else." She grinned, the expression sending a chill down my spine.

I was afraid to ask what it was that she needed, so I kept my mouth shut, hoping Ryvin and Laera would find me soon.

The goddess closed her eyes and tilted her chin toward the sky. All the chaos around us seemed to avoid us. Anyone in the labyrinth raced right by or turned around when they got near. She might not have her magic, but she was doing something to keep us from being bothered.

"I need to find Ryvin," I shouted over the din.

Nyx didn't respond. She stayed where she was, her face skyward, her expression serene and unbothered. I wasn't even sure she could hear me.

I took a few steps away, but she reached out and grabbed me again, those bony fingers cutting into my upper arm. "Let me go."

Her grip tightened, and I was suddenly frozen in place. I yanked my arm, but I was stuck in her grasp. "Please, let me go."

"I found her!" Belan's voice made me gasp, and I turned to see all the remaining tributes standing in front of me. They piled into the space I was occupying with Nyx, pale and wide-eyed.

"Is this her?" Belan asked. "Are you Nyx?"

The goddess lowered her face and smiled sweetly at Belan. "I was and soon, I will be again. With your help. Now kneel. Show me that humans still know how to behave in the presence of a god."

Belan dropped to his knees, bowing his head. The rest of the tributes followed. I hesitated, not liking where this was going. "Nyx?"

She ignored me and breathed in deeply through her nose as she gracefully moved closer to the tributes. Her hand was no longer on me, but I was still frozen where she'd been holding me. Gritting my teeth, I tried to fight it, but I'd experienced this before at Ryvin's hands. It must be a gift from his mother.

"How wonderful to see that my name has not been forgotten," the goddess said in her hissing tone. "I do appreciate the sign of devotion, but I need something else right now. Tell me, would you all be willing to serve me? To show your devotion to me?"

A terrible feeling made my insides twist. "Please,

leave them alone. They weren't part of this. Let's find the king, find your son."

"We are at your service, goddess," the tributes spoke as one, their voices a flat and lifeless chant.

I struggled against my invisible bonds, terrified to know where this was going. "Nyx, please—." My voice stopped working, my words vanished. I could move my mouth, but nothing came from it. Panic seized, making my chest feel tight. I continued to struggle, then desperately looked around for Ryvin. Where was he?

I wasn't sure if it was my imagination or if Nyx looked healthier than she had moments ago. Her face appeared fuller, her eyes less hallow, her skin more lustrous.

She swept her arms up in a fluid gesture and billowing shadows traveled in their wake. I tried to yell as a blanket of darkness fell upon the kneeling tributes. My attempt at a warning was just as silent as my begging moments ago, my voice still missing. The tributes' screams cut through the din of the chaos around us, the sound making my bones rattle. I think I shouted with them, I think I tried to reach them, but I was unable to break the invisible hold the goddess had on me.

When the shadows cleared, all that was left of the tributes I'd tried so desperately to save was a pile of ashes.

"What did you do?" I demanded, as tears stung my eyes. My voice had abruptly returned and I could move again. I stepped closer to her. "How could you? How could you do that to them?"

How could this happen? After everything we'd been through? They were there and then suddenly, they were gone. Without warning, without a fight. After all the effort I'd put into trying to get them off this island, they'd died here, anyway.

Leara's words about Morta choosing those who weren't long for this world flashed through my mind, but I shoved it away. If I believed that, it meant I believed that it was supposed to end like this. That there had been no other way. That they were always meant to die. It was too gruesome, too heartbreaking.

My lower lip trembled, and I looked at the goddess. Her dark hair was glossy and thick, her eyes sparkling, her body soft and curvy. Gone was the skeletal figure I'd found in the cave. "Why did you do that?"

"With their sacrifice, I am whole. Wasn't that why you got me out? So I could retrieve my magic and help you get what you want? It had to be a great sacrifice to recover my stolen power. There wasn't another option."

"I didn't ask you to kill them. They didn't do anything wrong, there had to be another way," I said.

She shrugged. "Perhaps. But I was trapped in that cave, right under the humans. They knew I was there, and they did nothing."

"But they didn't know you were there," I explained. "We didn't know."

"Well, if they didn't know, they didn't bother to find out where I'd gone. One day I'm receiving offerings at temples and the next day I disappear. Not one of their kind sought me out. Not one of them bothered to find their missing goddess. All of them are selfish, terrible beings. Once I disagreed with my mate about how we should treat them. I cared for them, in my own way, while he suggested we eliminate them. I'm starting to think he was right," she said.

I shook my head. "No, humans are worth saving. And your mate is a monster. We got you out so you could help us destroy him."

She cackled, the quiet hush of her voice was gone. She was loud and boisterous. "I can't kill my mate. If you were counting on me to get rid of him, you're going to be disappointed. Though, I would like to watch someone else do the task. After what he did to me, I hope it's slow and painful."

Lightning flashed, and the gray sky darkened. I couldn't help but look up just as the sun was swallowed by the moon. Without warning, it was night and the clouds that had covered Konos my entire life parted, leaving a sky dusted with stars.

"What's happening?" I asked.

"I'm just getting started. It's time for all those who helped keep me prisoner to pay for their crime." She straightened, as if hearing something far away. Then she turned her dark eyes on me. "You should run. The gods are on their way here and they're looking for you."

"Ara!" Ryvin called, then he stopped and stared at Nyx. "Mother?"

The goddess walked over to him and stroked his cheek. "You grew up so handsome." Then she looked at me. "You better say your goodbyes. They're here for her blood. And I'm guessing they're not going to be happy with me for hiding the sun."

Shadows twisted around Nyx, and when they dissipated, the goddess was gone.

"Was she telling the truth?" I asked Ryvin. "Are the gods really here?"

"I couldn't find you after you went into the portal. I've been so worried. Are you hurt?" He approached slowly.

"I'm alright. I just want to get out of here before the gods find us," I said. "What are we going to do?"

"I need you to trust me, alright? Please, trust me." His brow furrowed slightly and there was a pleading look in his eyes. He gripped my upper arms with his large hands, smearing the still damp blood coating my skin.

"I trust you." It took everything inside me to admit that, but he'd proven it over and over again. He'd protected me even if his methods weren't exactly things I'd approve of.

The ground shook, and bits of the walls around us crumbled. Lightning flashed, and the air felt charged. A feeling I'd noticed too many times before terrible things happened. "What's happening?"

"Zeus," Ryvin whispered. He ran a hand through his hair and his body seemed to tense. "I don't have a choice. There's no other way."

My brow furrowed, and I opened my mouth to ask him what he was talking about, but he leaned in, claiming my mouth with his. The kiss was frantic and desperate. Like a farewell. He pulled away before I could deepen the kiss to take that uncomfortable edge off of it.

"I love you, Ara. Please forgive me." He tightened his grip and heat seared through my insides. My knees buckled and stars exploded in my vision. I cried out as agony unlike anything I'd felt before tore through me. It was as if my body was being torn in half; like my soul was being cleaved from me. My body contorted as shockwaves of pain pushed me to the breaking point. Everything went dark, but I fought, trying to maintain consciousness. I'm not sure if I succeeded. I might have blacked out.

When I could breathe again, I was in Ryvin's arms, but I was so weak I couldn't even support my own weight. He held me, cradled like a child. I tried to lift my head; I tried to speak, but it took all of my energy to simply keep my eyes open.

Blurry figures stood in front of us. People I didn't recognize. They were glowing. Or maybe I was hallucinating. I couldn't even feel my own body.

"Hand over Ceto's child and we'll be on our way," someone demanded. The voice was deep and masculine. So loud it made my head throb.

"She's no threat to any of you," Ryvin replied.

"We felt her use her magic all the way on Olympus," the voice boomed. "You may be part god, but you're not one of us. We will kill you both if necessary."

"She no longer has any magic," Ryvin said.

Something prickled along the back of my neck. I wanted to say something, to defend myself or speak up or demand to know what was going on, but I couldn't move.

There was a long pause, and I tried to make myself wiggle my fingers. I couldn't even tell if they were moving.

"You're her mate," the voice said.

My heart kicked against my ribs. *My mate.* Ryvin was my mate. Which meant if my magic was gone...

"There is no rule saying I can't have her magic. I am not a child of Ceto," Ryvin said, his tone defiant.

My breathing increased, and I think I was trembling. Ryvin took my magic. Without asking. Without warning. He stole it from me. The very thing he despised his father for doing to his mother. I tried to speak, but my lips wouldn't move. Was I going to stay this broken forever? Was this what Nyx had to overcome?

The voice made a sound like a growl. I wasn't sure if it was a sound of approval or anger. Perhaps it was simply annoyance. I couldn't turn my head to get a better look so all I had to go on was the sound.

"I'll be watching you, Prince of Death," the voice said.

It was the last thing I heard before everything went black.

ALSO BY ALEXIS CALDER

Rejected Fate Series

Darkest Mate

Forbidden Sin

Feral Queen

Royal Mates Series

Shifter Claimed

Shifter Fated

Shifter Rising

Academy of Elites Series

Academy of Elites: Untamed Magic

Academy of Elites: Broken Magic

Academy of Elites: Fated Magic

Academy of Elites: Unbound Magic

Brimstone Academy Series

Brimstone Academy: Semester One

Brimstone Academy: Semester Two

Romcom books published under Lexi Calder:

In Hate With My Boss

Love to Hate You

ABOUT THE AUTHOR

Alexis Calder writes sassy heroines and sexy heroes with a sprinkle of sarcasm. She lives in the Rockies and drinks far too much coffee and just the right amount of wine.

- facebook.com/AuthorAlexisCalder
- instagram.com/author_alexiscalder
- tiktok.com/@authoralexiscalder
- amazon.com/stores/Alexis-Calder/author/B07TP5VCGZ

Made in the USA
Las Vegas, NV
23 December 2024